D1650424

Split Image

Split Image

Male and Female After God's Likeness

Anne Atkins

HODDER AND STOUGHTON
LONDON SYDNEY AUCKLAND TORONTO

British Library Cataloguing in Publication Data
Atkins, Anne
  Split image : male and female after God's
  likeness.
  1. Interpersonal relations—Religious
  aspects—Christianity   2. Women—
  Social conditions   3. Women in Christianity
  I. Title
  248.4   BT738

  ISBN 0 340 38341 0

*Copyright © 1987 by Anne Atkins. First printed 1987. Second impression
1988. All rights reserved. No part of this publication may be reproduced or
transmitted in any form or by any means, electronically or mechanically,
including photocopying, recording or any information storage or retrieval
system, without either the prior permission in writing from the publisher
or a licence, permitting restricted copying. In the United Kingdom such
licences are issued by the Copyright Licensing Agency, 33-34 Alfred Place,
London WC1E 7DP. Printed in Great Britain for Hodder and Stoughton
Limited, Mill Road, Dunton Green, Sevenoaks, Kent by Cox & Wyman
Ltd., Reading, Berks. Typeset by Hewer Text Composition Services,
Edinburgh.*

*Hodder and Stoughton Editorial Office: 47 Bedford Square, London WC1B
3DP.*

For Shaun
(*Proverbs 11:22*)

Contents

Acknowledgements

I would particularly like to thank Michael Green.

I would also like to thank Elizabeth Crofts, Jill and David Ridgewell, Michael Griffiths, my brother Andrew Briggs and his wife Diana, Jonathan Fletcher, my parents, my grandfather-in-law Austin Fulton, Carolyn Armitage, Elaine Storkey, Colin Wilcockson, Caroline Standing, Chris Ellse, and Chipping Barnet Public Library.

And of course I would like to thank Shaun. After all, a husband "is a man who stands by you through all the troubles you wouldn't have had if you'd stayed single".[1]

Foreword

I first met Anne when she was an undergraduate. Beautiful. Artistic. Dynamic. When she joined the Christian scene in Oxford the *avant-garde* gasped in amazement, and so did the God-squad. This arresting, happy, extrovert, and exciting personality threw into high relief the somewhat lack lustre lives of many of the Christian Union. Its president realised that something fairly exceptional was around – and promptly decided to marry her. It was the best and most far-reaching decision of his year of office. Shaun went into the Anglican ministry and, trailing clouds of the Old Vic, Anne went with him.

Given all that, you would expect something exceptional in this book. And you will not be disappointed. The verve, the humour, the controversial pungency, the love, the laughter and the sheer ability of Anne the personality has gone into Anne the writer. The book is every bit as arresting, as wholesome and as controversial as its delightful author.

Her thesis is bold and simple. Contrary to general misunderstanding, the Bible teaches the complete equality of man and woman, their difference but complementarity. She cheerfully takes on the extreme feminist camp and the extreme Evangelical camp, though she has strong affinities with both. Scripture does not teach male supremacy in work, marriage, authority, worship or preaching: man without woman is incomplete. At the

9

same time, feminist chauvinism is strongly repudiated. We need each other. The "image of God", male and female in interdependence, has been disastrously split. The cry of the book is (hilariously) enshrined in the last brief chapter: it is "get back to the image". Singleness and marriage, feminism and male dominance all receive fearless handling.

It is a superb first book, forceful, well researched, bold, unconventional and in places breathtaking. And above all it seeks to read the thesis of male and female interdependence out of scripture itself. The "fundamentalists", Catholic and Protestant alike, will have trouble dealing with this sharp exposé of some of their dearest shibboleths. The general Christian reader, who has a nasty suspicion that the Church has kept women down, will gain enormous insight from it. And single people and marrieds alike will thank God for its positive radicalism, its candour, and its warmth.

I know of no book on this subject which has affected me more. Buy it. Give it away. And then invite Anne and Shaun to speak. You will find "the half has not been told you".

MICHAEL GREEN

Imago Dei

> *"So God created man in His own image; in the image of God He created Him, male and female He created them."*

Genesis 1:27

We are made in God's image. We are also made male and female. And though the writer of Genesis does not spell this out any further, there is surely some connection between these two things.

God is One. So we, the human race, are first described as one: "He created *him*." But God is also "three". And immediately this first statement about us is followed up with a second: "male and female He created *them*." The suggestion is surely that we as male and female – one race in two sexes – are in some ways a reflection of Him as Father, Son and Spirit – one God in three Persons.

Now there are a number of things one can say about the Persons of the Godhead. They are different, obviously. They are also absolutely equal. But above all they are co-operative. They work together. They love, and serve, and exist for each other. This is what God is like. And it is also, surely, what we should be like. For as *inter*dependent vicegerents we can be a glimmer of that glorious Trinity. As two *in*dependent sexes we are merely a split image.

ONE

Splitting the Image

"There is no subject more charged with passion than the relation between the sexes. In one way or another, it lies behind most of the poetry and most of the crime, most of the sublimity and most of the cruelty, most of the ecstasy and most of the boredom in all our lives."[1]

A friend was telling me recently why he preferred an all male Bible study group as a teenager.

"We wouldn't have discussed our problems in front of girls," he said.

"Why not?" I asked him.

"We wouldn't have admitted our failings."

"But *why?*"

"Why?" He pondered a moment. "They're beneath us. They're lesser," he said simply. "That's what we really felt."

So what?

Some people will say that relationships between the sexes are much better than they were. In many ways this is true. Much sexual discrimination is illegal, many schools are co-ed., women and men mix freely with one another and equal opportunities are supposed to abound.

But these changes sometimes raise their own problems. The cures can be worse than the original diseases. To our shame, we Christians have been fairly apathetic about sexism. Consequently we have had little influence in finding the solutions. The world has been finding its own and they have not always been the best.

Instead of encouraging girls and boys to mix freely with each other, our society now encourages them to sleep freely with each other. Instead of elevating motherhood to the position it has in the Bible, society often implies women should not have to "suffer" it at all, so those who do are still more denigrated. Instead of showing that our differences do not make us unequal, some people try to pretend there are no differences at all. And instead of insisting that men should be less promiscuous, changing moral standards now pressurise women to become more so. It should hardly surprise us if the movement we think of as "women's liberation" sometimes seems unsavoury; it has had little Christian salt in it to save it from decay.

The fault is largely ours. Many Christians have had little to do with the recent feminist movement. The Church has often shown little interest in the *cris de coeur* many women have been uttering. Until a year or two ago the only books you would have found on your church bookstall on the subject would have been saccharine best-selling paperbacks telling you to "be a woman", by people who have tried.[2] They simply ignore many of the problems experienced by women – and men – today.

But so what? Why should we worry about the way women and men relate? After all, you may say, it is the world's problem; let the world solve it. But we are in the world (John 17:15,18). If our village has the plague we will catch it; if our country goes to war we do too; if our society embraces a philosophy we will come under its influence. It is useless to pretend we are not being radically affected by changing sexual patterns. They are altering our politics, our places of work, and the way we bring up our families. Unless we want to be helpless victims to the new philosophy we must know what it is saying. We must also be salt and light. We must shape the world. We must vote when there is an election and protest when there is injustice. And we need to understand changing trends in our society and know whether to resist or encourage them.[3]

I have heard it said that sexism is not an important issue. And in a sense, of course, this is true. It is not eternal. Sexual relationships and their related problems will pass away. So, indeed, will poverty. So will slavery. So will torture and war, capitalism and socialism. One can legitimately argue that none of these issues is of paramount importance. By far the most important thing in life is the gospel. Whether people are discriminated against, or happy in their marriages, or composing beautiful music is of no importance at all compared with whether their sins are forgiven. But Jesus nevertheless cared about these things. He still fed the hungry and healed the sick and wined and dined with the merry. He was never in any doubt that it was more important to save people than feed them, to teach them than heal them.[4] However, he did feed them and heal them. He did care about these things. We should too. Sexual disharmony can lead to unhappiness, frustration, or injustice. It may have comparatively little effect on our eternal destiny, but it certainly warrants our attention.

Nevertheless perhaps you think that it does not warrant yours. If you are a man you may feel these are women's problems, and you are not involved. Or, if a woman, that they are problems for other, "feminist", women but not the rest of us. Perhaps you get on perfectly with the opposite sex and never feel misunderstood by them; perhaps you do not mind who wears the trousers or even if nobody wears any at all. But we are told to love and honour one another. We are told to bear one another's burdens (Galatians 6:2). We are instructed to be a body (1 Corinthians 12:12,14). Some Christians are troubled by these issues. Some feel that our cultural, and Christian, heritage is deeply sexist. And we in the Church must nourish and care for each other: a few concerned people cannot overcome the sexism of the rest of us.

This brings us to the crunch. It is often glibly thought that Christian women are "happy and fulfilled" since Christian men are "unselfish and understanding". As a result we tend to think that these "feminist" concerns are not ours. Alas! all too often they are more ours than anyone else's. The Church seems, in many ways, to be one of the worst perpetrators of sexism. Many women feel that it is amongst fellow Christians, above all, that they are most devalued.

This has been my own experience. I reached the age of eighteen without ever noticing male chauvinism. Then I spent a weekend on a Christian holiday camp. In many ways it was an excellent and godly place; the people were kind, and the teaching, on the whole, was biblical. Yet the women were treated as inferior. We were kept apart from the men and given menial, domestic work. I was deeply shocked. For the first time I experienced that so-called "envy of men" which we women, according to Freud, are all supposed to feel. I caught myself thinking I would rather be a man. Not because I wanted to change sex, but because I would rather have played tennis in the sun than peeled spuds in the kitchen.

I have often found this kind of sexual inequality amongst Christians since. I know I am not alone. The most pernicious aspect of it all is that unashamed sexual prejudice is sometimes taught as a biblical truth. I have frequently heard frank male chauvinism presented as a creed of our faith.

The answer to heresy is truth. The answer to bogus biblical teaching is true biblical teaching. And the answer to sexism in the Church is a better understanding of what God says about the sexes. We are probably all agreed on this. Why, then, do we still find unbiblical attitudes, even unbiblical teaching, in the Church?

On some things the Bible gives us clear guidance. It is not difficult to see that murder and idolatry are wrong. On others, scripture seems harder to interpret. Are divorce and remarriage permissible? Should slavery be abolished? Sometimes the Bible does not directly apply itself to the issues we face. At other times the answers are staring us in the face, yet we find them remarkably hard to see. None of us comes to the Bible with an unprejudiced mind. Our preconceptions cloud our perceptions. And there are two main reasons for this.

Scripture twisting

The first reason is that we often *want* the Bible to say something. Take the question of divorce and remarriage. I have a friend who was deserted and subsequently, most unwillingly, divorced. He now needs to know whether he is free to marry again. He very much wants to believe he is and this makes his task of interpretation difficult. He will want to cling to the texts which suggest that remarriage is acceptable; he will want to "reinterpret" the texts which suggest the opposite if he can. Since he is aware of this, if he comes to a favourable conclusion he may wonder if he persuaded himself into it because that was what he wanted to believe all along.

And it is the same with the biblical teaching on the

sexes. It is tempting to ignore certain passages of scripture because they are unpalatable. Consider the usual under-standing of 1 Corinthians 11:2–16 (pages 105–106). There is an almost unanimous agreement that Paul is command-ing women to cover their heads in some way in worship. And yet there is also an almost unanimous conspiracy to ignore this command. It is disregarded as "culturally conditioned" and therefore irrelevant today. Of course there is common sense in this. However, I suspect the reason most of us interpret the passage like this is not because we have done some hard biblical thinking, but because we find the idea of compulsory headgear repellent.

This "culturally relative" approach is dangerous. If part of the Bible can be reapplied because it is "cultural" so can the rest. Much of it is. Paul's words on marriage, women's authority, and women's silence are all suscep-tible to similar treatment. Often he is written off as the last word in male chauvinism before he has been properly read. More striking still, his revolutionary support of women is totally ignored. All this is because people do not like what he has to say. It is difficult to come to the Bible with an open mind if it is likely to change the way we live. It is hard to be honest about 1 Peter 3:1 if you do not like the idea of submitting to your husband. Of course, much of the Bible may have to be reapplied today, but it is difficult to do this objectively because so much is at stake.

So this is the first reason biblical interpretation can be difficult: we all want the Bible to say certain things. The second reason is this: we all *expect* the Bible to say certain things. There are so many traditional understandings of the scriptures that it is hard to read them without preconceptions. Get a friend who does not know the story well to read through Genesis 3. Then ask her what the couple ate. She will probably say an apple. Get another friend to read Matthew 2. Ask him how many wise men came to see Jesus. He will probably say three kings. Yet the text makes no mention of an apple or any number of kings.

I have seen many examples of this phenomenon. I was studying 1 Peter with some friends and we started the evening by reading the book out loud. Chapter 3 verse 19 (RSV) goes like this: ". . . in which he went and preached to the spirits in prison . . ." Yet the person reading the passage read: ". . . in which he went *down* and preached to the spirits in prison". Though he had never heard of the tradition, he had subconsciously absorbed the patristic teaching that this verse is about Christ's descent into Hell. This influenced his, and indeed everybody else's, approach to the passage; almost all of us assumed that was what it was about, though the text itself hardly hints at it.

Another occasion was a talk about Paul's teaching on sex in 1 Corinthians. Most of the audience would have claimed to know the Bible fairly well and read it regularly. Yet when the talk was prefaced with half a dozen questions, almost everyone gave answers diametrically opposed to the biblical ones. "Who should govern your body?" it was asked. "Christ," they answered, though Paul tells them it is their spouses (1 Corinthians 7:4). "Is the body temporary or permanent?" To this the unanimous reply was "temporary", though the Bible clearly teaches that it will be raised immortal and incorruptible (1 Corinthians 6:13,14; 15:42). The preconceived ideas we have about the Bible often hinder our understanding of it. As we studied both the Petrine and Pauline passages, people read all kinds of implications into the texts that were never intended by the writers.

We have the same kind of preconceptions about the teaching on men and women. Read the account of Eve's creation in Genesis 2:18–25 (page 26). Who is presented as the weaker partner? Which of the two would be more helpless, more incomplete without the other? Who is to be the assistant, the follower, the "number 2" in the partnership? Why, the woman of course. It is clearly taught throughout the passage: she was made for man's benefit; she was a subsequent, junior, version; she was only a tiny bone out of his body; even her name is derived from his. In short, she owes her being to him and exists for his convenience. This may seem an extreme interpretation of the passage, but many of us believe it says something of the sort. We think the writer is saying woman is man's subordinate and created to be his assistant. Why? Is this what the passage actually says?

Try reading it the other way round. Suppose God had made the woman first, and the man out of her. Substitute the woman for the man and the man for the woman, and read the account again. Now who comes over as the helpless, dependent one, the weaker, inferior partner? Why, the woman again of course! She could not cope alone; man had to be made to bail her out. Part of her body was taken away to make him; she can never again be complete on her own. The man was made last, after the plants, after the animals, and certainly after the woman; he is the crown of God's creation. He was made out of human flesh; she is nothing but dust. Even her name ("man" now of course) is a diminutive version of his ("woman"). She is to "cleave" to him (and, as it happens, this word is "used almost universally for a weaker cleaving to a stronger";[5] no doubt a great deal would be made of this if the woman were to cleave to the man!). Most significant of all, she is to leave her parents and her way of life to join him and adapt to him; she was clearly found to be inadequate on her own.

If we think that the Bible says something we will probably find it there. Church and society have told us for centuries that woman is man's subordinate so we expect to find this in the Bible. And we are not disappointed. As long as we do not look too carefully it is precisely what we do find.

There is another example of this tendency in the very same passage. Again we have been told that woman was made as man's "helpmate". You may even, depending on your translation, think it is what you have just read in Genesis 2. The implication is that she is his back-up. He does the work, like an operating surgeon, and she is the nurse handing him the forceps. I know marriages which function on this understanding of the word "helpmate": vicars' wives, for example, who are expected to have little work other than that of promoting their husbands; whose chief (and often admirable) purpose in life is to facilitate their partners' existences.

And yet this extraordinary word "helpmate" never appears in the Bible. Eve was created as Adam's "help". This word does not imply subordination, inferiority, or in any way a secondary position. On the contrary, it is usually used in the Old Testament to refer to God, as man's help.[6] She is also to be "meet" for him. The word means "matching", "corresponding to", or "opposite to" the man. So the latter word implies equality, and the former superiority! Yet "helpmate" is presumably a corruption of these two words. And because of all the connotations of this unbiblical word, when we read Genesis 2 we assume all sorts of things that are not there.

There are numerous such examples. I have heard people ask "Why did Paul think women more sinful?", though he never suggests such a thing: or "What did he mean by the word headship?", although he never once uses it.

Conclusion

There is ample reason for addressing ourselves to the question of relationships between male and female, and how we should live together as the image of God. The human race traditionally tends to make a number of mistakes: we often tolerate and even encourage inequality and segregation between the sexes. Our own particular society, although beginning to combat these errors, is now adding more of its own; unless we want to end up worse off than we were before, Christians need to engage in the battle and direct some of the fighting. Lastly, and most to our shame, we in the Church are often the most to blame. Instead of being in the front leading the way, we are often miles behind the back line, dragging our feet unhappily and rather unthinkingly in the direction the majority are going. It is imperative that we study what God says about it all. To do this we must submit ourselves to His word.

But we need to be careful. We must be wary of what we want to find. Perhaps we want to believe that the sexes have different roles, or that husbands have a certain authority, or that marriage should be symmetrical, or women ordained. We may have to surrender cherished views. The Bible is not always a comfortable book to read.

And we also have to be wary of what we expect to find. We tend to think, quite sensibly, that the correct interpretation of the Bible is the most obvious one. This is usually true. However, the "obvious" can be determined and shaped by all sorts of factors. Sometimes we have heard something so often that it becomes "obvious". If we look a little closer it may not be there at all. It seemed obvious to our 1 Corinthians 7 study group that the body is unimportant: almost every other philosophy teaches it, so it was assumed that the Bible did too. It is only the careful reader who sees that this is not the case. We need to come to the Bible with a fresh mind. We must be ready to challenge things we have always assumed to be true.

With this in mind, we will turn to what God says about male and female.

TWO

Difference

*"The old war-cry of the sexists – **vive la différence** – actually implied exactly the opposite; the rigid division of an infinite variety of people into just two categories, male and female."*

Jill Tweedie, **In the Name of Love**.[1]

" 'All the women in history have been men.' Discuss."

1066 And All That.[2]

We are different. This is mentioned in God's first reference to the human race. We are not just people; we are male and female, and this means we are different. This would seem so obvious it is hardly worth saying, yet it is something people argue about all the time. We assert it. We refute it. Some say the differences between us exist in every sphere of life, others that they hardly exist at all. Whole books have been written insisting there are differences between men and women, as if that had ever been in doubt.[3] Other books are devoted to showing that the differences are culturally induced, as if that suddenly makes them irrelevant.[4]

And people get hot under the collar on this topic. "Of course, women are more emotional," someone says with confident omniscience. The particular woman opposite him, sensing some dangerous slight she does not even stop to examine, hotly denies it and passionately insists that women are not emotional at all. Somehow we feel that a great deal is at stake. But what? Why does it matter anyway?

It matters because we link "difference" and "discrimination". If two groups of people can be proved to be different from each other in some way that we think is important, we believe we can treat them differently. Some people like it when women and men are treated differently. Some do not. This is what motivates us to argue the case one way or the other. For years it was assumed that women were more stupid than men. It seemed logical for men to hold offices of government and power and authority. After all, you do not want your country run by congenital idiots. But if it can be proved that there is no significant difference between our IQs we might question a system which favours half the race at random.

Similarly the innate, rather than cultural, differences between the sexes are given importance. If it can be shown that girls are born more domestic and fond of babies than boys, and boys born more aggressive and competitive than girls (rather than both being trained to be so) we might assume that God has made women to stay at home with children and men to pursue competitive careers. The way we are created could be seen to reinforce the status quo. Again some people like the status quo; others do not. This is why they are keen to prove the issue one way or the other.

But there are really two questions. The first is *how are we different?* And the second is *so what?* Do sexual differences indeed mean that we should treat the sexes differently? It is the second question which is the important and interesting one. But we cannot answer it without considering the first. So what exactly are the sexual differences? The relevant text is Genesis 2.

(18) Then the LORD God said, "It is not good that the man should be alone; I will make a helper fit for him."
(19) So out of the ground the LORD God formed every beast of the field and every bird of the air, and brought them to the man to see what he would call them; and whatever the man called every living creature, that was its name. (20) The man gave names to all cattle, and to the birds of the air, and to every beast of the field; but for the man there was not found a helper fit for him. (21) So the LORD God caused a deep sleep to fall upon the man, and while he slept took one of his ribs and closed up its place with flesh; (22) and the rib which the LORD God had taken from the man he made into a woman and brought her to the man. (23) Then the man said,

> "This at last is bone of my bones
> and flesh of my flesh;
> she shall be called Woman,
> because she was taken out of Man."

(24) Therefore a man leaves his father and mother and cleaves to his wife, and they become one flesh.

(Genesis 2)

This passage tells us that the sexes are different. It is about the making of woman, which means, in effect, the making of sexual differentiation. God, suprisingly, did not make another man. Some theologians think he should have done.[5] But there it is. He did not.

So far so good. We are told that we are different. But that is all. The Bible gives us no clue at all as to what the difference is. A friend of mine spent an entire evening with her church study group, which included an outstanding biblical scholar, trying to discover what, according to the Bible, are the differences between the sexes.

They all drew blank. (And also, incidentally, got very cross with each other!)

Between every woman and every man

If the Bible does not tell us we shall have to work it out for ourselves. We must start with what we know for sure; before moving onto the controversial, we should state the undeniable. We are genitally different. Men beget children, or are designed to, and women bear them. There may be other sexual differences, but this is the only one on which everyone is agreed. It is the only one we can be sure of between *every* woman and *every* man.

And its relevance

Where does this get us? We now come to the second, more important, question: what is the relevance of this difference? The answer would seem to be, none. It does not in itself suggest that we should treat the sexes differently. There is no reason why those who conceive children should behave or be treated in any significantly different way from those who beget them.

We could say that the reproductive difference is created by God, so it is good. Attempts to tamper with it are suspect. Two men wanting to adopt a family together, or multi-parent families, as advocated by Greer[6] (not extended families, but households where children do not know which, of the many parents, are theirs), are not God's design. The same goes for the latest plan to do away with sex and reproduce by cloning, so men could be phased out altogether (however attractive some may consider the prospect!).

We can also see that a few occupations may be more fitting for one sex than the other: I personally think it is

appropriate that midwives, obstetricians and gynaeco-
logists should by and large be women; not because they
will do the job any better, but because the work involves
such intimacy. A woman doctor is obviously more
suitable for conducting internal examinations; apart from
anything else, she is free to show understanding and
tenderness without misunderstanding. Similarly I believe
a man should be offered a male nurse for bed baths and
other intimate services. However, even this much is
mere personal preference: Shaun tells me many men
would be far more embarrassed being nursed by a man.

So our reproductive difference could possibly make a
few specialised jobs more suitable for one sex or the other.
Women should care for rape victims, since they will be
more able to sympathise. Men should counsel young
boys with sexual problems, since they will be more likely
to know what they are going through. Common sense
tells us all this, and the fact that we are genitally different
does not take us any further.

Between "masculine" and "feminine"

There is a second kind of difference. I suggest it ten-
tatively: the Bible merely hints at it so we must use the
idea with care.

Male and female are simply genetic, biological differences. "Masculine" and "feminine" are more than this.
They are poetic symbols; they represent other things.
C. S. Lewis describes this well in *Voyage to Venus*. He
explains how masculine or feminine ("gender") encom-
passes far more than mere male or female ("sex"): "Sex
is, in fact, merely the adaptation to organic life of a
fundamental polarity which divides all created beings.
Female sex is simply one of the things that have female
gender; there are many others . . . the male and female of

organic creatures are rather faint and blurred reflections of masculine and feminine. Their reproductive functions, their differences in strength and size, partly exhibit, but partly also confuse and misrepresent, the true polarity . . ."[7]

The world is full of opposites. There are day and night, strength and weakness, logic and intuition. There are nature and artifice, spirit and matter; and there are male and female. Because this is the best example it is often used as a symbol for the others: earth may be seen as feminine and sky as masculine; or matter as feminine and spirit masculine; or the moon as a woman and the sun as a man. We can perhaps understand this better by borrowing from the notion of "yin" and "yang". In Chinese thinking these opposites are not categorised sexually. Night and earth, internal things, coolness and co-operation, are seen as yin. Day, heaven, external matters, warmth and competition, all belong to the yang. Feminine is also classed as yin; masculine as yang.[8] The significance of the idea is its illustration of harmony. Neither yin nor yang is good or bad in itself. What matters is the balance of these opposites, without which nothing can function properly.

This idea is also touched on in the Bible. As we shall see, there is a suggestion that God has made differences, which we call feminine and masculine as the Chinese call them yin and yang, but which are far larger than mere differences between a woman and a man. It is as if God has made principles of femininity and masculinity to express different things about Himself.

Look at it this way. God is both just and merciful. Suppose He were to make two kinds of creature, both in His image, each reflecting different aspects of Himself. Men might express His justice, for example, and women His mercy – or vice versa. In this way parents often complement each other, and give their children different images of God. But it does not follow that every man is more just than every woman, or any particular woman more merciful than a particular man. It is not so much that men are just as that justice, and men, may both be "masculine"; not so much that women are merciful as that mercy, and women, might both be "feminine". It is not really to do with individual men and women, but with certain principles which can be represented by gender itself.

If we pursue this idea further, we will find that "masculine" and "feminine" principles have different functions. For example a man represented the race in a way that a woman did not. It is in Adam we all die, not in Adam and Eve (1 Corinthians 15:22). It is in Christ we are all made alive, and Christ came to earth as a man (Romans 5:12–19). Some say He had to because of social restrictions on women at the time. Nonsense. When did Jesus care about social restrictions when important issues were at stake? This argument is as unconvincing as the claim that Jehovah revealed Himself as a male God because nobody was thinking in terms of female divinities: on the contrary, there were plenty of goddesses around at the time.[9]

There is more to this than mere coincidence. The fact that "man" can mean human beings in general, as well as a male human being, is no fluke. Nor is it an isolated flaw of the English tongue. French has the same characteristic. So does New Testament Greek. It could be argued that this, too, is simply another sexist quirk of "man"-made language. But at the beginning of Genesis we find the same idea, and this time consciously and deliberately expressed. "Adam" means the human race. The first mention of humanity goes like this: "So God made adam in his own image, after his likeness

he created him; male and female he created them."
(Genesis 1:27)

The word meaning the human race is thus deliberately
chosen as the name of the first man, as we all know. The
woman was called Life, because she is its origin: mortal
life in the form of the human race, and eventually eternal
life in the form of Jesus, are born through her. The man
was called "Humankind", because he *is* the human race.
(As Alex Motyer, an Old Testament exegete, is reputed to
have said, "In Hebrew thought man embraces woman . . .
Whoopee!!") So total is this identification of the male
with the whole race that it is hard to know when adam
has stopped meaning "humanity" and started meaning
Adam himself. The most striking juxtaposition of the two
uses of the word is in Genesis 5:2–3: "When God created
man, he made him in the likeness of God. (2) He created
them male and female; at the time they were created, he
blessed them and called them adam. (3) When adam had
lived 130 years, he had a son in his own likeness, in his
own image; and he named him Seth." It is no mere
linguistic mistake. The man, not the couple, represented
the whole human race.[10]

I am fully aware that "man"-centred vocabulary can be
used to degrade and ignore women.[11] But this is not the
fault of language so much as of male-centred thinking in
every sphere. It is true that when we hear the word
"chairman" we think of a man, not of a person of either
sex. But the same could be said of "MP", "doctor", or,
until recently, "prime minister". It is true that most of
us, when we hear of the descent of "Man", think of the
descent of a beefy, hairy hunter;[12] that when we mention
Neolithic "man" we envisage a Neolithic male. However, I suspect we would do this whatever we called the
species. Calling humanity "Man" is thoroughly biblical.
It has only become sexist because, in the impoverishment

of our language and the masculine bias of our culture, "man" has ceased to mean "male and female".

So the first human being, a man, represented the race. I can imagine steam rising out of the ears of some of my readers. Let me hasten to put the other side of the picture – for though the Bible shows ways in which the sexes are different, it also always shows, beneath the difference, a far more profound similarity. Humankind was represented by a man. But it is also, in a different way, represented by something "feminine". In its relationship to God the human race is frequently portrayed as a woman. All too often, alas, we are the faithless wife,[13] but we are also, often, called the beloved bride.[14] The way we respond to God is usually represented by a feminine image.

I know this idea might make some people even angrier. I suggested it once to a friend and she got very annoyed with me. After all, this "feminine response to God" business can be seen as more veiled sexism. By itself, one could argue, the fine, upstanding human race is masculine; in comparison with God it pales into the feminine.[15] This interpretation simply reinforces the idea that male means good, and strong, and self-sufficient, and female means sinful and weak and helpless. Some people seem determined to find any difference threatening and there is no need for such a tortured interpretation. The human race is neither fine nor upstanding on its own. It is singularly despicable on its own. It is only in its response to God, if you like when it is at its most feminine, that the human race can ever hope to be good, or fine, or upstanding.

(And perhaps at this point it should also be said that arguing God's gender is a singularly fruitless pastime. One can debate the question endlessly: God is always "He", and we are taught to call Him Father; on the other hand there are many instances of Him behaving to us as a mother,[16] and He cannot be more of one sex than another since male and female are equally in His image. And so on. But God is not any sex at all. Our gender is defined by our genitalia. How can we say that God is a particular sex? He is spirit: He transcends sexuality.)

Its relevance

Thus, as well as the obvious reproductive difference between every man and every woman, there is another, more pervasive but less identifiable difference between the principles of feminine and masculine.

And so to the more important question. What are the implications? Does this difference mean we should treat the sexes differently? It may be frightfully fascinating but will it change the way we live? The answer is no. The information is important, but not of direct practical use. There are two reasons for this.

First, as we have stressed, it is in the realm of abstract ideas, which are simply being expressed in sexual terms. It describes the principles behind gender, rather than people we know. It is concerned with the difference between masculinity and femininity, not the difference between Mr and Mrs Jones. It may tell us that a Man had to represent the human race in salvation because a man represented us in sin; it certainly does not tell us that men in general are more representative of us than women. It may tell us that our response to God can be described as feminine because Israel is described as a wife; it does not tell us that Sarah Smith is more responsive to God than Joe Bloggs. So it does not tell us how to behave towards the Joneses, or Smith and Bloggs.

Secondly, it is tentative. It is speculative. It is an idea which must be used with enormous care. Though the

Bible hints at it, it never states it categorically, and it certainly never applies it. God never says, "Because a man stood for the race so a man must stand for the country; you must have kings not queens." Nor does He say, "Because the church is my bride women make better Christians than men; you should have women doing Christian work not men." We will quickly get into trouble if we try to use these ideas, as C. S. Lewis does, to say women cannot be priests because they cannot represent God to man.[17] We could just as easily say men cannot be priests because they cannot represent the human response to God.

This difference cannot dictate our behaviour, but it is still important. Though it cannot command us, it can enlighten us. For example, if God tells us *elsewhere* that women must not be priests this difference could help us understand why not. It is not telling us what to do, but explaining why we might do it. When God comes to earth as a man not a woman this difference can help us see why, and why, as a man, He can represent all humankind. But it does not demand different behaviour or treatment for women and men.

Between the average woman and the average man

But neither of these is what is meant by the difference between the sexes. When people cry "vive la différence" they do not seriously fear a universal genitalectomy. They do not even consider the more philosophical differences. They mean all the rest. You know. Women are emotional; men are strong; girls are soppy; boys are made of puppy-dogs' tails, and so on. This is what people want to assert or deny – the popular generalisations.

A lot of them are obvious. Most men are taller and

stronger and hairier than most women. Some are less obvious. Many little girls like dolls, whereas boys often find them repulsive. Again, some of these differences are clearly and deliberately taught, not innate: in our society girls are brought up to take care of their appearance; boys are expected to be interested in sport. Some differences, on the other hand, have been with the human race so long it would take millennia to undo them: women may once have been as swift or as large as men, but they have surely been physically weaker now for several thousand years at least.

We could devote the entire book to arguing these differences – others do – and for our purposes it would be a complete waste of time. Even if it were conclusive (which is unlikely) the information would be useless because it would not answer the more important question. *So what?* Of what consequence would it all be? The answer is, absolutely none.

Its utter irrelevance

The trouble with these so-called differences is that they are sweeping generalisations. As such they are useless. We cannot discriminate on the grounds of generalisations. We must not treat all men and women differently on the basis of most women and most men.

For one thing it is unnecessary. If girls and boys are really different the differences will surface anyway. We do not need to give girls dolls and boys footballs: if we leave an assortment of toys in the nursery, the children (if they do have preferences because of their sex) will tend to choose appropriate playthings anyway. As J. S. Mill pointed out,[18] we are more likely to be fostering sexual differences because we fear they are *not* there than because we are confident they are!

For another thing, it is unjust. It may be generally true that girls are good at languages and boys at science. Is it therefore right and fair for boys to have better science teachers or more attention in the class? Of course not. *A few* of the girls may be brilliant: why should they suffer because of average statistics? Similarly, it might be possible to prove that more women than men enjoy homemaking, either because of the expectations made of them or the hormonal balance. Is it proper or logical for society to educate them for such a role or put pressure on them to adopt it? No. There are always going to be some women who do not like it at all. They are as much "women" as the others; why should they be made to feel unfeminine because they do not fall within the mean?

Someone who loves being domestic should, of course, be encouraged to run a home. This is not because she is a woman and other women have been good at the job before her, but because she, or he, has chosen it and is good at the job her- or himself. This is an important distinction. It is illogical to say (as I have heard some people do) that women should not be head teachers or barristers or vicars because their voices are not loud enough. Some women's are. On the other hand it may be perfectly reasonable to say that people with soft voices (many of whom might prove to be women) are not suitable for these jobs.

Many people think the Bible says women should not be ordained because they are not authoritative or objective enough. But some women are. If they should not be ordained it is for far better reasons. Some people think Paul says women should not teach or have authority because they are gullible (1 Timothy 2:12–14). This is ridiculous. Paul was a highly disciplined, logical thinker. If he had meant "gullible people should not teach or have authority" he would have said so.

To sum up then, there are three kinds of difference between women and men: undeniable reproductive differences between every woman and every man; a possible, almost indefinable difference between the "feminine" and the "masculine"; and probable, general differences between many women and many men. Again we ask the important question. What is the relevance of this? Can it be used, as is normally assumed, as a reason for different treatment?

The first can. It is a right and proper ground for discrimination. The biological difference between us rules some of us out for certain jobs. Men cannot be wet-nurses. Nor should they be employed to conduct intimate frisking of women. Nor can they earn money as surrogate mothers. Apart from these highly specialised forms of employment, though, there are few situations where the biological difference is relevant. I have been turned down for a role in a film because I was eight months pregnant and did not look the part. Fair enough. People who are eight months pregnant do not make very good athletes, ballet dancers, or in my case, anorexic teenagers. But when it comes to employing traffic wardens, prime ministers, nurses, miners, or indeed almost anyone else, the biological difference is completely irrelevant. It is a good reason for discrimination when it is appropriate. It is scarcely ever appropriate.

The next difference, as we have seen, is no reason at all. The difference between "feminine" and "masculine" does not dictate different behaviour or needs for individual men and women. Besides, the Bible never applies it. God suggests it exists. He never asks that it govern our behaviour.

And the third difference is more irrelevant still. Discrimination because of general and controversial observations – the usual grounds for any kind of discrimination – is nothing but unjust prejudice. Each individual must be treated on his or her own merits.

So the differences between the sexes do not mean we should treat the sexes differently. The only legitimate form of discrimination is one that common sense teaches us anyway: any fool can see that men cannot be wet-nurses. This aside, there is no reason why women should not be educated, employed, brought up and treated in exactly the same way as men.

Does this mean we have been wasting our time? If the difference between us is irrelevant, why have we spent a whole chapter on it? Actually, it is not irrelevant at all. It is important. As we said, God did not make a second man. He made a woman. There was a very good reason for it, but it was not the reason we have been pursuing.

The trouble is, we have been asking the wrong question. We have been asking how the differences might make us discriminate. We had to ask this question because everyone else is asking it, but it does not take us anywhere. Sexual distinctions, like racial ones, do not mean we should discriminate. They do not indicate that we should behave or be treated differently in any way. The question we now have to ask is: "if the difference does not mean we should discriminate, what does it mean instead?"

The answer is simple. It means we need one another. A singer and an accompanist need each other far more than two pianists do; a socket and a plug are far more use than two plugs or two sockets. We will probably never know all the differences. We do not need to. Their relevance is this: God made us different to complement each other.

We will come back to this in chapter 6. It is, after all, the central theme of this book. First, though, we will examine the other side of what we have been saying. We are obviously different. But we are also equal.

THREE

Equality

"Both sexes are equal, but one is more equal than the other."[1]

Equal in theory

We are equal. This is the second thing God says about us. Although we are different, He has given us the same value. And, biblically this is more important than our difference. Turn again to Genesis 2:18–25, the account of Eve's creation and the making of sexual distinctions. The difference is merely implied. The equality is stressed three times, and in three different ways.

It is first stated in God's purpose. He wants to make someone suitable for Adam, someone fit for him. As we have seen, the word means appropriate (page 21). She had to be right for him in every single way. In other words God wanted someone to balance Adam, to complement him, to be his partner. Someone above him or below him would not be perfectly "meet". He needed an equal.

This notion is then illustrated by contrasting the future woman with the animals. Verses 19 and 20, when God brought the other creatures to the man, is placed here as a vivid contrast. It is a graphic example of the wrong thing. The whole point of the naming of the animals at this juncture in the story is that the animals would not do. They were simply not meet. Adam was over them; he was, if you like, their "superior", just as God was his. But he was in need of help, not another creature to govern; the animals were rejected. He needed an equal.

Lastly, this interpretation is confirmed in God's method. Because the animals were not right for what He had in mind, He decided to create the man's partner in a new way. He would make her out of him. They would be naturally equal. They were made of the same stuff, the same flesh and blood. The similarity between them was profound, as the man recognised as soon as he saw her. "At last!" he said, "this is flesh of my flesh." At last he had an equal.

So the correspondence between the sexes is more important than the distinction. It is given more emphasis by the writer. This is true to our experience: striking though some of the differences between men and women might be, they are superficial when compared with the similarities. The ways in which we are the same run far deeper, and this essential similarity is what makes us equal. We are equally human, and equally valuable in the eyes of God.

How can we be different but equal? People who are different seem unequal. They may not be equally old, or dark-skinned, or good at football. And men and women are not "equal" in this sense. But two siblings can be very different, yet equal in their family standing. One is tall and blond and stupid, and the other is short, dark and clever. Nevertheless, they share the same parents, so they are equally members of the family. It is in this way that women and men, blacks and whites, the handicapped and the able, are equal. We have things in common which are more important than our differences. This lesson is taught throughout the Bible.

We are, male and female, equally good. We are equally created after God's likeness. It is wrong to suggest, as some have done,[2] that a man on his own can be in God's image but a woman on her own cannot. His image is to be restored in woman and man alike.

We are equally bad. We both disobey God, so we are equally sinful (Romans 3:23). The woman took the initiative, but they both ate the fruit (Genesis 3:6). After the act was done they were both in the same fallen state. It is also wrong to suggest that woman is more – or less – sinful than man.[3]

We are equally judged. We are equally mortal as a result of sin ("for the wages of sin is death" for everyone alike, Romans 6:23). As a result, we are considered equally responsible. I have heard a preacher say that when you marry a woman you must answer for her sins (to which a friend of mine replied that he had quite enough of his own without multiplying them by ten!). This is not biblical. As God gives us the same punishment, He considers us equally answerable.

We are equally saved. Paul makes this point in his letter to the Galatians. He is primarily talking about the difference between Jews and Gentiles, which seems to have troubled the Galatians, but he shows how salvation ignores other barriers as well: "There is neither Jew nor Greek, there is neither slave nor free, there is no male and female, for you are all one in Christ Jesus" (Galatians 3:28).

It is indeed true that men and women, blacks and whites, children and the very old are equal in the sight of God.

Equal in practice?

I doubt if many people would disagree with this. A theoretical and spiritual equality is something we now find quite easy to accept. But a belief is useless unless we act upon it. When God informs our minds it is because He wants to transform our lives. Doctrine is never of mere academic interest. If we believe we are equal we must live according to this belief. This is where we fail. I know of nobody who denies the sexes equality when the subject is being discussed. Yet I know plenty of people who deny it in the way they think and act and feel. We must change our behaviour to match our beliefs. We know we are equal; we must treat one another as such.

The Church is not good at this. The following are all comments I have heard, from different women of different churches and different backgrounds, about attitudes encountered among their fellow Christians. None of them was a woman of "feminist" leanings.

"Being a woman on the PCC is worse than being a worm."

"His (the vicar's) attitude to women is – well, awful really. Women are expected to make the tea and cook the harvest supper, but they're not expected to think."

"He (another vicar) wouldn't dream of asking a woman's opinion; they wouldn't have a contribution."

"He sort of writes off women. He thinks in terms of men. Everything's very male."

"I was never expected to have an opinion. I was never expected to think."

Clearly these people feel they are treated as inferior to men. The Christian doctrine of the equality of the sexes is, in practice, being denied. How can we overcome this?

Indiscriminate treatment?

Should we treat everybody the same? This must be the most obvious way of equalising everyone, but is it necessarily right? Parents who have several children know that loving them all equally may mean treating them differently. Because they are not the same they do not have the same needs: one will be reduced to tears by a cross word; another will grin through a thrashing. The older one might want an expensive motor bike for his birthday; the younger one would rather have a box of pencils. In loving them equally, a wise parent will treat them differently.

People sometimes look back in anger on the history of our country and say women were treated as inferior. This accusation needs careful thought. True, until this century they did not have the vote. Until the last they lost control of all their property at marriage, and so on. But this is similar to the way in which we treat children. They do not have the vote. They have no power to dispose of any property they may own. They are not allowed sexual relations. They may not go to pornographic films.[4] Does this mean we consider them inferior, less worthy of happiness, or inessential to the welfare of the country? Surely not. We regard them as important. We believe (for some reason!) that they are equally human and have equal human rights. We genuinely think their best interests are served by these restrictions. We may be mistaken, but we are sincere. Although we do not recognise them as full citizens with all the civic rights, we are certainly not trying to oppress them; we are aiming to respect them and treat them as equally valuable by giving them different treatment.

Similarly, cultures which treat women differently do not necessarily hold them in less esteem. It would be rash to assume that Victorian England (for example) did not value its women; in some ways they were looked up to as men's superiors. Nevertheless, there are a number of things which need to be said about treating people differently if we want to maintain their equality.

The first is that they must be treated *on an equal basis*. The parents who treat their children differently are nonetheless treating them on the same basis. They have not said one will be punished through life and the other rewarded; they are acting on the belief that everyone is equally in need of punishment for misdemeanour. They are disciplined differently because they respond differently. Basically, they are being treated in the same way.

This takes us on to the second point. You can only do this with *individuals*. Parents can do it because they know their own children. You cannot do the same with Jews, for example, or with women. It is mistaken to expect women to have different needs from men, and to treat them differently as a class, just as it would be wrong to say that all oldest children must be beaten, and all youngest children merely given a mild ticking off.

But the last and most important point is this: different treatment *must be reasonable*. Children are not given the vote for a reason: we believe they are not yet equipped to use it. They are not allowed sexual experiences for many reasons: quite apart from any moral considerations, they are seldom capable of saying "no" to an adult, however much they might want to.

It is true that women – and working-class men – did not have the vote two hundred years ago for a reason: only property-holding men were thought to have a stake in the nation. The question is whether this was a good enough reason; for we saw in the last chapter that there is hardly ever a good reason to treat women differently from men. Occasionally our reproductive functions preclude one or other of us from something. That is all. Otherwise there is no reason to treat the sexes differently. So there is no adequate reason not to give women suffrage. There is no biblical reason why a wife should not control her estates.

There is no satisfactory reason why women should be discriminated against in any of these ways.

We must indeed treat the sexes the same. This is the first way we should give men and women equality. We must be like God. He treats everyone on the same basis (Acts 10:34). So must we. He shows no partiality (Romans 2:11; Ephesians 6:9). Neither must we. His Justice is the same for everyone. Ours must be too. We cannot expect God to use us fairly if we use others unfairly.

I have been told by a clergyman that I do not suffer as much from unemployment as a man does. (He is quite safe in saying this: it would be almost impossible to prove him wrong. Or, indeed, right.) The implication is that it does not matter as much if women are unemployed, so we need not do so much about it. This is not treating everyone on the same basis. It is not just. I have heard another clergyman say we could solve much unemployment by preventing married woman from working. (By contrast this is so obviously true it would not need proving. We could also "solve" much unemployment by having the same policy towards Pakistanis, or people with red hair, or anyone under five foot four.) Such discrimination against people as a class is injustice, and should never be practised by Christians. We are not to be subject to prejudice (James 2:1–10). We are to be like God. We are to treat everybody the same.

If we look at the examples of sexism quoted earlier (on page 42), we can see the same tendencies emerge. Women are treated differently. For example they are not listened to in public. Many a woman has had a suggestion ignored, only to see it taken up later as a man's idea and adopted with enthusiastic praise. It has certainly happened to me. Or they are not taken seriously. Their problems are belittled or ridiculed. A friend of mine found it difficult being married to someone more successful than she. A man in her situation would have received sympathy and counselling. She was just "being silly". Again, expectations of women are lower. I was at a dinner party recently and asked my host a question about his work. Because the answer was vaguely technical he addressed it to Shaun (who, having missed the question, was mystified). One incident like this is amusing; an accumulation over the years is first disconcerting and then undermining. It makes one feel puzzled, ill at ease, and eventually simply inferior. These things are all symptomatic of an un-Christian attitude. Women are frequently treated as unequal to men by women and men alike. Sometimes they are simply ignored. A friend of mine was giving a talk for a Pathfinder service. The hero of the story was "Peter Pathfinder". I asked him why he invented a character called Peter rather than Polly, and he said it would be impossible to base the talk on a girl: the boys would never relate to her. It never occurred to him that the girls might have difficulty relating to Peter – or even, it seems, that it mattered whether they did or not.

All this can cut both ways. Just as women are sometimes expected to be all-round idiots when it comes to anything academic, so a man is often assumed to be inept at the most simple matters relating to his own family. Soon after our first daughter was born a woman in our church was playing with her when Shaun told her what his baby tended to like and dislike. She was indignant. "How would you know?" she said. "You're a man!"

All these are examples of people being treated in a particular way because of their sex. Jesus did not do this. In a sense He treated everybody differently. He would sometimes say one thing to one person and the opposite to somebody else (compare Luke 8:38–39 with Luke 9:59). He behaved towards people as if they were all unique. But He never treated a woman "as a woman", as some people do. As Dorothy Sayers said, "Nobody could possibly guess from the words and deeds of Jesus that there was anything 'funny' about women's nature."[5] He did not behave differently towards someone because of her sex. Nor must we. A friend of mine had lost her job and was receiving pastoral advice from her bishop. "Never mind," he said glibly. "God is calling you to be a woman, a wife, and a mother. You don't need to be anything else." He would never have dreamt of offering a man a similar platitude. (How do you "be a woman" anyway? It tends to happen whether you will it or not.) He was ignoring her individual need and treating her in a certain way because she was a woman. Jesus would not have done this. He treated everyone as an individual. We must do the same.

The simplest way to do so is to ask yourself, in your dealings with a woman, "Would I treat a man like that?" (or vice versa, of course). I have a friend I am very fond of, whom I tended to call on when I was working near his house. We had many interesting afternoons and conversations and meals together. He was treating me like a normal person – or as he would treat a man. A few months later my situation changed. My job ended. I also became pregnant. His attitude towards me changed completely. I was no longer an ordinary person doing a job of work ("like a man"). I was a Future Mother. Suddenly he started treating me like a woman. We seemed to have nothing in common any more: he would only talk to me about Shaun, and Shaun's work, and any other domestic concerns he could think of. It was months before I could persuade him to have an interesting conversation with me again!

We can apply this rule to any group of people we tend to treat as a class. Children are often at the receiving end of the most extraordinary bad manners: they are ignored in conversation, lied to, laughed at in public, or rushed over their food. We need only ask ourselves "Would I treat an adult like that?" to see how badly we are behaving.

We must treat everybody on the same basis. When dealing with large groups of men and women we must give them all the same treatment. When dealing with individual men and women we must give them individual treatment. This is the first way we must treat one another as equal. When Christians have learned to do this, we will have done away with almost all the sexism in the Church.

Protection

Much discrimination is unconscious. If the buttons in a lift are five foot off the ground, children (and dwarfs) cannot use it. Many groups of people are vulnerable in some way – because they are physically weaker, or in a minority, or poorer, or less articulate – so their needs are often neglected. Society tends to arrange itself around its stronger members, around the middle-class, able-bodied, white, adult, educated male. If the rest of us are to be treated as equals our interests must be protected. If handicapped people are to be treated as equal to the un-handicapped, we must have wheelchair ramps at regular intervals along the kerb. This takes some thought. We usually need to listen to disadvantaged people to discover their particular needs.

Women are vulnerable in some ways. There are obvious and terrible abuses, like rape, which women are subject to; clearly, if women are to be treated as men's equals, rape laws are very important. But there are numerous, less dramatic ways in which women may need protection, or simply consideration. A church I was in had a number of breast-fed babies. Because of the scruples of various members it was inappropriate for the mothers to feed them in church. This meant the women were disadvantaged. They might not be able to attend a church service for weeks if their babies needed feeding in the middle of a Sunday morning. Nobody was deliberately discriminating against them, or indeed treating women on a different basis, but the church should have catered for their needs (perhaps by providing a screened-off area) if it was to treat them as equals, equally in need of Christian teaching and fellowship.

Men also face disadvantages. It is often harder for them to attend church – perhaps because of an outdated image of Christianity; perhaps, under pressure to be "macho", it is harder for a man to admit that he is a sinner; or perhaps it is simply because parish timetables are arranged around those who work at home. Whatever the reason, men need more encouragement to come to church. Yet our congregation does the opposite. Each week there are three or four meetings exclusively for women. There are none for men.

So in order to treat people as equals it is not enough simply to treat them as the same, important though this is. We must protect those who are vulnerable in any way, and look to each other's interests.

Positive discrimination

I have a friend who insists he does not want to treat women as inferior. He follows this up by saying "though I won't have discrimination in their favour". Nevertheless, there is a place for positive discrimination. It must be used with great caution, and almost always as a temporary measure, but there is a place for it.

In the past, for example, engineering was considered an unfeminine subject. Women suffered a disadvantage:

they would have to cope with others' implicit disapproval and their own reluctance to be "unfeminine" if they were to succeed in the field. Obviously this is wrong in itself. It is unjust. (The fact that it is not deliberate does not make it any less so.) But there is another aspect of the situation which makes it highly undesirable. The real loser is not the individual woman. If she wants to be an engineer she probably will anyway. The loser is society. We are short of engineers, and have needlessly halved our supply. This is often the case: discrimination or prejudice may be as harmful to the society as to the individuals concerned; if we make it difficult for Africans or Indians to become doctors, we are going to deprive ourselves of good doctors.

The engineering industry has had the sense to spot this problem. In order to redress the balance some engineering firms give women particular encouragement: promising sixth-formers are invited on conferences to promote their interest in the work. Boys are not allowed. This is positive discrimination. And girls are beginning to apply for engineering in larger numbers. Firms and universities now have more good engineers.

There is a place for this in the Church. We suffer from a dire shortage of good biblical teachers. Our need is far more important than that of the engineering industry, yet we have halved the resources available to us. Women have been discouraged from studying theology or teaching the Bible. Almost all the promising young Christian men I know have been encouraged at some stage to consider full- or part-time Bible study and teaching work; I know plenty of equally competent young Christian women who have never had the suggestion put to them at all. If the Church exercised a little positive discrimination we might persuade some of them to take the idea seriously, and the benefits could be enormous. Whether or not we would allow *men* to take advantage of their skills and be taught by them is another issue (and one which we will come to later), but young Christian *women* could certainly be reaping the benefits. The engineering world has seen that talent is being wasted. It has made the effort to redress the balance. We in the Church have not.

To summarise, there are three ways we should treat people as equals. First, we must treat everybody on the same basis. Women and men should be treated the same. Individuals should be treated as individuals. This is by far the most important point. *Different* treatment accounts for almost all *unequal* treatment.

Next we need to protect disadvantaged members. Women must not be allowed to suffer because they are more vulnerable than men, or indeed men because in some ways they are more vulnerable than women. This is less important, but more likely to be ignored, so it is worth our attention.

Lastly, we sometimes need to use positive discrimination. Because of imbalances that have arisen, an individual may need particular help or encouragement. This is least important of all, and we should always be wary of it lest the pendulum swings too far the other way.

Equal in value

All these are ways of treating the sexes, or indeed anyone, as equal. They are important measures to take. In a sense, though, they do not quite get to the heart of the matter. To do this we need to approach the issue from a different angle. The essence of equality or inequality is not so much the *treatment* we give people as the *value* we put on them. The former is only, after all, an expression of the latter. The worst sexism of all is a failure to value the opposite sex.

I have a friend who is training for ministry in the

Church. Her fellow students sometimes tell her it is a shame she is not a man; and they are apt to say this when she has made an intelligent or pertinent contribution. This kind of attitude is far worse than treating a woman badly. The implication is that a man is more use than a woman. Her intelligence would be better employed in him: it is rather wasted on her!

This is worse because it is a criticism, not of women, but of God Himself. Man needed help, God said, so He made woman. To imply that men are more useful, or valuable, or make a more important contribution, is to imply that God made a mistake. He should have made another man. We could have designed the human race rather better than He did.

The most heartbreaking example of this I have heard was from a close friend of mine. He had been to a depressing and decadent party, and was burning with compassion for the people he had met.

"The only thing in life worth doing," he said with genuine feeling, "is preaching the gospel of Christ." Then he looked at his little daughter. "Next time we must have a son," he said to his wife, "so that he can do just that." In two sentences he had rendered the female sex useless.

So the heart of sexual equality, oddly enough, is the same as of sexual difference. We come to understand it when we realise our mutual need. It is enough for racial equality to follow the three rules set out earlier, and chiefly to treat blacks and whites, French and English, the same. Sexual equality goes much deeper. The races can survive without each other: the sexes cannot. And it is only when we realise this need that we will realise each other's value, and realise our equality.

Shaun and I are parents. The appearance of the thing suggests I am much more of a parent than he: I have borne them, given birth to them, and fed them for several months. Shaun merely had a few minutes of fun. My part seems more important. Yet this is a false conclusion. Shaun's contribution was different, but vital. We are both *equally* parents, because the part each played was essential. Yet society no longer treats the father as an equal parent (in reaction, it must be said, to the opposite imbalance of a hundred years ago): he is powerless to save his child from abortion (as a court case proved recently): if divorced it is far harder for him to win custody of his own children. And, sadly, I know a number of Christian women who treat their husbands as incompetent morons when it comes to the care of their children. "I can't leave them with him," they say. "He won't change their nappies", or "feed them properly", or something. But they are his children too. He has as much right to decide what they should eat or when they should be changed as she. It is quite out of place for the mother to assume this superior role, and she has only herself to blame if the father then abdicates from his job.

So this is what equality is really about. It is about recognising the other's value, the other's contribution, indeed realising our helplessness without the other. This is what it means to be the body of Christ: the eye cannot work without the brain, nor the foot without the heart. It is especially true of the sexes. It was not good for man to be alone, so God made a woman for him. She will do things differently, which is why we are indispensable to one another. Because we are both indispensable, we are equal. We must constantly bear in mind our utter dependence on the opposite sex. If we do this, it will be impossible to treat its members as inferior.

And it is this dependence we will now go on to consider.

FOUR

Interdependence

"(11) . . . there is no woman without man or man without woman in the Lord, (12) for as the woman is of the man, so the man is through the woman – but all things are of God."

1 Corinthians 11

"I was a better man to you as a woman than I ever was to a woman as a man. If you see what I mean. Now I've got to learn to do it without a skirt on."

Dustin Hoffman in *Tootsie*

The sexes are interdependent. This is the third, and most important, thing God says about us as male and female. We are designed to work together. This is the essence of the biblical teaching about the sexes.

Let us look once more at the account of Eve's creation, at the second half of Genesis Chapter 2. That we are different, and that we are equal, are implied or suggested by the writer. That man needs woman is explicitly stated. This is the heart of the account. It is the reason given for making a second sex. "It is not good for man to be alone." Man himself was insufficient.

The way this is put is striking. Over and over again, God said He was pleased with creation. He contemplated each new stage and saw that it was good (Genesis 1). When he had finished everything, including the male and female human race, He saw "it was *very* good" (verse 31). So it comes as quite a shock to hear God say, "it is not good". Something was bad. It was the only thing, before the Fall, which was. God had created the garden, the plants, and the animals; He had made man; he had given him work to do and a commandment to obey. It was what some people would think of as a haven of perfection, but it was still not good. Man needed help. God made her.

The teaching in Genesis is reinforced by Paul. Man is not independent of woman (1 Corinthians 11:11). He is born through her (verse 12); every man alive owes his existence to a woman; even the Son of Man Himself entered life on earth through a woman. In a sense, man owes woman everything. The message is quite clear: he cannot live without her; nor should he try. Man without woman is not what God intended.

His need of her is clearly announced in Genesis 2. Her need of him is not. Nonetheless, it is assumed by the text. He is to work alongside her; that is why she was made. Adam is the reason for her creation; he is her partner. And she was formed out of his flesh; indirectly she owed him her existence, as he now owes his to her.

Again Paul stresses this to the Corinthians. She is made "because of the man" (1 Corinthians 11:9). She is "of the man" (verses 8 and 12), as the man is "through the woman" (verse 12). She is not independent of him any more than he is of her (verse 11). And again the message is clear. Woman is made for man. She is not created to live in isolation from him. We are made in need of each other.

It must immediately be said that our mutual need does not mean that we must all marry. This can hardly be stressed strongly enough. Our need for each other is a biblically taught principle, but so is our freedom not to marry. Paul goes to great lengths to establish this before he talks about our interdependence (1 Corinthians 7). The fact that men and women need each other must mean something else. This is obvious as soon as we consider Jesus. He lived in perfect accordance with God's will; he is the very image of God (Colossians 1:15). Yet he never married.

Jesus's example

Indeed it is from His example, even more than from direct teaching on the subject, that we see God's design for us as male and female. There is something remarkable in the way Jesus related to members of the opposite sex. The impact tends to be lost on us because of our ignorance of Jewish society, but in first-century Palestine His behaviour was extraordinary.

By the time He was born, there was a rigid segregation of the sexes. Jewish society aggressively divided men from women. Twentieth-century "problems of communication" are laughable by comparison: first-century Jews were told not to talk to their wives at all. "Talk not with womankind," said the Mishnah.[1] "They said this of a man's own wife: how much more of his fellow's wife! Hence the sages have said: He that talks much with a woman brings evil upon himself . . . and at last will inherit Gehenna." A woman could be divorced for talking to another man.[2] Rabbis would normally avoid speaking to women at all (presumably again including their own wives). Some Rabbis today still continue this practice to some extent.[3] There was even a particularly diligent group of misogynists called the "Bleeding Pharisees": to avoid seeing women at all they walked around with their eyes fixed on the pavement; the more street corners they walked into and the more black eyes they acquired, the more pious they were deemed. Clearly the society in which Jesus lived did not believe in the sexes mixing freely. The segregation was extreme.

It is important to point out that none of this was scriptural. Any sexual apartheid which existed by the time Jesus was born was the result of man's law, not God's. So how did He react to it? Did He approve? Did He consent by silence? Did He go along with it because it was not an important enough issue to offend people over, because He had better things to do with His time than worry about sexual harmony? On the contrary, although He gave no direct teaching on the subject, the way Jesus behaved towards women was revolutionary, and sometimes shocking. Even today, His freedom and intimacy with them might raise an eyebrow. Then it must have been bizarre in the extreme.

It is sometimes said Jesus could not, in that kind of society, have chosen women as His apostles: it would have been quite improper, it is claimed, for women to have travelled and worked, and certainly lived, alongside Him. The evidence is that this did not trouble Him at all. The appearance of impropriety did not deter him in the slightest. On at least one occasion he took a number of women with Him as He travelled (Luke 8:1–3). Mary Magdalen, Susannah, and Joanna, who had presumably left her husband at home, were among the many women who went with him from town to town. I can think of Christians today who would frown at such an arrangement; then it must have seemed unprecedented licence.

Later on in His travels, Jesus stopped at Martha's home (Luke 10:38). No doubt there were others in the house, including perhaps her brother, but it seems to have been Martha who was Jesus's particular friend since it is she who is mentioned and she who welcomed him in. It was also at this house, to her astonishment, that Jesus encouraged her sister to sit at His feet and learn like a man (verses 39–42). Again no woman would normally have been granted such intimacy or, indeed, such a privilege.

This was not the first time Jesus had surprised a host with His freedom with a woman. Simon the Pharisee was shocked by the freedom Jesus allowed to the prostitute who had managed to gatecrash his dinner party (Luke 7:36–50). Despite her profession, Jesus let her kiss His feet over and over again and stroke them with her hair. Again this kind of liberty would have been unheard of between a Rabbi and even a virtuous woman. (Apart from anything else, loose hair was seen as extremely indecent.[4]) It is not surprising that Simon had second thoughts about Jesus. Many Christians today would too.

On another occasion He was touched by an unclean woman. This would have rendered Him unclean himself. When she was caught out she fell terrified at His feet, presumably expecting him to be angry as any other man would have been. Instead he praised her for her faith (verse 48). He did not seem at all bothered to have been touched by an untouchable woman.

Perhaps the most telling comment of all is the reaction of the disciples when Jesus, again most unconventionally, had a long conversation with a woman (John 4:6–30). She herself was surprised, particularly as she was a Samaritan as well as a woman (verse 8). And when the disciples came across them both, "they marvelled", not because he was talking to a Samaritan, but "that he was talking with a *woman*" (verse 27).

In all His dealings with the opposite sex Jesus was extraordinarily uninhibited. At a time when most men were ignoring women altogether except for the purposes of reproduction Jesus frequently included them in His life and work. He was prepared to depend on them for financial support and hospitality. Although He was single, and although the society around Him was extremely strict, He was easy and open with women, and allowed them to touch and even to kiss him. He talked with them, walked with them, worked with them and stayed with them. He even taught them. He revealed His identity to a woman early on in His ministry (John 4:26). And it was to women, not men, that He first made the most important revelation in history (Matthew 28:8–10, and parallels). Indeed, He ensured that they were included in the Church from the beginning by making their testimony indispensable to the apostles.

It is clear from Jesus's attitude towards women that they are not made to exist in isolation from men. Everything in His behaviour towards them militates against sexual segregation. Everything in His attitude suggests we should be in close partnership with one another. The first Christians clearly were. They worked together as brothers and sisters (Acts 1:14; 16:40, and 1 Timothy 5:1,2, just to name a few of many such examples). We should do the same.

So this is our ideal. Clearly it is not always wrong for men to be alone together, or women to meet without men. There are inevitably occasions, as there were in Jesus's ministry, when the sexes work separately. And clearly too there is a place for common decency. Just because we want schools to be mixed does not mean we want dormitories, changing rooms or showers to be so too. Just because we want men and women to share facilities at work or university does not mean that we want them to share bathrooms or loos. I hope this is common sense.

Sometimes in the name of evangelism we appeal to one sex or the other. Some churches hold meetings for men only as it is the only way they can persuade them to come and hear the Gospel. Obviously if this works it is an excellent idea. It is a form of positive discrimination:

holding meetings exclusively for men is a way of helping them overcome their image of church as for "women and children". (I know of one church, though, which holds a men's prayer meeting for the same reason: apparently they are less likely to come if women are present. Now an evangelistic meeting like this is defensible. A prayer meeting is not. Once people are Christian, they should behave in a mature Christian way!) So naturally there can be a place for men's and women's gatherings; the important thing to remember is that the segregation at such events is not good in itself. It can sometimes be a means to a good end.

Similarly, there is evidence that girls are held back, particularly in science and maths, if they are taught in the same class as boys.[5] So it may be advisable to teach them on their own. Again it needs to be said, though, that the segregation itself is not good: ideally it should be solved by treating all the pupils in the same way.

Another reason the sexes are sometimes separated is in an attempt to avoid promiscuity. This was the reason that Jewish society was so strict: the rabbis believed lust could only be controlled by hiding women from sight. But Jesus assumed that it can and must be controlled by an effort of the will (Matthew 5:27–28). Of course He is right. This kind of segregation never works. Any man who has been to a boys' boarding school where homosexuality thrives knows that sexual segregation merely results in another kind of promiscuity. Any woman who has travelled alone in a Moslem, or even strongly Roman Catholic, country knows that it is often more hazardous than being in a more lax environment.

We need to weigh each situation carefully. This teaching, that we are interdependent, could easily be pushed to silly extremes. There is nothing wrong with women going out for a meal together or men playing rugby together, or girls sharing a house. All these things are good. We occasionally need the company of our own sex, undiluted. Such activities become questionable when people start to *prefer* a single sex society, as a general rule, to one which is mixed.

This teaching could also make individuals feel unnecessarily guilty: I know of women so disillusioned by our masculine-biased society that they choose to work in female co-operatives. I know of men who have had ten years of single sex education and inevitably prefer the exclusive company of men. This is a great shame, but hardly the fault of the individuals concerned. So there are a number of things our interdependence does not mean. We are not to conclude that men and women should never be apart. Nor should we make people feel unnecessarily guilty. Aiming to work in sexual harmony does not mean these things. What then does it mean?

Interdependence

First we must *acknowledge our need* of the opposite sex. It is possible to behave as if the opposite sex is unnecessary for almost all aspects of life. Until recently, most Oxford and Cambridge colleges were monuments to that arrogance. Many businesses still are. Schools, universities and firms have been run as if women did not exist. And it is a tragedy of the feminist movement that, despairing of correcting men's follies, it falls to aping them: "These days," said Gloria Steinham, "a woman without her man is like a fish without a bicycle."[6] If she means by this that the female half of the race can exist in isolation, she is being as idiotic as ever the men have been.

Secondly, we must be prepared to *mix* with the opposite sex. Occasionally there are particularly strong reasons for not doing so, as we have seen, but these are not the norm. We should take it for granted that boys and girls are educated together, that men and women work together, and that we mix for recreation and business alike.

Thirdly we need to *listen* to the opposite sex. It is possible to work with women, and yet continue to work in an exclusively "masculine" way. Paul Tournier believes our society has put far too much emphasis on what he considers the masculine attributes.[7] About four hundred years ago, he argues, our society chose to go in a particular direction. We decided to value the qualities men tend to have and ignore those more often found in women. Some time after the Renaissance, according to Tournier, women were pushed out of public life and men began to run society; consequently they ran it for men and in a man's way. Our culture, he continues, has become increasingly concerned with logic and reason, with things and machines, with the broad scope of life without attention to the little details. We worship science. We breathe bureaucracy. We ignore people, despise intuition, and chase after materialism at the expense of the quality of our everyday lives. This, Tournier asserts, is because we value men's contributions and have no time for women's.

He may overstate his case, but his theory makes good sense. If women and men are different – and we must agree they are – our difference has a purpose. We must have different contributions to make. We express God's image in complementary ways and these two ways are equally important to His purpose.

Fritjof Capra argues a similar thesis.[8] He uses yin and yang for illustration. We can do the same; it is not uncommon to find biblical truth echoed in alien philosophies; and listening to foreign ideas sometimes helps us understand the familiar. The particular concept of yin and yang is helpful for two reasons. There is no suggestion, in the Chinese philosophy, that men ("real men") have certain attributes, and women ("ladylike" women) have others. "All people, whether men or women," says Capra, "go through yin and yang phases." So there is no implication that a woman who has yang qualities is "butch" or a man with yin qualities "effeminate" – as there might be if we said they had masculine or feminine characteristics.

More important, however, is the teaching that "what is good is not yin or yang but the dynamic balance between the two; what is bad or harmful is the imbalance". Capra's diagnosis of our society echoes Tournier's. He too thinks we have become unbalanced. He too sees excessive emphasis placed on the masculine qualities (and incidentally on the scientific and technological approach to life). Once again the problem with this is not that masculinity is not as "good" as femininity, but that, as God says in Genesis 2, "it is not good" on its own.

And of course if feminine and masculine are created by God to complement each other, it is essential that they work in harmony. Let us take an obvious example. Intuition is one of Capra's yin qualities and rationality is one of his yang ones. Since women are supposed to have more yin strengths, we may find their intuition tends to be sounder than many men's. Men may sometimes be brought up to think more logically. The observation is often crudely made: "men are logical, women intuitive." Its importance is overlooked. Reason and intuition are of very little use without each other. When Western society decided, two centuries ago, to value its own human reason above every other form of enlightenment it led, not only to a further devaluation of women, but also to the conclusion that there is no God. Of course. How can God be proved by human logic?

The limitation of masculine logic was well illustrated at Simon the Pharisee's dinner (Luke 7:36–39; 44–50). Simon's logic was not at fault. He knew the woman was a sinner, he knew she must be condemned by God; he also knew a prophet should have discernment and should judge as God would judge. And yet Jesus did not condemn the woman. There was only one possible logical conclusion: Jesus could not be a prophet.

But the woman's intuition summed the situation up better. She sensed her hopeless condition. She sensed she had good cause to mourn. And somehow she instinctively sensed that Jesus would accept and forgive her; she realised how much she would owe him, and she poured out her gratitude in love and tears and ointment. Nobody explained anything to her. As far as we know no words were exchanged with her at all until Jesus forgave her sins and dismissed her. Yet she had saving faith while Simon doubted. On this occasion a woman's intuition got the better of a man's logic.

Jesus possessed these two qualities in perfect balance. He read people's hearts with unerring intuition (Matthew 22:18), and sprung their traps with faultless logic (verses 20, 21). We should be combining these gifts in the same way. God has made excellent provision for us to do so. If one of these talents is largely found in one sex and a complementary one in the other it is clearly important that men and women work in harmony. When they do their matching gifts will harmonise.

Shaun and I have seen this graphically illustrated. If "masculine" characteristics do indeed exist, we should expect a profession dominated by men to be influenced by masculine values. It will perhaps tend to be efficient in a rather analytical, bureaucratic way. (This, according to Capra, would be a yang approach.) A field dominated by women, however, is likely to be shaped by "feminine" qualities, and may have, for example, a more personal, caring touch. (This gentler attitude would be described by Capra as yin.)

Almost everything in our society is run by men. But there is one profession which has retained a strong feminine influence. It is midwifery; throughout history most midwives have been women. If there is such a thing as a feminine approach, we are likely to find it here. Doctoring is traditionally done by men, so masculine methods, if they exist, are likely to have thrived amongst doctors. An increase in women doctors is unlikely to change this. (Like women prime ministers and executives, they have to behave like men in order to succeed in a masculine field.)

We noticed a significant difference of approach when we had our first child. We wanted her born at home. The doctors all disapproved. This is quite sensible if you view people en masse: the policy of encouraging everyone to have her baby in hospital has no doubt saved many lives; it can be safe, efficient and easy to organise. The midwives, on the other hand, were enthusiastic. Again this makes sense if you regard each person as an individual: in my case a home birth was perfectly safe and likely to be far more enjoyable. One approach deals with people in their thousands, the other with one person at a time.

This difference was noticeable throughout the births of all our children. Because they were all at home they were supervised entirely by the same midwife. And because of this they were conducted according to her intelligence, intuition and experience rather than a set of hospital rules. Medical guidelines lay down how long it is safe to be in labour; this is obviously important and useful information, but it is bound to be based on the average woman and the average labour. Our midwife, however, knew exactly how long would be safe for me. Her "personal touch" seemed infallible. She would say we needed some music. She suggested a pot of tea. She told Shaun to go downstairs and have a drink with his mother. These details would be beneath a doctor's notice; he is concerned with the technical safety of his "patients". But the details are important: a relaxed and confident mother is far more likely to give birth without complications. This approach was much more pleasant for us than the official, clinical way in which some labours are apparently organised.

There are two things which need to be said about our experience. The first is fairly obvious: this "feminine" aspect of midwifery is a good thing. When competent midwives are not interfered with, they can treat people as people and give them individual and intuitive care. Labour can be easier, less frightening and safer. If a large number of men become midwives, or midwifery becomes more institutionalised, it may lose this "feminine" characteristic. We may all be made to feel we are giving birth to our babies as machines do to sausages. This would be a great loss. We must struggle to preserve the feminine approach.

The second thing which needs to be said, though, is every bit as important. Midwifery owes a great deal to the "masculine" contribution to medicine. Men may have institutionalised labour, but they have also made it a far less terrifying, and painful, and dangerous business. Some time ago midwives may have held sway in the matter of childbirth. A great many women and babies suffered terribly under their care. A great many died.

Both contributions are vital. We were lucky: we had the full benefit of the masculine mastery of science and the feminine care of me as an individual. Both are of limited use on their own. Together, they are the perfect combination, the partnership envisaged at creation.

Again we see in Jesus's life and example the essential value of both. Because He was perfect Man (by which I mean of course perfect humanity) He had all human characteristics in perfect balance. There is a tendency in rather hearty brands of muscular Christianity to react against the "gentle Jesus, meek and mild" of our Sunday School days. But He *was* gentle meek and mild. Though He could be a ravaging scourge (Matthew 23:23–36), He was also the epitome of patience and humility (Luke 2:51). He was tough, living among wild beasts without food or shelter (Mark 1:13): but He was protective, longing to care for Jerusalem like a mother bird (Matthew 23:37). He endured a succession of tortures which would kill many hardened warriors, and was still able to think and speak clearly (John 19:26,27): but He delighted in little children, going quite against "manly" Jewish behaviour (Mark 10:14,16). He courted violent death (John 8:58,59): He cooked breakfast (John 21:12). He fought (John 2:15): He wept (John 11:35).

Throughout His behaviour we find this balance. And of course Jesus ought to contain such harmony, since God made both sexes in His image. Both feminine and masculine characteristics have their origin in Him, so we would expect Jesus to exemplify both.

We might go on to think we cannot hope to imitate this since we only have the gifts we think appropriate to our sex. But the fruit of the Spirit includes a list of qualities normally thought of as feminine (Galatians 22,23): patience, peace, gentleness, faithfulness and self-control. Christian men are to have these so-called "feminine" qualities. Perhaps we should each try to copy Jesus's blend of masculine and feminine strengths.

Where it matters most

The importance of masculine and feminine is that both are vital. Women and men should be partnering one another in everything they do.

Yet look around you. Is this what you see? We have girls' schools, gentlemen's clubs, ladies' coffee mornings, men's training colleges, Women's Institutes and Boys' Brigades. And we show great reluctance to change this. For over twenty years my father ran a boys' preparatory school. For more than half that time he battled to turn it co-ed. His experience in education had taught him that to separate girls from boys was as illogical as dividing redheads from blondes (and rather more harmful). He was resisted on all sides: governors, onlookers, and most of all the pupils themselves were passionately against it for no better reason than it had been this way for five hundred years. Ten-year-old boys lay down in the school drive in protest. What is amusing in prep school boys, is ridiculous in adults, but sadly it is often as rife: many people cling to sexual division because "it has always been this way".

And this is nothing. Every afternoon outside my window I see armies of women, their pram wheels glinting in the sunlight, mobilising at the school gates opposite. These women never get the chance to share a day's work with men. When Shaun went to theological college there was not a single female student. Those men were hardly ever able to work alongside women. From stockbrokers to infant teachers, nurses to car mechanics, people can be found in work which is the preserve of their sex. There are still many jobs in which the sexes work alone, though it is in work most of all that we are created to be together.

Work is the context of Eve's creation. It was in tending the garden that Adam needed help. "(15)The LORD God took the man and put him in the Garden of Eden to work it and take care of it." And then, two verses later, "(18) The LORD God said, "It is not good for man to be alone. I will make a helper suitable for him." It was in his labours that he was not to be alone. The Lord did not observe that Adam was sexually frustrated or lonely or unable to reproduce; He gave him work, and said he needed help. So Eve was not primarily created to be the man's friend or lover. First and foremost she was his colleague; his "helper", not his sweetheart. So segregation at work is the most serious form of segregation. Yet this is what we have. Although the law now allows both sexes to do most forms of work, custom still dictates much of our choice. Miners are men. Housewives are women. Politicians and professors are usually men. Cleaners and health visitors are women. Where is the "help" God envisaged for Adam? She is usually elsewhere, in the kitchen or typing pool.

As a result we miss out on the feminine angle. Many people, from Lysistrata to the Greenham Commoners, believe having more women in government would mean waging fewer wars; women are wary, it is argued, of sending husbands and sons to their deaths. Indeed, their influence would improve many other areas of life. Look at modern architecture. Who knows most about houses? And yet who designs most of the houses we live in? It is usually men, who spend far less time at home, who decide what our homes will be like. And we all know what the result is; my mother knows an architect who built a house with three floors and only two staircases. The examples could go on *ad infinitum*. It is impossible to know how much we have already lost by neglecting the feminine touch for so long.

How has this happened? And are we doomed to a masculine bias? If men are stronger and more forceful than women, are we bound to have everything run in a masculine way unless they are deliberately kept out of certain fields, as they were for some time from midwifery?

Tournier shows how we have become increasingly masculine in our outlook because women have been excluded from political and business life. Since our society has become industrialised and work has moved away from the home, men's and women's work has become more and more rigidly determined according to sex. Marxist feminists argue the same point. They criticise this divorce between public and private, where "public" work is recognised and paid for and "private" work is not even seen as work, and its essential contribution to the economy goes unacknowledged. In the public sphere so-called "masculine" virtues are rewarded and "feminine" ones penalised; it is no good hoping for promotion in some professions by being co-operative and sympathetic and gentle, however appropriate these qualities might be. Private work, on the other hand, requires what one thought of as feminine qualities: aggression and fierce ambition are not much use to a housewife. It is this division of labour into "men's" and "women's" work which has resulted in a widespread segregation of the sexes, and an accompanying division of masculine and feminine qualities.

Many people strongly believe in these divisions. Some say they are biblical. After all, there are two ways in which we can be interdependent. We can do the same work in different ways, by having male and female doctors; or we can do different work together, by having male doctors and female nurses (or vice versa). We can see our mutual need in terms of different contributions or different roles. Many Christians think the latter is more biblical. A man, they believe, contributes to the home by supporting it financially and imposing discipline; he needs to spend time with the family, but not nearly as much time as the mother. She contributes by feeding, loving, washing, and being a bosom and refuge from the world; she rears the children and runs the home. She needs him and he needs her; the children need them both. This is obviously a form of sexual interdependence. Is it the correct one? This is the next question we will consider.

FIVE

Work

"Home is the girl's prison and the woman's work-house."
George Bernard Shaw, **Women in the Home**.

"I don't want to play the pimp and educate her just for marriage. If I do that and she remains single then she'll just become one of those embittered spinsters. On the other hand I don't want to train her for some masculine vocation that'll take years of study and be completely wasted if she does get married."
Strindberg, **The Father**.

Shaun and I were on a weekend houseparty with some friends. Our host and hostess were talking about marriage, and giving us all some advice. Shaun asked how their ideas would work out in a family in which the woman was the breadwinner and the man the "home-maker". (Apparently "housewife" is now derogatory. Not that this is new of course: "hussy" is derived from it.) They were shocked at the idea. The biblical pattern, they said, is this: the man provides and the woman runs the home. They considered any deviation from this norm a perversion of nature; they thought it morally wrong and likened it to homosexuality.

Most of us in Western society expect men and women to adopt these roles. We assume a man's first commitment is to his job, and a woman's to her home and children. As a result she may be asked, when she has a baby, "Will you go back to work?" No one will ask this of her husband. She may face the agony, and the luxury, of choosing between work and home. He does not have the option. She will meet the child's needs first and only return to work if she can find adequate childcare. He will stay at work regardless. We are largely intolerant of the sexes "swapping roles": a man who stays at home with young children is freakish; a woman who does not is still frowned on in many circles.

Because we live in society we Christians have absorbed its assumptions. Indeed, they are often presented as biblical teaching. Some Christian books state categorically that a woman's first duty is to the home.[1]

Is this true? Does the Bible teach that there are different roles for women and men?

Before we address the question we must admit that these so-called "traditional" roles are no longer entirely successful. This is not to say that they cannot be, nor is it to deny that some couples are blissfully happy with them. But they do present us with serious difficulties in the modern world.

If earning a living is to be a man's career it is easy to prepare him for it. You train him for a job and he does it till he is sixty-five. He will probably marry and support a family but it does not matter if he chooses not to do so. His life has been a success. Of course, if he fails to find employment he is not a "real" man, and after sixty-five he is no longer seen as useful. But apart from this, the system can still work quite well for men.

If running a home and rearing children is a woman's natural sphere she should be prepared for it too. She should be taught to cook and be domestic and love babies. She will also, in this egalitarian age, be given an education – just in case she wants to become a career-girl, or find a part-time job when her children are grown up, or by some misfortune fails to marry. Nevertheless, her schooling is not seen as so important or vocational as a boy's, and her parents quietly hope she will "settle down". So she reaches her teens and marriage becomes her ambition. She shows interest in the boys. One of them is to be her ticket to success: without him, she cannot do *real* woman's work.

Now suppose she meets the man of her dreams, gets married, and starts a family. She is happy. She has "arrived". Naturally, she invests more of herself in her marriage than her husband does. His work is to earn money, win promotion, and be a success outside the home; his marriage is a pleasant bonus. Her employment, though, depends on him; her marriage is vital to her work. Without her, he would lack a little something; without him she would lack purpose and meaning and usefulness.

This puts pressure on them both, since the partnership means more to her than to him. He has to make an effort to remember wedding anniversaries, to come home when he would have liked to stay working, to make a fuss of her. She must try not to be "clingy", or jealous of his time. But they ride these minor irritations, and when the children are born the situation becomes more balanced; she spends her time and energy on them, and has her own work – as he has his. The serious problems start when their youngest leaves home. Suddenly she faces virtual unemployment for the rest of her life. She may be under forty, and her working life is over.

She is the lucky one. Another girl may not have "made it" at all. Like her sister, she wanted to marry. Unlike her brother, she was unable to do anything about her ambition. She had to wait for her work to materialise. It never did. She is not only a failure, but also out of place; she is a woman, but she is not doing women's work. She is doing third-rate men's work.

For if homemaking and childrearing are a woman's work, marriage, of necessity, becomes her aim. Not only can this put a strain on those women who do get married, but it can also have a devastating effect on those who do not, or on those who cannot have children, or whose children leave home. A man can prepare for, and do, man's work all his life. A woman's usefulness is seen to depend on catching her man. We have enslaved women in a situation from which Paul says explicitly he wanted them freed.[2]

It is also difficult for a woman to train for her working life. If she prepares for domesticity she may be disappointed all her life. If she prepares for "man's work", and succeeds and does well, she faces an impossible choice; she must either forego what most human beings long for – a lifelong partner and children – or the work she is doing so well. If she decides on some kind of compromise she may be mediocre in both roles.

In addition, our society offers those of us who work outside the home an increasing variety of choices. We no longer have to do the jobs our parents did; we can do other things if we enjoy them more. There is a lot of status in many of these jobs: by and large, the harder the jobs are to do or get, the more money they bring with them and the higher the status they carry. However, a housewife is always a housewife is always a housewife. She receives no pay. It is an easy job to qualify for (though not to do). Any woman is considered capable of it. The status is almost nil. Small wonder, then, if women are heard to say "I'm just a housewife".

And "woman's work" can be lonely work. As Genesis 2

makes clear, for most of us work needs to be a social thing.
It is not good to do it alone. One of the satisfying things
about work is the fellowship it gives us with others.
Housewives work with no one but their children and
Hoovers. The children are often at school and not their
mothers' workmates anyway. It is not much use to say they
could chat over the garden fence and pop in on each other
for coffee:[3] housewives can mix together, but they do not
work together. Two businessmen, or MPs, or miners, are
working on the same project, but two housewives are not
cleaning the same house. They share this problem with a
number of others: research students, clergymen and
gardeners, writers and road sweepers, can all find
themselves working alone; some of them, like some
housewives, can be the loneliest people in the world.

This analysis may seem simplistic and hopelessly
old-fashioned. Many girls are ambitious, successful and
accomplished. Many men do some of the household
work. But the underlying expectations are still there.
There is more of a stigma attached to spinsters than
bachelors, and to unemployed men than women. I have
often witnessed tensions resulting from the above
assumptions.

A veterinary student asked me recently if she should
throw in her training, which she enjoys and is good at, in
case she might one day get married. My best friend at
university believed women should not receive higher
education: they are likely to waste it when they have
children. A teenager told me she does not know how to
plan her future: should she take up a career at the risk of
losing it at marriage?

It is hardly surprising many people are re-evaluating.
Some women have expressed discontent. Many are
frustrated. They feel torn between work and home. They
may find a single life difficult: society persuades them

they have "failed". They can find married life worse: they may be given low status, and either stuck in domestic work which might not suit them, or doomed to mediocrity in the office because of their extra duties at home. On paper, we may have sexual equality. In reality, it is difficult for women to work alongside men.

Of course it can work well for some people. And it can work in certain cultures. In a society where no one has a choice about employment, "women's work" need not be unprestigious; where families live in extended households several women can run a house together, and those who are single or past child-bearing can look after other people's children; where polygamy is acceptable, or men have a duty to marry (as in Islam or ancient Judaism) every woman can get married. In some societies it can work beautifully. But in ours it does not.

These problems do not mean that we can necessarily abandon the roles. If, as is often taught, they are the biblical pattern, we must embrace them; but we must also make them work. It is not enough simply to tell women to get back into the kitchen. We must solve the problems which have driven them out.

However, there is one more objection which cannot be so easily dismissed. Under the present system many areas of work are dominated by one sex. This does mean the sexes are depending on one another, which is biblical: if an office is managed by men and dusted by women, both men and women are needed for the business to function smoothly. But it also means we are often segregated, which is not biblical: the men run the business between nine and five; the women clean it after six. This division is not God's plan for us. Jesus did not encourage it. Yet it is exactly what we have created. Men work largely with other men; housewives work on their own. The work is bound to be impoverished. Governments are run along masculine lines. Homes are dominated by femininity. Business standards conform to men's ideas. Children are moulded and shaped by women. This is a more serious charge. It is difficult to see how this shortcoming can be solved at all if men and women are to be in completely different spheres of work.

But we must leave the problems on one side for a moment and return to the question. Are these supposedly "traditional" gender roles designed by God?

NATURAL?

Your reaction to this question may well be a "gut" reaction. You may "feel" it is right; you "sense" it is proper. If pressed further, you may say it is "natural". Our feelings, our instincts, are not necessarily to be despised. They often tell us when something is right or wrong. On the other hand, they can also easily lead us astray. If you are angry with someone it may feel right to give him a black eye: this is also "natural", but it is seldom right. The fact that we are moral beings means we are capable of moral decisions: if we are to decide whether something is right or wrong we must examine and question the "natural".

Poor Nature is often given rather vague responsibility for a great many things. What exactly do we mean when we say it is "natural" for women to be domestic, to rear children and to run the home?

The animal kingdom

We may mean "natural" is what the animals do. I have heard this argument used to persuade women to care for their children. "Females of other species do it" the

argument goes, "so human females should do so too."
The fact that females of many other species totally ignore
their young is overlooked. So too is the fact that females
of some species eat their lovers after the sexual act[4] – I
have yet to hear this practice recommended as "natural".
Other animals do all sorts of things. In many species, it is
true, the females look after the young. In others it is the
males who have this responsibility.[5]

However the argument is not wholly ridiculous.
Amongst non-human primates (by which, of course, I
mean "monkeys", not "archbishops"), the group of
species considered nearest to our own, the care of
individual infants is almost exclusively the work of the
mother. She carries, suckles, feeds, loves. The males
merely tolerate.

Can this lead us to the conclusion that we must do the
same? Does it mean it is "natural" for us too? One could
conceivably argue this, but where do you draw the line?
Male gorillas and chimpanzees do not provide for the
females or the young. They do not recognise their own
offspring or show them particular affection. A male
orang-utan or gibbon may mate with one female one day
and another the next; if he is "top ape" he will probably
enjoy them all. Are we saying that this is "natural" and
therefore recommended for us too? And why, of all the
animals, should we choose to copy the apes? Other
species may be far worthier to set us an example.
Whereas apes are promiscuous, swans show a lifelong
faithfulness to their mates. Surely we would do better to
take our standards from them – yet swans share the care
of the young equally between cob and pen.

The trouble is, of course, we are turning God's creation
upside down if we start judging our behaviour by the
animals'. Yet this is what people are doing when they say,
as I have heard them do, that certain gender patterns are

"natural" (and therefore right) because they are found in the animal kingdom. Human dignity has sunk low indeed if the creatures who were put under us have become our teachers. If we decide what is right or wrong on the basis of animal behaviour, like a parent asking a baby for moral guidance, the whole of creation will be in a mess.

Human behaviour

What is "natural" could also be understood to be what human societies do. If women look after children in every culture perhaps we can conclude that it is natural because it is universally practised, and therefore essentially human. I have been told that every society enforces the sixth commandment in some form: there is a worldwide taboo against murder, though murder may be variously defined. If all peoples also have the same gender roles there may be a good reason for it.

But all peoples do not have the same gender roles. Alaskan Eskimos share the care of the children equally between mother and father; for them it is no more the woman's work than it is the man's. Male Cheju Islanders care for their children while their womenfolk go out to work.[6] The same is true of the Alor Indians.[7]

And which particular "universal" or "natural" trends are right? No doubt aggression and greed are found in almost every culture. No doubt they are often rewarded (as indeed they are in ours). Are they therefore good? We find the same problems in imitating other societies as we have in imitating the animals: which particular society do we choose as our model, and which of its qualities are we to value?

Again, of course, we are turning God's plan upside down. Just as it is degrading if we humans take our standards from the animal kingdom, so it is foolish if we Christians take our standards from non-Christian cultures. We are "not of this world" (John 17:16). This does not mean that we are not to be involved with this world, but we do not have to take our standards from it. We are not to be moulded by human mores (Romans 12:2). We are to be salt (Matthew 5:13). We should set the standards. The reason we do not kill is not because others think it wrong, but because God has spoken. The fact that others think it wrong too is an interesting incidental – no more. We decide what is right and wrong by what God has said, not by what others do. So this argument is as invalid as the first.

Biology

The third possible meaning of "natural" is what our bodies, our biology, can teach us. If God has created us a certain way it is because he expects us to function a certain way. This would not be taking our standards from others but from God himself. So what does biology tell us? That one man and one woman are necessary for conception. And that a woman will bear, give birth to, suckle, and incidentally quite often die from the birth of a baby.

That is all. It does not tell us who will clean the house. Or who will care for a three-year-old child. Or who will change the nappies. Nor indeed who will bring home the bacon. We assume that the parent that bears the child must do all the other things for it because that is how our society is structured. We also assume, for the same reason, that the other parent will earn money. Neither of these norms is biologically dictated, or "natural" at all.

Our biology also tells us a man can father twenty

children, by different women, at once. And that a
woman can bear children from different men. And that a
father can ignore his children, yet they can survive. It
tells us he can kill a woman with his bare hands. Or
impregnate her against her will. And so on. Do we
really want to be dictated to by our biology? We are very
foolish if we think that because something can be called
"natural" it must be right. Of course, the truly natural
must have been right, but the whole of nature is now
fallen, and we are not to be enslaved to it. God has given
us a moral law so that we can be freed from our fallen
"natures".

So whatever Nature says – and what she says is by no
means clear – we are free from her dictates. We are free to
make up our own minds on the basis of what the Bible
says. It is only there that we will find the answer.
Whether something is "natural" or not is quite beside the
point.

BIBLICAL?

So what does the Bible say? Are certain types of work
more suitable for one sex than the other?

Let us define, for convenience, three kinds of work.
"Breadwinning" is providing money or its equivalent
means to live; since industrialisation, Western middle
classes have largely considered this to be man's work.
"Homemaking" is turning this money into food and a
pleasant home; again, in recent history we have considered this to be woman's work. And "childrearing" is
caring for children; this can easily be combined in our
society with homemaking but not with breadwinning. So
it is also thought to be woman's work.

It is important to realise that these assumptions are

recent ones; they became necessary when work moved away from the home. Until industrialisation, work was not rigidly divided in this way. Men and women alike earned a living and ran the home.[8] And it was not until after the Second World War that a woman was likely to have the sole care of her children.[9] Many people think these roles are "traditional" or "universal", so there is a subconscious tendency to expect to find them in the Bible. But they are not. They have been with us for about two hundred years. If they appear to be in the Bible we must examine our interpretation carefully, in case we are making the kind of assumptions we noted in Chapter 2.

Genesis 3

The only biblical passage which might suggest that "breadwinning" is the man's job and "homemaking" and "childrearing" the woman's is the second half of Genesis 3. The woman and the man have disobeyed God's word and He pronounces judgement:

(14) The LORD God said to the serpent,
      "Because you have done this,
          cursed are you above all cattle,
          and above all wild animals;
      upon your belly you shall go,
          and dust you shall eat
          all the days of your life . . ."

(16) To the woman he said,
      "I will greatly multiply your pain* in
                                    childbearing;
          in pain you shall bring forth children,
      yet your desire shall be for your husband,
          and he shall rule over you."

(17) And to Adam he said,
  "Because you have listened to the voice
            of your wife,
   and have eaten of the tree
  of which I commanded you,
   'You shall not eat of it,'
  cursed is the ground because of you;
   in toil* you shall eat of it all the days
            of your life;
(18) thorns and thistles it shall bring forth to you;
   and you shall eat the plants of the field.
(19) In the sweat of your face
   you shall eat bread
 till you return to the ground,
  for out of it you were taken;
 you are dust,
  and to dust you shall return."
Genesis 3, Revised Standard Version.
(*"pain" and "toil" – which can also be translated as "labour" – are the same word in Hebrew.)

At first sight there seems to be an assumption here. The woman is cursed in her sphere, the man in his. Her "labour" is having children. His "labour" is tilling the ground and getting food from it. I have heard people interpret the passage in this way. God expected woman to be doing one thing and man another. This is what it might seem to suggest. But it suggests this to us largely because it is how our society is organised. If we read the passage more carefully we can see that the expectation is not there at all.

The two curses are not on the woman and the man in their spheres of work, their "labour". The curses are on the snake and the ground. The snake's curse is addressed to the snake (verses 14 and 15), and the ground's curse to the man (verses 17–19). The curse on the snake need not concern us here.

The curse on the ground is a curse on us all: the whole of creation is under it and we all suffer from it. We all die (verse 19). The man does not endure this any more than the woman. It is not a punishment on him in his sphere of work; it is a punishment on us all. It is simply *addressed* to the man. There is, as we shall see, a significant assumption here; but it is nothing to do with work.

The woman, on the other hand, receives individual treatment. She is given a specific punishment. Childbirth will be painful. This is relevant to her alone; nothing else in creation seems to be affected. She will suffer as much as the man from the curse on the ground; in addition, she will suffer her own punishment, presumably because she disobeyed first.

There are two assumptions here, though not about work. The first is that women have babies. Now I know of no one who seriously disputes this. We must confess they are better designed for it than men. But there is no assumption about housework, cooking, home management, or even child care. God, like our biology, says nothing about the nappies. However, when God assumes women have babies we jump to the conclusion that they run homes and families too. This is ludicrous. Everybody knows women have babies. It is all the other jobs we are trying to find out about, and there is no mention of them here.

The other assumption, though, is often missed. God addresses to the man the curse which affects us all. Not to the whole of creation, or even to the man and woman together. Only to the man. The assumption is that he is responsible. It is because he fell that the whole world is fallen (verse 17). He represents the world. This follows the point made in chapter 2, that the man was deliberately named with the name of the human race. He stands for us all. It is not clear whether this was God's original plan or the result of the Fall; now, though, the man is addressed in place of all of us.

Whatever the implications of this may be, they are nothing to do with work. They do not tell us about the man's particular occupation. We all eat in toil. We all find life a struggle. We all go back into the ground, and we all return to dust. The animals also suffer and die. We all find work spoilt by this curse: it is frustrating, unpleasant, and often meaningless for us all. There is no assumption that the man does any more work, just as there is no assumption that he is going to do any more dying. So there is no suggestion in these verses that "work" is a man's responsibility, and "domesticity" a woman's.

So what does the rest of scripture say? It is often thought that the overall biblical picture is that women do indeed run homes and care for children, and men provide for them. These roles are often vaguely connected with the idea of the man being the "head of the household". If pressed, no one seems quite sure what the connection is. As we shall see in a later chapter the idea of a husband's "headship" is often associated with a number of concepts which are not biblical at all. One of these is that "headship" is something to do with making money. This idea is not found anywhere in the Bible. An unemployed or incapacitated man can be fulfilling his duties as a husband and a father just as faithfully as a man on £20,000 a year. The biblical teaching that a husband is the head of his wife has nothing to do with breadwinning.

So let us see what the Bible says about each form of work – breadwinning, homemaking, and childrearing – in turn.

Breadwinning

Is this a man's domain?

We must immediately acknowledge that a woman who

earns money or works for a living is not condemned in the Bible. Lydia was a businesswoman. She is described as "a dealer in purple-dyed [clothes], and a worshipper of God" (Acts 16:14). There is no indication that this is strange, or dubious, or unwomanly. Nor that being a businesswoman and worshipping God are incompatible. Nor that when she was converted to Christianity she changed her lifestyle and became more domestic. (Nor, incidentally, that she was a widow or unmarried. Her household was baptised with her, as the jailer's was with him (verse 33). It is sometimes assumed with spectacular male arrogance that because her husband is not mentioned he did not exist – no one makes the same assumption about the jailer's wife!)

Priscilla was a tentmaker (Acts 18:3). She and her husband Aquila were in the trade together; the account specifically says "*they* were tentmakers by trade". This is how Paul became friendly with them: he was a tentmaker too, so the three of them worked together. Again, there is no suggestion this is inappropriate for a wife and a Christian, or that she would have been better employed running a house or caring for children.

Lydia, presumably, provided for her household. Priscilla and Aquila earned money together. These women are in no way criticised for the work they do. However, neither are they held up as examples for us to follow. There is a difference between tolerating the occasional businesswoman and expecting or even commanding women to provide for their families. After all this is surely what men are told to do. Paul says "anyone who does not provide for their own people, and especially their family, has denied the faith and is worse than an unbeliever" (1 Timothy 5:8. I am afraid I have sacrificed English grammar for the sake of a more accurate translation of gender). This is usually taken to mean that a man must provide for his wife and children. In the context this meaning is forced, to say the least.

For one thing the Greek has no suggestion of the sex of the person described. To translate it as "he" throughout (as is normally done) is to assume that then as now men were thought of as the providers. A few verses later Paul shows that this is not his assumption.

For another, Paul is not thinking in terms of exclusive "nuclear" families. He is saying Christians must support widowed mothers and grandmothers (verse 4). He is not talking about a man working for his wife and children.

Lastly, Paul makes clear that he expects women to provide for their families. Indeed he commands them to do so. "If any believing woman has widows [related to her] let her relieve them, and not let the church be burdened" (verse 16). Those of us who are able-bodied are to support those in our family who cannot support themselves. We are not to sponge off the Church (or perhaps in our case the state). Women are in no way exempt. They are to provide for their families.[10]

But the best example of biblical expectations of a married woman is found at the end of Proverbs (31:10–31). She is called the "good wife". She is the ideal. She has all the best qualities a wife could ever have. (It is amusing, because of this, that people sometimes quote this chapter and say, "You see! the ideal woman is domestic." This hardly follows: she is the good *wife*, not the good woman. The ideal husband would also be seen in terms of his domestic contribution since this is what would make him a good husband.) So if a man were to dream up the best wife money could buy, this, according, to the Bible, is the woman he would come up with.

I am reminded of a recent talk about men's and women's roles. By and large the audience believed a good wife stays at home while her husband goes out to work. We turned to this passage. Members of the audience were asked to read it through carefully and say what struck them about her. Which of her qualities is most often mentioned? What seems to be the talent for which she is valued most?

There was a stunned silence. One could see most of them coming to the same conclusion.

"She works."

"She earns money."

"She trades."

It is impressive. The ideal wife is a working wife. Her husband trusts in her "and he will have no lack of gain" (verse 11), presumably because her business deals are successful. She buys a field and plants it "with the fruit of her hands", money she has previously earned. She is strong (verses 17 and 25). She is diligent (verse 27). She gets up early in the morning (verse 15), and works well into the night (verse 18). She negotiates with merchants (verse 24), sells them her own produce (verse 24), and makes sure she is making a good profit (verse 18). She is generous (verse 20); she can afford to be. She is a worker.

The first thing that is said about her is that she is valuable (verse 10): her husband will never be poor (verse 11). The last thing said about her is more noteworthy still. "Give to her the fruit of her hands," says the writer, "and let her works praise her in the gates." Let what she earns be her own reward, and the work she does her own eulogy. The ideal wife is a working wife.

We must not be anachronistic. Of course this does not mean careerists are praised and housewives condemned. Housewives are some of the hardest workers in the world. Nor does it mean women, or men, must rush out to work in droves and leave their children inadequately cared for. The "good wife" did some of her work at home; and besides she had a house full of servants (verse 15). But it does mean that "breadwinning" is a feminine role. It means that women are expected to earn a living. It means that they, like their husbands, are to support their families.

So much for breadwinning.

Homemaking

What about "homemaking"? Which sex, in the Bible, is expected to run the home? Is it the man or the woman who is to manage the household affairs?

There is no doubt that a woman is to care for her home. She is responsible for the welfare of her children, her guests, and her employees. Again the "good wife" of Proverbs 31 is exemplary. She provides food (verses 14 and 15), clothing (verses 21, 22), and work (verse 15) for her family and her servants.

Paul, in his letters to Timothy and Titus, is unequivocal about the duties of married women. A widow is not to be supported unless she has performed certain duties, which include showing hospitality and bringing up children (1 Timothy 5:10). He goes on to say a married woman should rule, master, or be the head of her household (verse 14).[11] To Titus he says young women should be taught to love their husbands and children and to be "home-workers" (Titus 2:5).[12] Since we do not know what the household work would have been, or how many servants the women in Titus's church would have had, we must assume they were to ensure that their houses were smoothly run. Like today, for some women this probably meant doing every chore themselves, for others (like the woman in the Proverbs) it meant ensuring that the work was done by employees or servants. It is not clear precisely what work each woman would have done. But it is clear that a married woman is considered by the biblical writers to have a duty to her home. She is to make sure it is properly organised, well managed, and hospitable. She is to be a "homemaker".

So is a man. One of a married man's duties is to see that his household is managed. Like a woman, he is also to run the home and bring his children up properly (1 Timothy 3:4). Paul specifically says that he is not fit to be an elder (or bishop) unless he copes with his household duties (verse 4). He then says the same thing all over again with reference to deacons (verse 12). If we took these commandments more seriously, quite a few of our clergy might be defrocked!

This is remarkably similar to what he has said of a woman. It is clearly a married man's responsibility, as it is a married woman's, to organise his household. This does not necessarily mean each husband and wife must perform identical functions. To a large extent this depends on the culture and personality. I, for example, cannot pack. Neither can my father. Nor could my grandmother. We depend on our spouses to do this for us. Some Arab couples I used to teach assumed that men should do the shopping; they would not have dreamt of exposing their women to the public eye. Until recently, many English couples would have assumed the opposite. We do not know how Paul's readers would have divided the household jobs. It does not matter. The point is that both sexes are responsible for the home. They are both to manage it, rule it, and make sure it is well and hospitably run. Married men and married women alike are to be "homemakers".

Childrearing

Finally what about the most important job, the care of the children? Who is responsible for them? Are they largely the work of the mother, as our society has for some time assumed? We have already touched on their care in discussing the running of the household. Women are to "bring up children" (1 Timothy 5:10). Men are to manage, or care for, or rule their children (1 Timothy 3:12),[13] and have them in subjection (verse 4). Again, we are not told what this will entail. Different things will be appropriate for different cultures. The important thing is that both are responsible.

But it is in the Old Testament that we find the bulk of the teaching about mothers and fathers. When it comes to the duties of respective parents the differences are imperceptible. *Hastings' Dictionary Of The Bible* says "the constant co-ordination of father and mother in such passages" (references to parents in the Bible) "practically" (i.e. in practice) "places the mother on the same level as the father with regard to the children".[14] Throughout the Old Testament mother and father are mentioned together, or in the same way (for example "honour your father and mother, that your days may be long in the land . . ." Exodus 20:12). Both are to be given honour and respect (Leviticus 19:3; Deuteronomy 5:16). Both are to be obeyed (Proverbs 6:20; 30:17). Both parents teach and instruct their children (Proverbs 1:8; 6:20; 4:1; and 31:1). As Hastings says, "the utmost respect and obedience to both father and mother are insisted on".[15]

If anything is equally shared between the sexes it is the duty of being a parent. Again, this does not necessarily mean both parents do the same for their children or even spend the same amount of time with them. However, their care, discipline, and teaching is the job and responsibility of both.

There is not the slightest suggestion, when we are told to multiply and subdue the earth (Genesis 1:27) that one job (multiplication) is the responsibility of one sex, and the other (subduing) the responsibility of the other. The idea is not a biblical one. There is no biblical reason why the woman not the man should wash the clothes or do the shopping, or why the man not the woman should earn the higher or only income. In fact one could go so far as to say that these ideas are often anti-biblical. They are responsible for many men's abdication from their God-given work of running their homes and caring for their children. They are responsible for many women's feelings of guilt at their natural desire to work and provide for their families.

Before we conclude there are one or two important things which must be said about our labour. We are all created to work. So we all have a duty to work. But we do not have a duty, or indeed a right, to a *career*. This is a totally unbiblical concept. We are expected to do an honest day's labour and support ourselves and others. We are not expected to scramble for a place in the rat-race, put in overtime instead of coming home to our husbands or wives or children, and agonise over whether we are in the most fulfilling job possible. Plenty of men have sacrificed their families to their careers. If women start doing the same they will merely be adding one disaster to another. We are to *work*, not be promoted or successful or careerist.

As we have seen, there are different kinds of work. It can be paid (breadwinning) or unpaid (homemaking, childrearing, and of course voluntary work). For some time now our society has equated "work" with breadwinning. Those who are not paid to work are assumed not to work. As a result people are sometimes asked the absurd question "Do you work, or are you a housewife?" A previous vicar of ours honestly believed that seventy-five women on the electoral role "sat at home all day doing nothing". The distinction made is not between work and idleness, but between a pay packet and lack of it.

This attitude is disastrous. Those who fail to secure the wages are made to feel unproductive. Christians must fight this wholeheartedly. The "unemployed" must be supported in any work they do; whether it is housework or helping neighbours, mowing the lawn or writing poetry, it must be taken seriously as work. Increasingly, housewives also need this kind of support. This is where feminism has sometimes failed. Women who stay at home to raise a family are given little encouragement: they are doing unpaid, sometimes lonely, and usually exhausting work. Consequently they often suffer depression brought on by low self-esteem, fatigue and "loneliness, frustration and boredom".[16]

Christians must never allow housewives or the unemployed or the retired to feel inadequate, insignificant or guilty because they are not being paid. The involuntarily unemployed support their families with money from the state to which they are entitled as members of it; nobody should ever be made to feel a "failure" for providing in this way. Housewives support their families not only directly by the work they do, but also indirectly by freeing their partners to work full-time. Nobody should ever be allowed to feel inferior for giving this kind of provision: housewives do some of the hardest, most important, and often most unrecognised work in the country.

Conclusions

What does all this mean in practice? The most significant implication is the wide range of choices it gives us. Society can be a tyrant, and on this issue it has done its best. My brother tells me that where he lives (amongst Oxford intelligentsia) it is not really acceptable for a young mother to stay at home. Where we live (North London suburbia) it is barely acceptable to do anything else. I realised this when I visited him carrying a baby on my back; I was introduced to an academic who asked me "What do you do?" Such a question would be inconceivable where we live in Persil Country. Wherever one lives one is liable to be bullied by expectations. These are not necessarily biblical, and when we realise this we can cease to be dictated to by them.

Some friends of ours recently wanted some advice. They had postponed the idea of children because he had been hoping to study for three years. His plans had fallen through; he would not be able to do the course for several years, if at all. Should they wait so long to start a family? Should they contemplate it now? They were put off by the uncertainty of his position: he had taken a job but might lose it at a moment's notice.

But her job is completely secure. She is a doctor. So in fact there is little problem. If he is still working when the baby is born she can either leave medicine and become a housewife, or stay at work and employ a nanny. If he loses his job they will not be able to afford help, but then he will be free to stay at home himself and look after the baby while she returns to work.

This latter choice had not occurred to them, although it is a perfectly legitimate one. It is just as much his job as hers to bring up the family. It is as much her job as his to provide for them. Because she has secure and well-paid work he will be set free to stay at home if he wishes. Of course this choice, like others, is not without its hardships. Society does not encourage the option: if he takes his child into a public lavatory to change a nappy he will find no facilities to help him. Christians may not be supportive either: some will tell him categorically that he is abdicating from his "headship". And he may well find his task frustrating and even humiliating (as many women have before him) so he will need support and encouragement from his partner, just as many women do.

Another couple we know, on the other hand, have made a different choice. They are both highly qualified scientists, and they have two tiny daughters. They too each have a duty to bring them up, to manage the home, and to provide. It would be difficult for both to do all three. They have made the conventional choice: she is a housewife and his work continues as before. Temperamentally they are well suited to this, and they had no reason to opt for anything else. Yet this too is not without its difficulties. She will never again be as high-powered as he. He may not be as close to the children as she. They have halved their income; she has a low status; he is no doubt tempted to work long hours and neglect his other duties; she will need appreciation and company from him since she may not get enough from anyone else. And so on. These difficulties can also be overcome, but he will need to give her much of the support which society has taken away.

It is often the parent who stays at home who has the harder time. This is particularly true of certain professions. Some housewives undoubtedly have more rewarding jobs than their husbands. Others experience considerable frustration, even if to work at home was a voluntary choice. So the "breadwinning" partner has a responsibility to the other. He (for it is still usually he) must provide much of the company, stimulation and support other people tend to receive from their colleagues.

It is not always necessary for either parent to be the sole housewife. A lecturer at a theological college near us shares her job with her husband. They both teach, and they both look after the children. In many ways this is ideal: both are enjoying the wide variety of work for which they were created; the children (and indeed the college) are getting the benefit of both, including the different contribution each sex brings to a job; and they will be able to understand each other's setbacks and joys at work. They are true "helps" to one another.

There are many possible combinations, and we often give ourselves unnecessary problems by conforming to certain patterns. A couple told us of their dilemma about starting a family. She is a solicitor and he a clergyman.

She is reluctant to become pregnant because she is fond of her work. It would be almost impossible to find part-time work and difficult to return to law after some years' break. Someone asked if it had occurred to them to get an au pair or home help.

He objected. "You can't push your children out on others."

"You wouldn't be pushing them out," it was pointed out to them. "You work at home most days. You have afternoons free because you work in the evenings. You could look after the children much of the time. The au pair would free you to work, but you'd often be around if you were needed. If you still disapprove, *you* could work part-time. It would be easier for you than for a solicitor!"

He laughed. "My mother would be horrified!" he said. Again, it had not occurred to them that they had so many options.

We have not addressed ourselves to the question of nannies and childminders. It is not the place of this book to do so. The Bible does not tell us much about them, other than suggesting that Rebekah was closer to her nurse than to her mother (Genesis 24:59). Despite this, many people think parents who employ professional help are abdicating from their responsibility. This may sometimes be the case but is not necessarily so. There are three things which need to be pointed out.

First it is preferable and biblical for parents to be the main influence on their children. Their upbringing is chiefly the responsibility of the mother and father. This is a God-given responsibility, and for those of us who have children it is perhaps more important than any other work we do. There is no excuse, for men or women, for neglecting our children because we have taken on other work which is too demanding.

Secondly, though, parents are never going to be the only influence on their children unless they live on a desert island: grandparents, godparents, teachers, and society itself are also responsible. Schools have a large part to play. The good parent is not necessarily the one who minimises other influences – for example by teaching the children at home – but the one who chooses it with great care. The same applies to nannies, au pairs and childminders.

Thirdly, being a good parent cannot necessarily mean being a full-time one. It is impossible for every parent to be full-time: someone has to earn a living. A man can be a superb parent even if he only spends evenings and weekends with his children; the same must also be true of a woman. So it is perfectly possible for parents to employ professional help in caring for their children and still to be the best of parents.

Christians sometimes talk about "different roles" for the sexes. It is thought that the Bible says we have particular parts to play. No one seems to know exactly what those different roles are. People are either vague about them or else claim, as biblical, certain rather dated cultural trends.

But "roles" is a misleading word which means different things to different people. Some people mean we have different contributions to make. This is absolutely true. God made us different to complement one another. But other people mean we have different jobs to do. This is false. The Bible does not suggest different work for the sexes. Except for those which are biologically defined in reproduction, the tasks are not different for women and men; the ways of doing them may be different. We play our respective parts by doing the same work in different ways, we do not need to know what the respective roles are. They will come quite naturally to us because they depend on the way we are created.

Are there any exceptions to this? It is sometimes thought that in two areas, the Church and the family, God has given the sexes particular and different duties to do. Let us look at these in turn, beginning with the Church.

SIX

Authority

"Woman taught once and ruined all."
St John Chrysostom[1]

MAGISTRATE: I'd rather die a thousand deaths than obey someone who wears a veil.
LYSISTRATA: If that's all that's bothering you, here, take my veil, wrap it round your head and shut up.[2]

I must confess I am uncomfortable writing this chapter. On certain topics in this book the Bible is clear. On some (sexual difference) it says little. On others (interdependence) it leaves us to apply the principles. On a few (marriage and singleness) we are given practical, unambiguous commands. On this topic alone, the teaching seems opaque if not downright contradictory.

It has traditionally been understood to say that women cannot have authority over men. But society now says that they can. Women are trained, educated and expected to do jobs the Bible has been thought to forbid. And they have proved themselves competent. Some women, like some men, are clearly gifted in positions of leadership. They can teach and govern and direct. If the traditional interpretation of the Bible is right then these particular skills should not be used. It is difficult to know what to make of this: to us it seems like a waste.

We have also learned to accept certain inconsistencies. We tolerate women in schools, business, and Parliament, but when it comes to preaching or parochial administration we go into paroxyms of verse-quoting indignation. We accept a woman as Supreme Governor of the Anglican Church, with authority over every man in it. Yet we baulk at a woman running a parish. Again this is confusing. Why should talented women be allowed to run the government or publish works of theology, but not preach the gospel? Why should the world, not the Church, be allowed the full benefit of their skills?

I find myself, I suspect like many others, caught between the devil and the deep blue sea. The Church seems to be ignoring abilities, embracing double standards, and presenting a sexist image. I am bound to appreciate a society which allows my sex to lead government. I naturally feel deeply uneasy when I hear people say women should not lead the church. I cannot help noticing a few women who would make far better vicars than some of the vicars I know. And yet there are Christian leaders I greatly admire who say the traditional view is right.[3] The last thing I want is to be in disagreement with them, but I have yet to be totally convinced by their arguments. The last time I heard a sermon on the subject, the speaker made three points: first, women have an important ministry in the Church; second, they must be encouraged to exercise it more than they have been in the past; and, third, we have no idea what it is since they cannot do anything involving authority. I have heard from several eminent Christians that women have a vital contribution, different from a man's. I have never yet heard what that contribution is. It seems to me we have more thinking to do. I do not know if my interpretation is right either, but perhaps, at least, it will contribute to the debate.

There are three possibilities. The first is that women should never, under any circumstances, have authority over men. That is, at a glance, what the Bible seems to say (1 Timothy 2:12). Yet I know of no Christian since John Knox[4] who has had the courage to say so: after all, it would mean we should object to policewomen, women doctors, the Prime Minister and indeed the Queen.

The second possibility is that there is more than one kind of authority. There is "secular" authority which women may have over men: they can be monarchs and generals and surgeons. And there is "spiritual" authority, which they may not: they should not preach, run a church, lead a Bible study, or even pray or prophesy if to do so involves authority over men. This is the position many Christians have adopted.

The third is that God makes no sexual distinction when it comes to authority. He can give it to people regardless of sex (or race or skin). If this is true, then those who object to women's ordination on the grounds of authority are mistaken.

So we must ask whether God allows women authority over men. If He does, we must then ask what kind of authority it is.

The nature of authority

We cannot consider the question until we have a biblical understanding of authority. There are three things we must get clear.

First, authority comes from God (Romans 13:1). Most people assume it comes from man. Authority gets confused with an "authoritative" personality. Some people are born authoritative, as others are born red-haired.

This is a good quality in a leader but it is not the same as authority. Authority comes from above. A soldier, no matter how "authoritative", has no authority over his commanding officer. Both men are under a higher power, and if one has command over the other it is because he has been given it from above, not because he has a forceful personality. So authority is like grace. It is not something we have by nature or right. God can give it to anyone, and sometimes he gives it to people who seem wholly unsuitable (Exodus 3:11 and 4:10,13; Judges 6:15). He can even give it to people who do not have qualities of leadership at all.[5]

Secondly, it is given for a purpose. Moses was given authority to lead the people out of Egypt; the apostles were given it to preach the gospel; at one point seventy disciples were given it to cast out demons. It is always given to do a job of work. So two people can have authority over each other. When you leave your place of work, your boss loses authority over you. If he plays in the cricket team you captain, you sometimes have authority over him. There is nothing contradictory in this. And two people can have authority over each other simultaneously. A man may be ordained in his parent's parish: he and they will both, in their respective roles, have authority over each other. The Queen may submit to Prince Philip as her husband, while he submits to her as his monarch. The authority goes with the job and "you salute the uniform, not the wearer."[6]

And thirdly that job is servile. True authority always involves service. If you have authority over someone it is for his or her benefit not yours. You must put their interests first; you must become like a slave. Jesus was given all authority in heaven and on earth, and He knelt down and washed our feet. Those of us in authority must be prepared for the most unpleasant and humiliating of jobs; one of the first tasks a parent learns, after all, is to change a baby's nappy.

When we have a biblical understanding of authority, we can see a number of things.

Authority can be given to anyone: it does not depend on personal qualities. That some men may or may not be more "authoritative" than women is neither here nor there. That some people may find it harder to obey a woman is the most irrelevant of objections; you would hardly be prepared to face a court-martial because you think your sergeant-major lacks a bossy enough personality. You "salute the uniform".

All authority is "spiritual". It all comes from God. A traffic warden or a prime minister ultimately receives power from Him (Romans 13:1-7). Anyone disobeying an individual within the confines of that authority is disobeying God. It is a spiritual matter.

Authority is not something we are born with. It is not part of our natures, an abstract quality endowed on some of us for no reason. No man simply "has authority" except Christ Himself, its origin. So it is unbiblical to suggest that authority resides in one sex or the other. God gives it to us for a purpose and to do a job. Men will not have some vague or permanent authority over women. Whether husbands have authority over their wives is another question, and one which we will turn to in the next chapter. If so, it will be for the particular job of loving their wives and will not affect the issue any more than a mother's authority over her sons or a queen's over her subjects: neither of these relationships suggest that women in general have authority over men.

And authority is not enviable. This is the last and most important implication. If God never asks women to exercise authority this should pose no threat to us at all. Because it is given as a responsibility not won as a prize, having authority does not mean we are better people than those who are "under" us. Because it goes with a job and does not rest in a person it does not mean we are any more important in ourselves. Because it means slavery to those in our care it is not something we need ever covet. It is perfectly possible to believe God never gives authority to women without abandoning the biblical doctrine of the equality of the sexes.

Now we can address the question. What kind of authority, if any, does God allow women over men?

WOMEN'S AUTHORITY – CAN WE FORBID IT?

Scattered throughout the Bible are a few verses which suggest limitations on women's authority. It is usually these, rather than the broad sweep of scripture, which cause people reservations. They are not numerous, so we can look at them each in turn.

Genesis 3:16

The first is Genesis 3:16. It is after the Fall. God is telling the woman the consequences of her actions. Childbirth will be very painful, but she will desire her husband and "he shall rule over you". The comment is sometimes taken as an indication that women are not to be in charge: God specifically gives men authority over women for the rest of time.

In fact the verse implies no such thing. For one thing, God tells Eve her husband will rule over her: there is no suggestion that every one else's husband will too. Your mother rules over you: does that mean every other mother in the world should too? This verse is set in the context of marriage; and it does not necessarily refer to the relationship between the sexes in general.

For another thing, there is no indication whether this arrangement will be good or bad. We do not know whether the man's rule is a merciful provision or a disastrous result of the woman's sin: whether God has just arranged it or is merely warning her it will happen. (If you shoot yourself you will die: you can hardly say I am killing you simply because I have warned you what may happen.) The suffering in childbirth is God's work (as he says) yet we use all our scientific knowledge to overcome it. We do not know whether the husband's rule is God's work or not, but it is assumed we cannot improve upon it. We give women drugs for the pain of childbirth, but nod approval when their husbands rule over them. This is illogical.

So Genesis 3:16 tells us that a husband will rule over his wife. It does not tell us whether he should or not, and it does not say that men in general will rule over women.

Isaiah 3:12

The next text in question is Isaiah 3:12, sometimes translated as follows: "Youths oppress my people; women rule over them." The context of this verse is a list of disasters. Women in authority are seen as another misfortune of the people and a sign that they have turned against God. The situation is clearly seen as undesirable.

But to argue from this verse that women should never have authority over men is to stretch the text to breaking point. Isaiah is referring to Ahaz, the contemporary king. Ahaz was probably twenty when he came to the throne (2 Kings 16:2) and strongly influenced by his mother and the other women of the court. Isaiah frequently criticises him; he saw the kings as weak and compromising, and the whole nation as idolatrous (see, particularly, Isaiah chapters 1–8). It is as if a prophet in the 1940's had said, "Germans oppress my people". He would not necessarily mean a German should never have authority over a Jew.

God is not saying that young men, and women, should never be in authority. No criticism is implied of Josiah because of his age ("Josiah was eight years old when he began to reign . . . and he did what was right in the eyes of the LORD." 2 Kings 22:1,2). Timothy was another young man; and in Paul's first letter to him, in which the apostle clearly expects him to command and teach in the church, he tells Timothy to let no one look down on him because he is young (1 Timothy 4:11,12). And yet if we understand this verse in Isaiah to be saying women should not have authority we must also understand it to mean young men should not have authority. We cannot use it to question a woman's authority without also questioning Timothy's authority.

In any case, the verse is sometimes translated completely differently: "Money-lenders strip my people bare, and usurers lord it over them". One text (the Hebrew) talks about youths and women. Another (the Greek translation, the Septuagint) mentions money-lenders. Scholars and translations disagree as to which version should be preferred.[7] So we could not rest any case on the basis of this passage anyway: we cannot have Christian doctrine founded on an uncertain translation of one text.

1 Corinthians 11:3–15

The next relevant text is in 1 Corinthians 11:

> (3) . . . but I wish you to know that every man's head is Christ and a woman's head is the man, (or

"husband") and Christ's head is God. (4) Every man praying or prophesying with anything over his head shames his head, (5) but any woman praying or prophesying with an uncovered head shames her head, because it is one and the same thing as a woman who has been shaved. (6) Because if a woman is not covered, let her be cropped as well, but if it is a disgrace for her to be cropped or shaved, let her be covered. (7) For indeed a man ought not to cover his head, being the image and glory of God, but the woman is the glory of a man (or "husband") (8) because man is not of woman, but woman of man; (9) for indeed man was not created because of the woman, but woman because of the man. (10) Because of this the woman ought to have authority (or "power") over the head because of the angels. (11) Nevertheless there is no man without woman or woman without man in the Lord, (12) for as the woman is of the man, so the man is through the woman as well, but all things are of God. (13) Judge among yourselves: is it appropriate for a woman to pray to God uncovered? (14) Does not nature herself teach you that, indeed, if a man wears his hair long it dishonours him, but if a woman wears her hair long it is a glory to her, because the long hair has been given to her as a covering?

Pauls's message here was no doubt crystal clear to the Corinthians. To us it is like mud. Hardly a commentator approaches the passage without some excuse or apology; it is common to claim that this is the most obscure passage Paul ever wrote.[8] The interpretations are numerous. Some say all women should be "covered" by a man's authority.[9] Many have believed women should wear hats in church. One has recently asserted that women should have longer hair than men.[10] All this should make us wary: as with the verses in Isaiah, though for a different reason (here it is not the text's reading which is in doubt but the interpretation), we should be slow to claim anything dogmatically from a passage over whose meaning there is so much disagreement. However there are a couple of things we can say with reasonable certainty.

Women do have authority to pray and prophesy (verses 5,13).[11] Praying in public means to some extent representing the church to God. Prophecy is harder to define: it is not always easy to know what is meant by New Testament prophecy, but it surely involves bringing God's word to his people. It is for upbuilding and encouragement (1 Corinthians 14:3). It edifies the whole church (verse 4). It convicts. It judges (verse 24). It necessarily implies some authority over its hearers: when God speaks, we must listen. So women can have a certain kind of authority over men.

And they are to have authority over their heads (verse 10). In "popular" interpretations of the passage this verse has often been grossly misunderstood. Paul says a woman "ought to have authority . . ." Whenever this Greek idiom is used, in the New Testament or anywhere else, it always means possessing authority. It cannot mean being under authority. Even the most conservative scholars[12] insist that the Greek cannot be twisted into such a meaning. Such a "grammatical distortion of exousia" (authority) "to mean not power . . . but powerlessness" is condemned by commentators.[13] M. D. Hooker criticises interpretations in which exousia "is . . . given a very strange meaning, since the head covering is not being understood as a symbol of authority but, quite the reverse, as a symbol of subjection."[14] W. M. Ramsey called such an abuse "a preposterous idea which a Greek scholar would laugh at anywhere except in the New Testament, where (as they seem to think) Greek words

may mean anything that the commentators choose".[15]
No reputable scholar takes this sentence to mean a
woman must be under someone else's authority. The
only authority mentioned in the passage is that which is
hers. Whatever we make of the rest of Paul's argument,
we can be sure there are occasions when a woman
"ought to have authority" (verse 10).

For the purposes of our present enquiry it is not necessary to examine this passage any further. When seen as
restricting women's authority it is usually because of a
misunderstanding of the Greek idiom in verse 10.
Nevertheless, it is interesting to pursue Paul's idea. He
says a woman should "have authority over her head".
What did he mean by this and why is it so important?

We must read the passage in the light of the first
premise. *"I want you to know"* he insists (verse 3), that
man's head is Christ, woman's head is man, and Christ's
head is God. If we forget this series of metaphors we
are likely to miss his entire meaning. Throughout the
passage we must be conscious of the meaning of the
"head" which Paul has taken such care to establish.
When the man's head is referred to, we must remember
his head is Christ. When the woman's head is mentioned, we must remember her head is the man.

In verse 10 Paul tells us "the woman should have
authority *over her head*". He has told us unequivocally
(verse 3) that her head is the man. Surely he is telling us
therefore that the woman ought to have authority over
the man?

And, indeed, when one pursues Paul's argument
carefully it is not difficult to see why. What does he tell us
about the man? First, his head is Christ (verse 3) and,
second, that he is the image and glory of God (verse 7).
As we saw in chapter 2, man and woman represent the
race in different ways. In Genesis 2 (to which Paul is

referring in verses 9 and 12) man stands for the whole human race; his very name means "Humankind". It is in this sense that he is God's glory. He is His representative on earth, and the crown of His creation.

So, Paul tells us, man should not cover his head (verse 7). This is logical. He is God's glory. To cover his head would presumably be to hide that glory. When a man prays or prophesies (verse 4) he should not cover himself and thus hide the glory of God. And man's head is Christ. Unlike the woman, he should obviously *not* have authority over his head. He should not cover himself, because this would shame his head (verse 4).

So much for the man. He should pray to God uncovered. What about the woman? Again Paul establishes two things. First, her head is the man (verse 3); secondly, she is man's glory (verse 7). She presents a different aspect of the human race. She is the crown of man himself, the glory of the glory, as it were. As (dare one say it?) the more glorious member of mankind, she shows forth its glory. After all, says Paul, she was made for man, just as mankind was made for God: she was made as his glory, as we were all made as God's. As one commentator has said, "Of all the lovely things in this world of beauty, the loveliest of all is a woman. In a world of beautiful things which proclaims God's love of beauty, she is the crown."[16]

So, Paul says, she should be covered in worship (verses 5 and 6). Again this is logical. She is man's glory (verse 7). If she is praying or prophesying (verse 5) she should not be glorifying the human race. She should cover herself, lest she give glory to man, not God. In addition, her head is the man. Whereas it would be quite inappropriate for him to have authority over his head, the woman, according to Paul, *should* have authority over hers.

It is not difficult to see why a woman should have

authority over her head. Anyone praying or prophesying must do so with the appropriate authority or not at all. If a woman has distractingly lovely hair[17] the men in the congregation, in particular, are likely to be concentrating not on God, but on her; not on the divine, but human; not on the message, but on the messenger. Clearly this is wrong. She must have command of her congregation if she is to proclaim God's will. Let her hide her own glory, and have authority over her head, the man.

It is hard to see how this passage restricts women's authority. Any careful reading points us in the opposite direction. The only authority mentioned is the authority of the woman. And that authority would seem to be over the man, her head: there are times when women must have authority over men. So the authority in this passage cannot legitimately be taken to be authority *over* the women. Verse 10 does not speak of her subordination at all.

1 Corinthians 14:34–35

But this does give us problems three chapters later! If nothing else, Paul has surely been endorsing women's vocal contributions. They can hardly pray or prophesy without speaking. And yet we read:

> (34) As in all the churches of the saints let the women in the churches be silent, for it is not allowed for them to speak, but let them be subject, as even (or "also") the law says. (35) But if they wish to learn anything, let them question their own husbands at home, for it is a shame for a woman to speak in church.

Again we must be careful. This passage is almost as ambiguous as the last. It offers at least six interpretive problems in about as many lines.

First there is a textual question mark over these verses. A few manuscripts reproduce them later in Paul's argument (after verse 40), which might make the emphasis slightly different.

Secondly he quotes the law; but he does not say which one. Bibles with cross-references usually mention Genesis 3:16. There is no good reason for this. Presumably it is done because no other text fits better. Nowhere does the Old Testament say that women should not speak; it is certainly not to be found in Genesis 3:16. Nor, as we have seen, does this verse say women *should* be subordinate (simply that they will be), but if it did, it is not clear how this would support the case. Subordination does not easily suggest silence: you are subject to your parents, but I hope you talk to them. There is no law in the Old Testament relevant to Paul's argument.

Then he does not say to whom the subordination is to be. It is automatically assumed that he means subordinate to men, or perhaps to husbands. Again there is no good reason for this. If he had said "men should be subordinate" we would never have dreamt that this would mean subordinate to women. Paul may be talking of subordination to God. Perhaps he means subordination to the Church?

Fourthly, we do not know which women are included. All of them? We know some were not married (1 Corinthians 7:8); how can they ask their husbands? Or does he mean only married women? We know some were married to non-Christians (1 Corinthians 7:13); how can they ask them questions about the faith? Or only women with Christian husbands? Why should they be silent and not the others?

And what kind of speaking is forbidden? "Laleo", the word Paul uses, can mean idle, empty chatter; perhaps the women were simply gossiping. But Paul also uses "laleo" throughout the letter when referring to the spiritual gift of languages; this usage, some say, would make him unlikely to use it for something so trivial.[18]

And lastly, of course, these verses seem to contradict the assumption three chapters earlier. How can women pray or prophesy if they are not allowed to speak? To resolve this, as some do,[19] by saying that they can speak as long as they do not exercise authority makes little sense. In chapter 11 he says they *should* have authority. Here he says they should be absolutely silent, not simply quiet or respectful.[20] This is the most puzzling problem of all.

The trouble, of course, is that we rip these sentences out of context and apply them to an issue they did not address. That is why we have such difficulties with the sense. Here, Paul is not concerned with the rights and wrongs of women in authority, as he was to some extent in chapter 11. Throughout chapter 14 he is talking about Church order.

The Corinthian services were a riot. They were babbling in unintelligible languages (verses 6–12). They struck outsiders as crazy (verse 23). They all came with different contributions (verse 26). Several people would speak at once (implied, verse 27). They even brought their dinners to the communion table and some of them were getting drunk (chapter 11:20–22). We would never call it a dead church, but it was a hopelessly chaotic one. Paul was making a perfectly reasonable attempt to check the spontaneous racket and confusion which would erupt in place of a sober Sunday service.

So grow up, he says (verse 20). Don't talk languages which no-one understands. Build the church up. Do things for edification. Don't have more than two or three people speaking languages, and don't let them all talk at once. Let someone interpret. If no one can, let the language speaker "be silent in church" (almost exactly the phrase he uses to the women). Don't have more than two or three prophecies, and then think about them and weigh them up. And if someone else gets up to say something "let the first (speaker) be silent". It is all common sense and decency. And don't let the women chatter interminably, as they could when they sat apart from the men and were not taking part in the services. Don't let them interrupt with endless questions they could just as easily ask at home. Paul implores them, "Let all things be done decently and in order" (verse 40). This is the context of verses 34 and 35. As Calvin said, "The discerning reader should come to the decision, that the things which Paul is dealing with here, are different, neither good nor bad; and that they are forbidden only because they work against seemliness and edification."[21] In the light of this can we resolve our earlier questions?

First, the textual uncertainty need not really concern us. We certainly would not wish to dismiss these words in verses 34 and 35 as un-Pauline since they appear in every manuscript. If they were indeed written after verse 40 this makes little difference (though it would render even more far-fetched the already unconvincing explanation that the women can speak as long as they do not judge the prophets.[22])

Secondly, why did he quote the scriptures if they did not support his case? In Pauline usage, "the law" does not necessarily mean the Torah, the first five books of the Old Testament, or even the Old Testament as a whole. Sometimes it can mean a secular law, or even an accepted custom.[23] Here, in fact, he is quoting a non-biblical rabbinic law. He repeats almost verbatim a tradition of the Pharisees: "It is a shame for a woman to let her voice be heard among men."[24] The suggestion he is making is that "even" or "also" – in addition to common sense or decency – "even (non-scriptural) law says you should be quiet". He is not quoting the Old Testament at all.

So, thirdly, he is not referring to subjection to men. Nor does he suggest it. The most natural reading is that women should be subject to the Church, and to church order. After all this is the only subordination which would suit Paul's purposes and induce the women to be quiet. In the same way, those who speak in languages must submit themselves to the Church, and to the interpreters. Those who prophesy must also submit themselves to the Church, and to those who judge.

Similarly, women should submit to the Church. It is reasonable for Paul to tell them to be silent, just as he tells prophets and speakers of languages to be silent when they, too, are being disruptive. It is part of the mutual submission of all of us to one another (Ephesians 5:21).

But it is not reasonable of us to take this as a contradiction to his earlier assumption that women will pray and prophesy. Women are not *always* to be silent, any more than the first speaker in verse 30, who is told to be silent in church, is expected never to speak again. We cannot push Paul's words to such extremes or we will find ourselves with absurd questions like "can unmarried women speak since they have no-one to ask at home?".

Some understand Paul to be saying here, on the basis of Genesis 3:16, that women as a rule should be in subjection to men. This is not the case. He does not refer to Genesis 3; he does not mention subjection to men; he is insisting on orderly services for "God is not a God of tumult but of Peace" (verse 33).

So far we cannot say that God restricts women's authority.

1 Timothy 2:11–15

But the passage which persuades many people that women should not be in authority is still unexamined.

It is the last and most frequently quoted text on the subject:

> (11) Let a woman learn in quietness and all subjection, (12) but I do not allow women to teach or use authority (or domineer) over a man, but to be quiet, (13) for Adam was formed first, then Eve, (14) and Adam was not deceived, but the woman, being deceived, came into sin; (15) but she will be saved through childbirth, if they remain in faith and love and sober holiness. (1 Timothy 2:11–15)

At last something directly on the subject! It looks as if Paul has specifically addressed himself to the question of women's authority. And the prohibition seems clear enough. The text certainly appears to say that women, at least in church (since corporate worship is the context) should not have the authority over men.

The popular understanding of the passage goes something like this. Women should quietly give way to men and never be in charge. This is argued from creation and the Fall, so it is not culturally conditioned, and it is still binding on us today. There is even, for good measure, a suggestion thrown in that women's proper occupation is not trying to take over the men's role but being loving and good and having babies.

On closer examination, however, this interpretation is not without its problems. It leaves a number of questions unanswered.

What does verse 15 mean? Some take it that good Christian women will not die in childbirth. History can quickly prove this wrong. The Greek wording suggests that women will be saved by having children. Common sense and the rest of the gospel tells us that this must be nonsense. The traditional interpretation does not adequately account for this verse.

Then, we can see that Paul argues something from creation. But what? The fact that Adam was formed first does not seem to support his case. It is possible that his seniority implies authority. But this is not immediately apparent here, or even hinted at in Genesis 2: the animals' seniority over Eve certainly suggests no such thing.

Lastly, her deception seems even more of a red herring. Is she more culpable than Adam because she sinned in ignorance, while he knew what he was doing? Surely not. As we have seen, it was Adam not Eve who was blamed for the fall of the world (1 Corinthians 15:21,22). Even less likely is the idea that Paul thinks all women are gullible. It is patently not true. And if this were his argument we should have to allow any exceptions, any discriminating women, to have authority after all.

So it is a little too facile to claim that Paul must be talking about permanent gender patterns because he mentions creation and the Fall. We must discover *why* he mentions them. What is he saying about Genesis? What point is he illustrating, and how?

It is also all too easy in this "straightforward" interpretation, to ignore one or two details of the Greek text which might be significant.

Paul says he does not allow a woman "authority" over a man. But what kind of authority does he mean? He has not used the noun (the "exousia" of 1 Corinthians 11:10) which is normally translated as "authority". Here he uses the verb "authentein". This word appears nowhere else in the New Testament. Elsewhere it can refer to a prostitute's authority in the latest techniques of sexual naughtiness.[25] If this is what Paul means it is hardly surprising he is unenthusiastic about it. Many believe a better translation would be "domineer". The noun from this verb originally meant suicide or murder, and the verb still had the suggestion of "self-willed arbitrary behaviour".[26] So a woman should not be bossy. But neither should a man. No Christian is to lord it over another (Mark 10:42–45). Church leaders in particular are not to domineer over their flock (1 Peter 5:3). It should not surprise us then that women are also told not to domineer. And it does not necessarily mean they should never have authority over men if they are mature and responsible about it. In other words, it can be argued, "the manner in which the wife should not instruct her husband is the subject dealt with. It is not the question of instructing or teaching him, but the manner of doing it."[27]

This quotation brings us to another point. The words given as "woman" and "man" can equally legitimately be translated as wife and husband. The words "wife" and "woman" are the same in Greek, as are "man" and "husband". (There is another word for man which can also mean mankind; it is not used here.) The sense of these words is determined by the context. Unfortunately in this case the context does not make it clear. The mention of Adam and Eve may suggest Paul is thinking of a "wife" and "husband" though the fact that he has been talking about men and women in general (verses 8–10) might imply that he means "woman" and "man".

Most translations tamper with the text slightly in order to enforce the latter meaning. The Greek is: "I do not permit a woman/wife to . . . have authority over a man/husband." The RSV translates this: "I permit no woman to . . . have authority over men." This suggests a different situation: no longer two individuals (who may have a particular relationship) but a blanket prohibition on any woman having charge of a group of men. (Small wonder if it sounds, from this translation, as if women should not be Church leaders!) The Good News version similarly changes both words to the plural, thus moving from the individual to the universal. However, not allowing a wife to domineer over her husband is very different from never allowing a woman authority over men. The former may be all Paul means.

There is another characteristic of Paul's wording, however, which is not lost in translation. It so clearly throws doubt on the traditional application of the passage that I am astonished it is not usually mentioned. Paul says he "does not permit" (or "is not permitting") a woman to do so-and-so. He is not saying that it should never be permitted. Whether he is talking about women or wives, sexual licentiousness or authority in the pulpit, wholesome Christian leadership or selfish domineering bossiness, in his words to Timothy Paul does not forbid it. He does not tell us to forbid it. He does not say it is wrong. He simply tells us what he does. It is descriptive, not prescriptive. An observation, not a command.

Come now, you may protest: that is splitting hairs. No it is not: not at all. If we have any kind of belief in the inspiration of scripture, we must surely believe its wording is inspired. Paul was perfectly capable of saying "they must not have authority" or "do not let them have authority". He does not. He says, "I do not permit it". What we have here is an account of Paul's practice. He tells us what he did in the circumstances of the time. It is not necessarily what he would do today, or what he would have done in his own day had the situation been different. He does not tell Timothy he is necessarily to follow Paul's example.

Now of course we are to imitate Paul. Of course we must follow his example. Of course, as an apostle, he is a model for us. But we are to imitate him *intelligently*. We are not all to be single (1 Corinthians 7:7b). We do not all speak in languages (1 Corinthians 12:27–30). We know this because he says so. But different circumstances can make us depart from his practice too. Paul sent an escaped slave back to his master (Philemon 10–16). If we lived in the eighteenth century Deep South we would not necessarily do the same. He told Timothy to drink wine as well as water (1 Timothy 5:23). Living, as we do, in an age when alcoholism can be crippling, we might not necessarily insist that all Christians do so too.

We must of course be very careful of this kind of hermeneutics. We want to be obedient to scripture. If we start saying God's people avoided certain practices only because of current cultural taboos we may soon (albeit illogically) be allowing adultery, occultism, homosexuality, and even stealing from the DHSS or the tax man. But we must be careful in the other direction too. If we believe unthinkingly that because the apostles did something then we must too, we would have to conclude that no Christian should eat black pudding because the first Christians were not to eat blood (Acts 15:29).

There is clearly a wide difference between God saying, through Moses, "you must not commit adultery", and saying, through Paul, "Take a little wine for the sake of your stomach". We need to work out which kind of statement this one to Timothy is. It will help to know why Paul behaved as he did, and what he was conveying to Timothy; whether he intended a permanent restriction on the Church, and if not, why he said these words at all.

Let us attempt to look at the passage afresh. When you read it before, what struck you? What, to your twentieth-century Western eye, was the statement which seemed most memorable and important? I imagine it was that a woman should be quiet and submissive and not "teach or have authority over a man". This is what we think of when we mention this passage; it is this pronouncement for which it is well-thumbed. In a society which is beginning to take for granted women as professors, judges and prime ministers this is bound to jump at us out of the page as the heart of Paul's meaning.

But this is anachronistic. It ignores Paul's main concern. What was likely to have been going on in Timothy's church? Consider this:

"It was debated whether or not a man should give his daughter a knowledge of the Law . . ."

"Not only was a woman not to be instructed in the Law, but the rabbis made it explicit that her obligations to it were limited."[28]

Women could depend upon men for guidance: "The husband seems competent to transmit the knowledge of the law to his wife." (Hypothetica 7:14)[29]

These attitudes were not unusual. It never really occurred to anyone that women should be taught: "Women were not subject to education in the ancient pagan world. Although the Greeks had the highest standard of culture, they did not educate their women."[30] The Jewish rabbis went further, expressly forbidding women any direct access to God's law. They are not commanded to study it, says the Talmud, which then continues "the wise men have commanded that no man should teach his daughter the law for this reason, that the majority of them have not got a mind fitted for study, but pervert the words of the law on account of the poverty of their minds. The wise men have said 'Everyone that teacheth his daughter the law is considered as if he taught her transgression'."[31]

Rabbi Eleazer added, "Let the words of the law be burned rather than given to a woman."[32]

This is the context in which Paul wrote. These are the assumptions of his day. It is hardly likely, in view of this, that Timothy's church would seriously have been considering a teaching or authoritative ministry for women. Indeed "rabbinic prohibitions even ruled out a mother's teaching the Torah to her own children".[33] It would surely not occur to them that women would take any important part in the life of the Church at all.

Now read Paul's words again:

> Let a woman learn quietly in all submission. But I do not allow women to teach or have authority over a man, but to be quiet. For Adam was formed first, then Eve, and Adam was not deceived, but the woman was deceived and entered into sin; but she will be saved through childbearing, if they remain in faith and love and holiness with sobriety.

What is the heart of his message, the surprising – even extraordinary – idea, indeed the only *commandment* in his words to Timothy here? Why, *let a woman learn!* This is what is important. At last the barriers are down (Galatians 3:28); even women can be full, baptised members of God's covenant. And the equality must go all the way. They must indeed have access to God's law and learn along with the men (as, indeed, they did in the past before men started adding to God's commandments – for example in Deuteronomy 31:12).

When we realise what would have struck Paul's contemporaries on reading these verses, rather than what strikes us in completely different social context, the whole passage suddenly makes sense. Everything falls into place.

"Let a woman learn", Paul is saying. What immediately follows now sounds like a caveat. She must do so "quietly and submissively". Indeed anyone should learn quietly and submissively; rowdy pupils are a thorough nuisance. And "I do not allow a woman to teach or domineer over a man, but to be quiet". Of course. Most women at the time were ignorant, illiterate and strangers to any form of education. It would be thoroughly inappropriate for them to teach or have authority. Paul is being reassuring.

He is firmly, but very gently, insisting that women learn; nevertheless, he is not going berserk. He says he does not use them as teachers or leaders (although in fact he sometimes did, as in the case of Priscilla and Phoebe). Not yet: it would be crazy, as anyone who thinks about it will realise.

Now he returns to his real theme. Let a woman learn. Why? "Because Adam was formed first, then Eve . . ." The traditional interpretation is that Adam, not Eve, came first, so he not she must be in charge. The Genesis writer does not suggest this. Nor in fact does Paul. He does not say "Adam . . . not Eve", but "Adam . . . *then* Eve". Look at the sequence of events in Genesis 2. God made Adam (verse 7). He commanded him not to eat out of the tree (verse 17). *Then* he made Eve (verses 18–22). As far as we know, she did not hear directly from God the warning about the tree. Presumably she only heard through Adam. She may not even have received the information accurately (Genesis 3:3). Similarly, many women in Paul's day would only pick up what teaching they could glean from their husbands. But the result of this was disastrous: ". . . and Adam was not deceived but the woman was deceived and entered into sin". So, from now on, let a woman learn! Teach women as well as men.

Alternatively, Paul may simply be drawing attention to the fact that Eve was created at all. As we have seen, contemporary men behaved largely as if women did not exist. But after Adam came Eve, says Paul: "Adam was formed . . . then Eve". Mankind did not stop at man. Jewish education was conducted as if it did. The importance of learning had long been recognised, and rightly so: to some extent it is what our spiritual lives depend on; we cannot obey God unless we know what he has commanded. But it had only been recognised for men.

Paul's insistence on Eve's creation reminds us that women exist too; they need teaching just as much.

Either of these interpretations is reinforced by the next verse. Eve was deceived. This is an inevitable result of ignorance. So she sinned. This is the result of deception. The solution is obvious. Let women *learn* and they will not be so easily deceived. They will be better equipped to recognise sin. Paul's logic is clear. Teach the women. And teach them directly, not just through their husbands. Let them have open access to God's word.

He sums up with what is almost an aside to his argument. His mind is still on Genesis, but now on chapter 3. Sin came into the world through woman. "But she will be saved through childbearing." He is surely thinking on to the promise of Genesis 3:15. Salvation will also come into the world through a woman, through the birth of the Christ to a young girl or virgin (Isaiah 7:14). And that salvation is available to all, to men as well as women, "if they" (there is no gender here) "remain soberly, in faith and love and holiness". So in case we should be tempted to blame women because their ignorance helped cause the Fall, we should be quick to thank women because their childbearing helped bring salvation.

Paul may even see this as an additional reason for their learning: creation, the Fall and redemption all argue for women's spiritual education. She was made, as man was, so she should learn. She was deceived, as man was not, so she must learn. She gave birth to the Son of God Himself, as man could never do, so she is even entitled to learn; what excuse could we possibly have for keeping the mother of Jesus in ignorance?

This, I believe is the correct interpretation of the passage. Paul is one of the few men of the ancient world to insist on women's education. He argues it logically and consistently from Genesis, and does not impute back to the Old Testament a meaning which did not appear to be there.

Seen in this light, verse 12 is almost in parenthesis. It is still there and we must not lightly ignore it, but we may apply it differently now we can see Paul's real concern. There is often tension between God's ideal at creation and what the restrictions of society may make desirable; so Moses allowed divorce, and Paul, prepared to oppose Peter in order to abolish circumcision, still had Timothy circumcised. We can see this tension illustrated by the fact that, some years earlier (1 Corinthians 14:35), Paul had suggested that women asked their husbands for answers to their questions. The ideal is that they should be properly taught like the men. Until they are, and to avoid the assemblies getting out of hand, let them also be helped at home by their husbands.

Paul insisted on a slave's obedience. Yet it is generally agreed that it was the underlying principles in the New Testament which eventually overthrew slavery and made his words unnecessary. Can we not hope for the same for women? He was cautious about their leadership, but dare we not believe that the principles he laid down about their equality and the importance of their education might, some day soon, render such caution superfluous?

Summary of the texts

None of these passages definitely prohibits a woman's authority. The one which most strongly suggests restrictions is the last one. Yet even with this text there are other possible and equally legitimate interpretations. He may be talking of a husband and wife. He may mean bossiness, not true authority. He never categorically forbids it anyway. And the force of his argument is elsewhere. So to say on the basis of these verses that women should not teach or lead in the Church (or in the world) is to hang a great deal on a very thin thread.

To be fair, the texts often used to claim that women *should* be given authority are ambiguous too. Some say 1 Timothy 3:11 is talking about women deacons. This is probably the most natural reading of the text: the context is deacons' qualifications; the phrase is, "Similarly the women . . ." But, as we have seen, we often cannot distinguish between "wives" and "women". So "deacons' wives", not "women deacons", may be the intended meaning (although we certainly have no right to translate the word "wives", as many versions do).

We do know that Phoebe was a deacon (Romans 16:1), but this does not necessarily tell us she was in authority. There is no job description for the office: the word simply means one who serves. (Though again there is no reason for translating it as "servant" when it refers to Phoebe, but "deacon" or "minister" when it is Paul or Tychicus!)

Junia was "notable among the apostles" (Romans 16:7). Some take this to mean she was an apostle herself. This is not necessarily the case. We are simply told she was notable among the apostles. In Greek, as in English, this may mean that as an apostle she was notable; or it may simply mean she had a good reputation in the apostolic circle. We cannot argue anything from this. (Besides, as the critics never tire of telling us, she may have been a man . . . like all the other women in history!)

It all seems fairly inconclusive. We have not proved women can have authority in the same way as men. All we have shown is that we cannot be dogmatic in saying they cannot. Yet this is important. Those who disapprove of women's authority on biblical grounds can sometimes be very dogmatic. They can also be self-righteous: there is a tendency to think that those who hold firmly to a traditional interpretation of scripture are holding more firmly to scripture itself; that those who exclude women's authoritative ministry are being more obedient or biblical. This is not necessarily true. There are sincere and intelligent people on both sides of the debate. Both are equally trying to understand and obey scripture. So there is no room for arrogance or even assurance on either side: from the texts examined so far, we simply cannot say whether women should or should not be in charge of men.

WOMEN'S AUTHORITY – CAN WE PERMIT IT?

So we can have no certainty that women should not be in authority. There is no text which absolutely forbids it. But have we any reason to believe that they should? If we can find any examples, however rare, of women in the Bible being allowed or commissioned by God to hold positions of authority over men then we will know that it cannot be wrong.

And as well as knowing *whether* women can have authority we will also want to know *what kind* of authority it may be. As we have seen, authority is always given for a particular function. If women can have authority over men, the next question is naturally going to be "to do what?". The reservations people most frequently have – no doubt because of 1 Timothy 2:12 – are whether women can have authority to teach and lead in the Church. Let us now look at these questions in turn.

Authority to teach

We certainly find women teaching men in the Bible. Chapter 31 of Proverbs presents a woman's teaching (see verse 1). Timothy received the faith from women (2 Timothy 1:5). And Priscilla taught Apollos. Apollos was a fine speaker, accurate teacher, and zealous Jewish convert to Christianity who was "well versed in the scriptures". But he did not know the whole gospel (Acts 18:24,25). So, along with her husband Aquila, Priscilla took him and "expounded the way of God to him more accurately" (Acts 18:26). It is not unseemly then for a woman to correct and instruct a man. But Priscilla's authority in this instance was limited. Though Apollos owed her respect, he was under no obligation to obey her. And authority to correct him in private as a friend is not the same as authority to do so officially in public before the Church: the Princess of Wales correcting her husband over the breakfast table is not the same as her doing so at a press conference. Thus Priscilla had informal authority to teach and instruct but, as far as we know, no formal authority demanding an immediate response, or public authority as a Church representative.

But women also had authority to teach their sons, and not only to instruct them but also to expect obedience to that instruction. A man is not at liberty to reject his mother's teaching (Proverbs 1:8 and 6:20). Nor, indeed, is he at liberty to disobey her. Throughout the Bible we are told to honour our parents. It is one of the Ten Commandments (addressed incidentally to adults not to children: Exodus 19:25; 20:12). And Paul lists disobedience to mothers with crimes like murder and hating God (again referring to adults, since he has just mentioned their homosexual activities: Romans 1:26–30). So a mother had fairly extensive authority over her grown sons. Her teaching is to be listened to and she is to be obeyed.

A mother's authority to teach is formally instituted, and much more far-reaching than Priscilla's. But to us, in a society which has greatly "privatised" the home (compared with a tribal society where family life *was* public life), authority in a domestic sphere will still seem limited. Could women have authority over men on a scale we could call "public"?

Authority to lead

We can see from the case of Deborah that they could. She was judge over Israel (Judges 4:4). As such she would have had authority not only to judge, but to lead in war, govern in peace, and keep Israel faithful to God. Judges were chosen by Him and representative of Him. They were deliverers as well as rulers, like the king. Indeed, "we may see in them a type of Christ, who came to be our Saviour, is with us as our leader, and will come to be our judge".[33]

Deborah was one. Throughout Judges 4 we hear of her using her extensive authority to save Israel. She summoned Barak, commander of the Israelite army (verse 6). She commanded him (verses 6 and 7). She told him when to attack (verse 14). And the result of her leadership was superb victory (verse 23).

I have occasionally heard the insinuation that there was something "second best" about Deborah as a leader of the people; that she was only chosen because there was a shortage of suitable men; or even that having a woman leader at all was a sign of Israel's hopeless degeneracy. There is no suggestion of this anywhere in the text. All the judges were raised up and chosen by God himself (2:16). They were God's answer to Israel's need (3:15). And Deborah is no exception: "The people of Israel cried to the Lord for help" (4:3), and He replied by giving them Deborah. There is not the slightest hint that His choice of Deborah was in any way different from His choice of any other judge. (Besides, He chose some very odd people as judges. Samson and Gideon are hardly what we could call "suitable". There does not seem to have been such a thing as a "suitable man" as far as God was concerned, so there can hardly have been a lack of one!)

Nor is there much evidence for the theory that Barak is criticised for bowing to Deborah's authority. In verse 8 he says he will not fight without her. She replies by promising to go with him, and adds that he will not win glory himself, since someone else, a woman, will kill the enemy commander. This is sometimes seen as a rebuke to Barak for not claiming his "manly" authority, and for wrongly wanting a woman by his side as his boss. Even if this somewhat forced interpretation were correct it simply reinforces Deborah's authority. What was Barak's fault but that of failing to obey her promptly? As we see in the gospels (Matthew 8:5–13), if someone has sufficient authority their presence should not be necessary for their word to be obeyed. If Barak was in the wrong it can only have been because Deborah's commands could just as well have been carried out in her absence.

So Deborah was given authority by God over the whole country, including an army of ten thousand men. A woman can therefore have full public and official authority to lead men on a large scale.

And there is one other element in Deborah's leadership which is very important. Israel's victory as a nation was directly dependent upon the Israelites' obedience as a worshipping people. Because of this, a judge's authority was not simply civil and military, but also religious. They were not only to save Israel from invasion but also from idolatry. Failure to listen to them resulted in a departure from the way of their ancestors, a breaking of the commandments, and widespread unfaithfulness (2:17). So, as a judge, Deborah was expected to be a spiritual leader as well as a temporal one. Indeed she was exceptional among the judges in being also described as a prophet (verse 4). Her commandments came directly from God himself. Her first words to Barak were "The LORD, the God of Israel, commands you . . ." (verse 6). She told him what God was going to do, had done and was doing (verses 6, 9 and 14).

From her example, we can see that a woman can be a political, military and religious leader of God's people. She can judge in law, command in battle, and proclaim God's will and message. As His spokesman she can insist on obedience from men. And she can do all this nationally, in a public, official capacity.

Authority to preach

Deborah's authority resembles what we would expect of a preacher. To expound God's will and Word to His people, and tell them what to do in the light of it, is surely what faithful preaching is all about. And in Huldah we have an even better example. She too was a prophet (2 Kings 22:15–20, or 2 Chronicles 34:22–28). She too was appealed to by men for her authority (2 Kings 22:15–20). In her case the chief man involved was a king; he sent a number of ambassadors to her, including his secretary and the high priest, to discover God's will for himself, his people and the whole of Judah (verse 13). She was expected to instruct the entire nation in its worship and moral behaviour. Nor is there any doubt that this authority was from God. The men were sent to "Go, inquire of the LORD" (verse 13); they immediately went and inquired of Huldah (verse 14). In her reply to the king, she said, "Thus says the Lord" four times in the same number of sentences.

In a sense, Huldah was preaching to the whole

country. As with Deborah, there was no suggestion that she was chosen only because there were no suitable men available. Indeed Jeremiah had already been prophesying for four years and was living only a short distance away in Anathoth; he could easily have been consulted instead. So we cannot say women were only given this kind of authority because there were no men around to exercise it. Huldah and Deborah were appealed to and obeyed regardless of their sex. It is also interesting that both of them were married. Their husbands must have come under their authority like anyone else in the country. So their marriages, like their femininity, were no barrier to their leadership or authority.

As prophets, then, women can preach God's will to his people on a public and official scale. And there are women prophets throughout the Old and the New Testaments. Miriam was not only a leader of the Israelites, along with her brothers Aaron and Moses (Numbers 12:2), but also a prophet. Anna was another (Luke 2:36). The Corinthian church presumably had several (1 Corinthians 11:5), and Philip had four daughters who prophesied (Acts 21:9).

Authority to lead worship

As we saw in 1 Corinthians 11, women were also expected to lead the Church in worship. Paul assumes they will be praying and prophesying, and says that they must have the proper authority to do so.

Therefore, according to the Bible, women are free to perform many of the functions often thought barred to them. They can teach, and expect their teaching to be obeyed; they can govern, judge and command as God's representatives; they can publicly preach and prophesy to His people; and they can lead the Church in worship.

God clearly chose women to have all these different kinds of authority over men and does not see this as in any way a contradiction of Genesis 2.

Nevertheless, there are one or two things we do *not* find them doing in the Bible. However much authority a judge or prophet may have had, she (or he) could not offer sacrifices. This was firmly restricted to the priests; Saul, who had considerable authority as a king, was condemned for usurping the authority of a priest in this matter (1 Samuel 13:8–14). And a woman could never be a priest. Nor, indeed, do we find that any of the twelve apostles were women. Jesus chose these people very carefully to pass on His teaching and history, and deliberately chose only men. Does this mean there are things that women should not have authority to do today?

We must first look at the functions of priests and apostles. Priests had various duties, including the teaching and instruction of the Law, but their one exclusive role was the offering of sacrifices on behalf of the people. And this is why the priesthood has now been abolished. The great Sacrifice has been paid; we no longer need priests to offer sacrifices for us. We have a perfect High Priest; we no longer need any others (Hebrews 7:11–28). And we do not have an exclusive priesthood any more: we are now a "priesthood of all believers" (1 Peter 2:5).

Similarly, apostles, in the way that Paul and the eleven were apostles, were appointed for a specific purpose. They were the foundation of the Church (Ephesians 2:20). They were to preach the faith to the world (Romans 1:5). And for this they were attested by "signs, wonders and mighty works" (2 Corinthians 12:12) and had to be eye-witnesses to Jesus and His resurrection (Acts 1:21,22; and 1 Corinthians 9:1, where Paul, in order to give weight to his apostleship, says he had seen the risen

Lord). Obviously then, just as we no longer have priests in the Old Testament sense of the word, we no longer have apostles in the sense that the eleven and Paul were apostles. They have founded the Church, given us their first-hand accounts and teaching, and left us.

We no longer need priests or apostles, but if we did, they would not simply have to be men. Priests were all Levites, members of only one tribe. No woman could offer sacrifices, but no male member of the tribe of Benjamin or Judah could either. Similarly, the apostles were all Jews. The old covenant was exclusive: it was made through circumcision, so only with male Jews. The New Testament repeatedly tells us this is over; the covenant is now made through baptism, so it is for anyone who believes. And yet Jesus chose for His apostles only members of the old covenant. He deliberately built the new Israel on the foundation of the old. So both priesthood and apostleship were considerably restricted.

There are denominations today which call their leaders "priests" or "apostles". Obviously these are not priests or apostles in the way we have just defined them. But it would be easy in such a church to think women cannot be Church leaders because they were never priests or apostles in the Bible. By this argument, however, the only priests we can have are Levites, and the only apostles, Jews. I doubt if these churches would find this acceptable. These restrictions are no longer relevant today; but if they were, they would not only rule out women, but most men as well.

There is one more position in the Bible which, it is said, women never held. This is the position of elder (or bishop, which was much the same thing, as is clear from Titus 1:5–7). Actually, we do not know that there were no women elders. When "elders" are mentioned the word is always in the masculine plural. But this is also true of "saints" and "brothers" (and the latter should usually be translated in the New Testament as "brothers and sisters").[34] Yet we know these terms included women. This is a feature of the Greek language, like modern French; a crowd of men and women, even if there are fifty women and only one man, is still referred to in the masculine plural. We cannot deduce anything from the fact that elders are referred to as masculine.

In Acts, when the Church was very young, the elders were all men. When Peter and James address them (15:7,14) they actually say, "Men brothers . . ." (*andres adelphoi*). But later on, in the epistles, we simply do not know if there were any women elders. It is possible that the "older women" of 1 Timothy 5:2 were elders since Paul used the feminine form of the word "elder" (*presbuteras*) rather than the word which can mean "older women" (*presbutidas*). The context, however, does make this extremely unlikely, since Paul seems to be talking about older and younger men and women in general.

The important thing is not whether there actually were any women elders at the time, but whether the practice is prohibited. Is there anything to suggest that they will always be unsuitable for eldership? We are told that elders and bishops are to be "the husband of one wife" (1 Timothy 3:2; Titus 1:6). This could mean that they should be male and married: I am told that in the Eastern Orthodox Church parish priests must be married men (though their bishops, strangely enough, have to be single!). It is more often taken to mean that *if* an elder is married he should only have one wife; he should not be polygynous, or divorced and remarried. In this case, Paul simply expected most elders to be married men, but was not insisting that they must be. Either interpretation is legitimate. Perhaps we should assume that elders will usually be married and male, but make exceptions in the case of outstanding women or bachelors, as Paul would probably have done himself.

We know there were no women priests or apostles. They could not be the former, and were not chosen as the latter. We do not know that there were no women elders. Even if we think it unlikely in the social conditions of the time, there is no restriction to suggest that they could not be elders when circumstances might make it appropriate.

Implications

Most of the teaching, preaching, leading, ruling, governing and prophesying in the Bible is done by men. But not all. Women are found doing all these things, and are approved by God in them. The implication is not that there should necessarily be *as many* women in authority as men, but that *it cannot be wrong*. Yet there are church denominations and individual Christians who forbid it. This is surely mistaken: if God does not disapprove of something, how can we?

So the most obvious implication is in the realm of church leadership. There is no part of a church leader's work which, on theological grounds, a woman cannot do. We find God commissioning women to rule, judge, command, proclaim His will, correct, reprove, teach, and train. It is hard to see what is left out. There is no prohibition or lack of example to prevent us ordaining women to teach and lead in the Church. Yet in many churches this is still not done.

Why is this? Why are some people still unhappy about it? Sometimes it is because of 1 Timothy 12. This is the most convincing reason for not ordaining women: Paul did not allow them to domineer, and this is seen as an indication that they should never have spiritual authority. However, though I respect this conclusion, in the light of the rest of the scripture I do not think it is right. Men are not to domineer either. And women in the Bible are seen to do plenty of things which involve spiritual authority over men.

Often, though, people are not even sure what their objection is. Sometimes it is only half-articulated, which makes it difficult to examine, but one frequently hears something like this.

"A woman can *help* run the Church or preach an occasional sermon, but she should not have ultimate authority." This may be argued from various notions about the family. It might be said that women have a limited authority over their children, not ultimate authority: this is in the hands of the father, so in the Church it ought to be in the hands of a man. Or it may be argued from a man's "headship": a man is the head of the household, so he ought to be the head of the Church; a woman cannot represent Christ in this way because she is not head of the home. Or perhaps it is claimed a woman always needs a man to submit to, a "head" in this sense, so she should never be at the top of any organisation; there should always be a man over her.

A number of different ideas often get mixed up in these kinds of arguments. Concepts about "headship", authority itself, the family and the Church can all become somewhat confused, so we need to examine each in turn. First we should dismiss once and for all the idea of every woman needing a "head" in the sense of someone to submit to. Paul's use of the word head has been grossly abused. It is given all sorts of meanings the apostle never gave it himself. A fashionable one at the moment is to suggest a woman needs a man, a "head" over her and responsible for her, in order to flourish and use her gifts and feel secure in the Lord. Not only is this an insulting and emotionally dangerous teaching for single women, but it is thoroughly unbiblical. In 1 Corinthians 11 Paul uses the concept to insist on a woman's authority, not her submission to or emotional dependence on men. And in Ephesians 5 he teaches quite clearly that a head should lay down his life for his body. No one suggests every bachelor should have a body, a woman to adore and give his life for, though people seem to say that every spinster needs a head. In 1 Corinthians 7 Paul is at pains to free single women from the pressure to marry. Do we want to enslave them instead to an equally tyrannical pressure: to find a head, though not a husband, and possibly even to share with him his rightful body, his wife? Whatever Paul may mean by "head" he never suggests a woman must have a man over her in this way. If Lydia was indeed single, who was over her in the church at Philippi?

The next question to answer is whether women should have ultimate authority. And of course the answer is no. No one should. God is the ultimate authority. Any authority we may have is derived from him for a specific purpose to which it is limited. Someone who has the authority to preach has no authority to book you for a parking offence, and vice versa. All human authority is limited. None is absolute or ultimate, nor should it be. This applies to men in leadership as much as to women.

Next, we should understand the family properly if we are going to apply it to the Church. We must know whether we are talking about a man as a *father* or as a *husband*. As a father his authority is the same as his partner's. There is little distinction – for example in the ten commandments, or Proverbs, or Paul's teaching about the family – between the authority of the two parents; both are owed equal honour and obedience, and a mother has as much authority as a father in this respect.

The Church is indeed the family of God. But we are not His aunts or uncles or grandmothers or cousins. We are His children. And we are all His children. We have all been adopted as His heirs (Galatians 3:26–4:7). It is almost blasphemous to suggest that a man, a mere minister or servant of the Church, is in some way the father of God's family. I hope most ministers would blush to hear it suggested. We are specifically told to call no man "father" (Matthew 23:9). God is now our Father, and this gives us a glorious equality (1 Peter 3:7). Paul, who was in many ways in the position of father to the churches he founded, and indeed to subsequent Christians since we owe so much of our faith to his writings, nonetheless calls us his siblings far more often than he addresses us as his children. We are the family of God, but we demonstrate this by living as brothers and sisters; it is in our love for one another, not our power structures, that the world will see we are His family (John 13:35).

On the other hand, when we talk of a man as husband, or *head*, we are referring to his relationship with his wife. As we shall see in the next chapter, Paul does not talk of a man as head of his household or children, or dog and car and four-bedroomed semi. In the context of the family, head is synonymous with husband. He is head *of his wife*. We must have this clear in our minds when we apply "headship" to Church structures. "Headship" is about the relationship between a man and a woman.

And the Church, like a woman, is also described as a bride and a body (Ephesians 5:22–32 and 1 Corinthians 12:12–30). As a wife, the Church does indeed have a husband. As a body, she does indeed have a head. But her head, her bridegroom, is Christ and Christ alone. Again it is verging on the blasphemous to say that a man can be the head (and therefore the husband) of the Church. A man's relationship with his wife is a picture of

Christ's love for the Church, but this does not mean that a minister is to behave towards the body of believers as if it were his wife! If we start drawing unbiblical principles from a biblical image like this we are asking for a Church in which there is one man at the top and lots of women in the pews. (And alas, all too often, we get what we ask for.)

These metaphors – the Church as the family, or the wife, or the body of the Lord – are never used in the Bible to maintain that a man should be in charge. They are used to teach almost the opposite: that God alone is head of the Church, and that we are equal and united in His service.

We must, of course, be sensitive to any uneasiness felt over women becoming bishops or elders in the Church. There are numerous other objections given by people who feel unhappy about it. I have heard many of them.

"I don't think it would be proper."

"I would feel very uncomfortable."

"It just smells wrong."

"I don't think they'd be any good."

Most of these come down to the same thing in the end. We simply would not *like* it. This is surely what C. S. Lewis is unwittingly referring to when he talks about "an inarticulate distaste, a sense of discomfort which [we] find it hard to analyse."[35] Many people would have felt the same two hundred years ago (and might even today) about a black clergyman, or a woman doctor. It is a gut reaction. And if we are truthful, it is often simply prejudice. This is why many of us object to clergywomen, but not to the Queen as Supreme Governor or to women working as missionaries in places men will not go. We are accustomed to those things; they seldom threaten us, so we seldom question them.

To be honest, many of the reasons on the other side spring from the same thing, too. We must be careful of going along with the spirit of the age. Our society is increasingly treating men and women the same; inevitably we are going to want to follow suit. Perhaps this is why I feel defensive when people say that women should not be in charge. Perhaps it is quite simply that I do not like the idea.

So the Church is right to exercise caution. We may be free to employ women as leaders and teachers in the Church, but we still have cause to pause. We may be free to. But we are also surely free *not* to. The issue is highly controversial. The relevant texts are difficult. I do not think they are usually interpreted correctly. I am uneasy to be in disagreement with Christians I respect, although I must admit I am more uneasy with their interpretations. However, I think there is more room for humility on either side of the debate; there are sincere, biblical, dedicated Christians in both camps. For this reason none of us should be dogmatic.

The Church has often survived without women's leadership. Though the New Testament allows and indeed I believe encourages it, it does not insist upon it. We must conclude that it is not essential. It may not even be of particular importance. Other things are more crucial. Church (or even Evangelical) unity is surely one of them. Women's ordination might split the Church. Unlike the authority of scripture or the lordship of Christ, it is hardly worth the bitter dissent. (It ought to be noted in passing, however, that it is not those in favour of women's ordination who are proposing the division. At present, at any rate in England, it is the others who are saying that the issue is more important than Church unity: the Movement for the Ordination of Women has been extremely patient in *not* leaving the established Church, but waiting until the Church as a whole is ready and in favour of it. It is those on the other side who say they will refuse to worship with Christians who disagree with them.)

In addition, one Christian's freedom should never cause another to stumble (1 Corinthians 8:9; 10:28–29). There are those who think the Bible forbids women's leadership. I think they are mistaken. But Paul was prepared to become a vegetarian for the sake of those with more tender – though mistaken – consciences (1 Corinthians 8:13); we should follow his example. The Bible can be seen to favour women's leadership. We could ordain women. Perhaps, in many ways, we *should* do so. But we should also be able to say, with Paul, that "we have not made the use of this right" (to earn a living preaching the gospel) "but we endure anything rather than put an obstacle in the way of the gospel of Christ" (1 Corinthians 9:12).

A few things should be said in conclusion. We have talked of sensitivity to those whose consciences will not allow women authority. But there is often very little sensitivity shown in the other direction. While we continue an all male "ministry" we should do so with far more love and concern for all those who find it difficult. Many feel deeply and strongly about the issue. Men often fail to sympathise with this.

I have heard many pragmatic arguments against women's leadership in the Church and they are often astonishingly sexist. "Men find it hard to listen to women", for example. This argument seems to assume there is no nectar sweeter to the female ear than the sound of a male voice. Is it inconceivable that some women might find it hard to listen to men all the time?

Or "men can't submit to women. It doesn't come naturally to them". Again, presumably, there is nothing a woman would rather do than take orders from a man in a dog collar. Or, "it would make evangelism to men even harder than it is. No man wants to come to church to be preached at by a woman". Such attitudes betray a total ignorance of the other side of the picture; how galling it can be to be under an all-male clergy; how infuriating to waste the abilities of some of our most talented members; how difficult it can sometimes make evangelism to many women with any guts. For I know plenty of non-Christian women who are thoroughly repelled by the Church's apparent sexism. So while we continue to be cautious about using women as teachers or leaders, we should be more aware of the difficulties this may present to some of us.

There may also be more serious issues to consider. Perhaps we should question whether the *authority* of the clergyman, rather than his faithfulness or his ability to teach, is as important as we think, anyway? When Paul was writing, the canon of the scripture had not been fixed. His authority was crucial. If he did not have apostolic authority then his writings were only a matter of opinion; if he did, then they were to be obeyed. No vicar (I hope!) makes this claim. Everything he says is to be tested by his congregation. It is the Word which has authority now, not the person who preaches it. We might come to the conclusion that women can have authority over men. We may also conclude that exercising authority is a negligible part of a Church leader's work. Clergy and congregation are both under scripture; if either strays from this they should be corrected by the other.

Surely it is high time we were asking whether our concept of ordination is right? Many who are questioning an all-male ordained ministry are also wondering about our very concept of ordination.[36] Is it biblical to give one person sole charge of the Church, whether a man or a woman? The New Testament pattern seems more often (though not always) to have been that of a shared leadership, a responsibility held by a number of elders. Instead of ordaining women, perhaps we should question the ordination of men (in its present form). In his essay against women clergy, C. S. Lewis makes a point and then says, "If that claim is false then we will not want to make priestesses but to abolish priests."[37] Exactly. A more pertinent word was never said on the subject.

And if we do find ourselves with more shared leadership we will surely want to say, in the light of all that has been said so far, that whether a woman should run the team or not, if it has no women on it at all it is most certainly inadequate. For we have established that men and women are equal in value before God. We have seen that they are different, and the contribution that each sex makes is vital. We have acknowledged that throughout the Bible the sexes are seen as interdependent in all aspects of life; and that they are also seen as necessary and able to do every kind of work. And yet it has been said of our present Church, "Men preach, women listen. Men pray, women say 'Amen'. Men form the clergy, the diaconate or the oversight, women abide by their leadership. Men study theology, women sew for the bazaar. Men make the decisions, women make the tea."[38]

This is surely not right. It does not speak of equality. It suggests that men are important and women supportive. It does not speak of interdependence. It suggests that theology, for example, can be perfectly adequately studied by men alone. (And some claim that this is why certain passages of the Bible are traditionally interpreted in a male-biased way.) It does not even speak positively of the sexes' different contributions: there is not much to be gained from a feminine approach to making tea.

A teacher of theology told me recently that she thinks the ordination of women is probably a side-issue. But is it? Does it not rather affect our whole attitude towards the sexes? If the Church – the family and army of God – is only to be taught and governed by men, does that not communicate a certain ideology? Does it not suggest that a perfect world is one in which men show initiative and women passivity? It is not, in effect, a denial of much of what we have been saying?

I said at the beginning of this chapter that there are those, whose opinions on most issues I greatly respect, who say that women have a vital contribution to make in the Church. I agree. I believe they should be teaching, preaching, leading, praying, listening, saying "Amen", making the tea *and* making decisions. They will do so in a woman's way and the Church will be greatly enriched. But some say women should not be doing many of these things. If they nonetheless believe that women have an important contribution to make, the burden is now on them to tell us what else that contribution might be.

SEVEN

Marriage

"Marriage is popular because it combines the maximum of temptation with the maximum of opportunity."

George Bernard Shaw, **Marriage.**

There is nothing more relevant to our theme than the biblical picture of marriage. Nor can there be any human relationship more exciting. And yet the subject has been overlaid with more prejudices, unbiblical assumptions, and just plain unnecessary conventions than almost anything else.

The other night we were talking to some friends about the pressures on marriage. We all agreed that the hardest thing to adjust to was other people's expectations. "Others have no right to tell you what your marriage should be like," says Patricia Gundry in *Heirs Together*.[1] And yet others are telling us all the time. Or, worse still, they do not tell us but then disapprove when we do not live up to their expectations.

In addition, many are saying that the biblical teaching on the subject is no longer relevant. If the Bible says wives are to be submissive we should dismiss it as hopelessly old-fashioned, goes the theory; they are no more to obey their husbands now than slaves their

masters. Now occasionally, it is true, reinterpretation
of scripture can be right. Elsewhere some understand
Paul to be giving teaching for a particular situation
(". . . because of the present distress . . ." 1 Corinthians
7:26); as we have seen he is also capable of making
pragmatic concessions which are in contradiction to a
more important argument (1 Timothy 2:12, or Acts 16:3).
But there is no suggestion of either in his teaching on
marriage. The real answer to this argument, however,
must come as we examine the teaching itself, and see
whether it is argued from contemporary circumstances
or from something more fundamental.

LOVE & EROTICISM – The Song of Songs

What marriage is

Perhaps the most beautiful and poetic book in the Bible is
the *Song of Songs*. It also strikes people as one of the most
problematic. The first remarkable thing about it is its
apparent immorality. It describes a couple making love
without any of the impedimenta we think necessary to
make love-making proper. They are not recognised as a
couple by society, they do not live in the same home,
they seem to have no plans for children, and they are not
bickering; by our standards they are not married. We
know God does not approve of extra-marital sex; how
can he approve of this?

Is it conceivable that our definition of marriage is
wrong? The most explicit biblical description of the
relationship is in Genesis 2:24. "A man leaves his father
and his mother and cleaves to his wife, and they become
one flesh" (verse 24). Our society has of course reversed
this, and expects the woman to leave and cleave. She is

supposed to adapt to him emotionally, psychologically, and domestically; I know someone who recommends that a woman should not marry until she has seen her fiancé "on the job" and knows what she is letting herself in for. This is not biblical: the writer of Genesis expects him to leave his family and his way of life and give himself to her.[2]

However, the climax of the wedding – "they become one flesh" – is mutually active. This is the essence of marriage. He has left those whose flesh he once was: he has joined her whose flesh he will become. The cycle is to be completed; the body which God divided will become one again. She was once part of him, his side: he will be part of her, her head. She once came out of him: he re-enters her. And the moment of marriage is the moment this happens, the moment they become one flesh, the moment they first make love.

Now of course there is true lovemaking, and there are many distorted imitations. Lovemaking as God designed it in Genesis 2 is heterosexual, exclusive, and lifelong. When it steps outside this definition in the Bible it is roundly and unequivocally condemned. But in its true form it is synonymous with marriage. Marriage is agreeing to make love to someone for the rest of your life.

Seen in this light, the *Song of Songs* is a glorious celebration not only of the erotic but of marriage itself – which is, of course, the same thing. The relationship is heterosexual. The couple's love is exclusive (the references to Solomon being surely poetic allusions, not serious suggestions that the woman is a member of his harem[3]). And they intend a lifelong commitment: for "love is as strong as death, jealousy is cruel as the grave" (8:6).

In God's terms the couple are married. The wedding ceremony is even referred to at the end of chapter 3, when the shepherd is described as a king coming through the desert with the crown with which his mother crowned him: "on the day of his wedding, on the day of the gladness of his heart . . ." And after this celebration he frequently refers to his lover as his bride.

There is nothing immoral about the poem at all. But because our marriages are plagued with convention, we do not see the Shulamite and her beloved as husband and wife; they do not appear to eat breakfast together or share a bank account. We burden ourselves with as many expectations and requirements when we get married. I know plenty of people who become overweight after marriage because they suddenly feel they must eat "properly"!

My sister once invited me out for the day with her and another girlfriend. Then she hesitated: "But you'll have to make Shaun's lunch," she said. Her friend had just as long-standing and stable a domestic relationship as mine; wouldn't she have to cook lunch as well, I asked?

"I wouldn't expect her to," my sister said. "They're not married; they're living together!"

Now of course cooking someone's lunch, or buying red roses, or giving up a lifetime's work to nurse someone through illness, is often part of making love as surely as having children is. But these things do not *make* a marriage. They are not an essential part of everyone's relationship. What makes a marriage is the commitment to be one flesh. This is given formal expression in our society through a church or registry office, and worked out year by year as a couple learn to give themselves to each other. The point is we do not necessarily have to invest in houses or washing machines together, or adopt certain domestic roles in order to be properly married, as many people seem to think.

What marriage illustrates

Even more important than what marriage is, however, is what marriage illustrates. For the other extraordinary thing about the *Song of Songs* is its apparent lack of reference to God. There is no mention of Him at all. Yet we are told all the scriptures speak of Christ (Luke 24:27). Dare we conclude that erotic love between a woman and a man can somehow, of itself, imitate Him? That it is, even unconsciously, a picture of the divine? C. S. Lewis suggests something of the sort when he talks of "'the Pagan sacrament' in sex".[4] We would perhaps not presume to pursue this idea were it not confirmed in Ephesians 5. Paul quotes Genesis 2:24, "'For this a man shall leave his father and mother and cleave to his wife, and the two shall become one flesh'" (verse 31); then he says "This is a great mystery, and I take it to mean Christ and the church" (verse 32).

It is perhaps the most exciting imagery in the Bible. It promises that the love between mere mortals can resemble an immortal relationship with God. So our concern must be how we can live up to this honour. If God has chosen erotic love as an image of divine Love we should not take our part in it lightly. We should be concerned that our eroticism is thoroughly Christian. For the world inevitably spoils and twists and distorts this "Pagan sacrament" as much as it can. There are obvious ways in which this is done, like rape and promiscuity, adultery and divorce, but there are also more subtle ways which Christians are more likely to fall for.

One of the most common fallacies to be found through-out Christendom is the view that sex is either not good or not important. The Corinthian church was suffering from this delusion, so married couples felt free to abstain

for no good reason (1 Corinthians 7:1–5), and extra-
marital sex was not seen as particularly serious (1
Corinthians 5:1). These are two sides of one coin: if true
lovemaking is not seen as important its abuse will not be
seen to be either. We have the same attitude in our own
society. We think we are "liberal" in turning a blind eye
to sexual immorality; in fact we simply do not see sex as
an essential part of marriage. I often hear people say that
an affair would not hurt their relationship; they would
still be best friends, which is the most important thing.
But if marriage is making love, an affair attacks its very
heart. Sex is important, says Paul. Married couples
should not abstain. (Unless they both agree to, for a short
time, for prayer. But even this, he continues, I only say
as a concession to you; you must come back together
again, or you are asking for trouble. 1 Corinthians 7:5,6)
Otherwise married couples are actually robbing one
another: they owe each other the "debt" of their own
bodies.

We must also realise that making love means giving
oneself away. Again, our society tends to think in terms
of self-gratification. Of course this is a pleasant bonus to
making love, but it is not the driving force. "I am my
beloved's and my beloved is mine" says the Shulamite
(*Song of Songs*, 6:3). They have given themselves to each
other. The entire poem is full of possessive pronouns:
"my sister, my love, my dove, my perfect one"; (5:2),
"my beloved", "my fair one", "my bride". This is the
desire behind their desire; a longing to give themselves
away. It is not difficult to see why Paul says a married
couple have authority over one another (1 Corinthians
7:4). If we bestow ourselves on each other as this couple
do we keep nothing back for ourselves at all. It is
inconceivable that these two would refuse one another
anything.

And their giving is mutual. We still tend to see sex as male-centred. He is taking; he is satisfied; he is the one who "has sex" while the woman acquiesces. Christians easily fall for this attitude too. In her book *The Mark of a Man* Elisabeth Elliot includes two chapters entitled "Masculinity means initiation" and "Femininity means response"; the man, according to many Christian books, is supposed to take the active role and the woman the passive one. Similarly, versions of the Bible which ascribe speeches in the *Song of Songs* to one partner or the other tend to call the man the lover and the woman the beloved; it is assumed that he does the loving and she the receiving. But this is not the picture of the goat swain and her shepherd at all. She starts the song. She frequently refers to him as her beloved, and as "him whom my soul loves". She searches for him repeatedly. She holds him and refuses to release him. She takes him to her mother's bedchamber. She woos him and makes love to him. He is not slow to respond, but the initiative is hers; she is the lover.[5] Our society puts great pressure on men to "perform" in bed, to be the expert and the one who does all the wooing; but (unless the one I know is abnormal) men sometimes long to be made love to, and to be allowed the passive, receptive role.[6]

Perhaps the most striking aspect of the song is the sheer delight of it all. Throughout the poetry there is an intoxicating extravagance of beauty and enjoyment. This is the overwhelming example they set us. They drown in the pleasure of one another's company: "Eat, O friends, and drink: drink deeply, O lovers!"

This is not merely a narrow kind of eroticism resulting in a momentary physical climax. It is also a deep and lasting friendship (5:16). And it is a fruitful partnership; there are several reminders of conception, the natural result of this kind of love (3:4 and 8:5).

For this is the love which imitates Love Himself. Doubtless it does this in many ways. God is all-knowing: in lovemaking we "know" each other. God is faithfulness: love stays faithful to the grave. He gave Himself up for us: we find sexual fulfilment in complete self-surrender. And God is three in one, three Persons in one Godhead: we become two in one when we make love, two persons in one flesh.

There is also something God-like about a couple when they have children. When God made the world, Father, Son and Spirit were all working together (Genesis 1:1–2; John 1:1–3). When parents have children, male and female work together. They have to. It is the only form of human creativity in which two people are absolutely and involuntarily dependent on one another. So, like God, when parents bring their own image into the world they do so as an interdependent team.

C. S. Lewis has said, when describing what he called "the Pagan Sacrament" of making love, that "within the rite or drama they become a god and goddess."[7] There is indeed truth in this. It is partly in what lovers receive from one another – a surrender no human being has a right to expect. It is partly in what they can create with one another – new human beings in their own image. But above all the similarity lies in what they give to one another; it is in its overwhelming self-sacrifice that marriage most nearly comes to resemble the divine.

LOVE ENACTED: CHRIST AND THE CHURCH – Ephesians 5

And for this the husband and wife are given different parts to play. For there is a sense in which, as well as the relationship imitating Christ, each partner in the relationship enacts a different role. "Husband and wife", said a friend of ours when preaching from Ephesians 5 at a wedding, "should be visual aids to each other of Christ and Christian discipleship." A husband should remind his wife of Jesus: she should remind him of the Church. As we saw in chapter 2, the idea that God and His people are like husband and wife is fairly common in the Old Testament. Paul is using an established biblical picture and taking it further: not only is Jesus like a bridegroom, but a bridegroom is to be like Him; not only are we like a bride, but a bride is to be like us, the Church.

Preparation

Our marriages will never illustrate God's Love if we ourselves do not. So before telling us how to live as Christian wives or husbands Paul tells us how every Christian must live.

First we are to imitate God (Ephesians 5:1). Whether we are husbands or wives, or slaves, or children, we are all to be like Him. We must immediately ask ourselves, *how* are we to imitate God? Are we to be an avenging, angry judge, as God undoubtedly sometimes is? Of course not. We are not to imitate God in every way. Paul tells us exactly how to be like Him. "Walk in love, as Christ loved us, and gave himself up for us as an offering and sacrifice . . ." (verse 2). We imitate God by imitating Christ, and we imitate Christ in self-sacrifice. Not by ruling over one another with any kind of authority, but by giving up our lives for one another in obedient humility.

So the first commandment to all of us is to be Christlike. This is a common New Testament command. It does not mean that we are to be in authority over one another, as Christ is in authority over us. As Paul clearly says, it means we are to lay down our lives for one another. It is important that husbands get this clear: Christlike love is singled out as a husband's particular duty. And he must know that by "love" Paul does not primarily mean "responsibility", or even sweet nothings or sexual desire. He means self-sacrifice.

The second command to us all is to submit. We are to be "subject to one another in the fear of Christ" (verse 21). Respect for Christ means submission to Christians. This is also essential to our Godliness: it is part of Christian wisdom and worship (verses 15–20).

So Christian marriage is set in the context of Christian love and Christian submission. The first is commanded at the beginning of the chapter; the second at the beginning of the passage itself. The two are different sides of one coin. Christ's own life was a life of submission; He was obedient to the Father in everything. It was also a life of self-sacrifice; He gave everything up for us. This is how we *all* have to be.

So, although we have our own individual roles to play, there is a sense in which we are also both to play both parts. All Christians are to be Christlike; all are to lay down their lives as he did. So – although a husband is specifically told to do this for his wife – simply by virtue of being a Christian a wife is also to lay down her life for her husband. And all Christians are to be submissive: all are to put other people's wishes first. So – although a wife is specifically told to submit to her husband – simply by virtue of being a Christian he is also to submit to her.

And God has provided us with an excellent preparation for this. "Children, obey your parents in the Lord," says Paul, "for this is right. 'Honour thy father and mother,' which is the first commandment with a promise, 'so things will go well with you, and you will live long on the earth'" (Ephesians 6:1–3). Every time we do something for our parents we are preparing ourselves

for marriage. As we put our wishes aside for theirs
we become more self-sacrificing. As we obey them we
become submissive. As we learn to please them we are
learning to please our partners. Good children are likely
to become good lovers.

Sociologists tell us that we will repeat our parents'
mistakes. If your father hit his wife you are likely to beat
yours. If your mother was unfaithful you will be tempted
to be too. But God's commandment carries a promise. If
you "honour your mother and father . . . things will go
well with you". Be Christlike and submissive, however
reasonable or unreasonable your parents are, and when
you marry a partner who makes impossible demands (as
every partner does) you will have been well-trained in
your role.

So this is how we prepare. Husband and wife are given
different roles to enact in "the Pagan Sacrament", but
first we are both to learn both parts. We must all be
like Christ *and* like the Church. Before we can hope to
be good husbands or wives we must learn to be good
Christians. We must all become self-sacrificing and
submissive.

Husbands

(25) Husbands, love your wives, as Christ also loved
the church and gave himself up for it, (26) so that he
might sanctify it, cleaning it by the washing of the
water by the Word, (27) so that he might present the
church to himself glorious, not with a spot or wrinkle,
or anything like that, but so that it might be holy and
unblemished. (28) This is how husbands ought to love
their wives, as their bodies. He who loves his wife
loves himself; (29) for no man ever hated his own flesh,
but feeds and looks after it, as indeed Christ does for

the church, (30) because we are parts of his body. (31) This is why a man shall leave his father and his mother, and cleave to his wife, and the two shall be one flesh. (32) This is a great mystery, but I say it is about Christ and the church; (33) nonetheless you should each love his wife as he loves himself . . . (Ephesians 5)

. . . In the same way, husbands, each of you live considerately with your wife as a weaker vessel, giving her honour as a co-heir of the grace of life, so that your prayers are not hindered. (1 Peter 3:7)

I suspect that most husbands, when they read the Bible and see that their wives are told to submit to them, are tempted to feel a slight glow: it is rather pleasant to think of oneself as the ordained recipient of such behaviour, and it is rather a relief that God does not demand such an attitude from you! The trouble is that we are all more interested in our spouse's obedience to the marriage teaching than our own; it is much easier to see how your partner would benefit from Paul's words than to see how you would. So it is worth bearing something in mind.

Paul seems far more concerned with a husband's behaviour than a wife's. He spends much more time on it. This could be because he thinks it more important. It could be because it is harder. I suspect it is partly because, then as now, the subject was superbly and successfully neglected. The question usually prompted by Ephesians 5 is whether a wife can still be expected to submit. But if we expounded the passage as we should we would be asking instead, mouths agape, whether a man could *ever* have been expected to love in such a way. Paul's emphasis is on him. We have cleverly drawn attention away from the husband's behaviour by making his wife's controversial. I noticed a similar thing happening recently during a Bible reading on Ephesians 5. Because Paul concentrates on a husband's behaviour rather than a wife's this talk tried to do the same. But when a friend was talking to me afterwards he let fall a couple of comments which indicated that he had simply received the same old message. All he had heard was "wives submit".

Husbands should beware! The weight of the Pauline teaching is directed towards them. Before a man worries about whether his wife ought to be submitting to him in this day and age he should ask himself whether he is behaving towards her as the Bible tells him to.

His duties are threefold. He is to love like Christ, care like a head, and honour as an equal. Before we turn to the practical implications of this we must get something absolutely clear. We must understand exactly what Paul means when he says a husband is *like* something. A wife is to be like the Church; obviously, though, I am not supposed to cultivate spottiness and wrinkles. Yet there are many popular understandings of a husband's role and duty which are just as inappropriate. Take an absurd example. A husband is a head; Paul says he is to cherish his wife as his own flesh, to care for her as a head does for its body. Elsewhere he tells us that he, Paul, treats his own body severely and subdues it like a slave (1 Corinthians 9:27). One would have a plausible case for saying this is how a husband should treat his wife.

Common sense shows us this is daft. Neverthless we constantly do the same kind of thing. Paul is quite specific in applying his images. A man should treat his wife as his body by nourishing her and cherishing her (Ephesians 5:29). If we ignore his specific application and invent our own then we can infer that a man should govern his wife and be in control of her, as he should govern and control his own body. Yet this is not Paul's use of the image at all. Similarly a husband, according to Paul, is to be like Christ (Ephesians 5:25). And again he is quite specific in what way he is to be like Christ. But it is easier to lord it over your wife than to lay down your life for her, so we ignore Paul's use of the simile and substitute our own: he has authority over her, and should rule her. Once again, this is not how Paul applies his image.

Of course when we start introducing our own applications rather than using Paul's the whole thing becomes controversial. We would all like to infer different things. Some say there are clear instances of the word "head" being used in the sense of "boss"; this is part of Paul's meaning in Ephesians earlier on when he refers to Christ as "head over all things" (1:22) as the context makes clear. So, argue some, the man is to be boss over the woman.

Their opponents point out that in the same letter, and much closer to the teaching about marriage, Paul employs the meaning "source" not boss, since he talks of "the head . . . Christ, from whom the whole body . . . makes bodily growth and upbuilds itself" (4:15,16); in this sense the source of a river is spoken of as its head. So it is argued instead that a man is merely the origin of his wife as Adam was the origin of Eve. This argument is attractive, but even more absurd than the last; how is a husband supposed to behave like the head of a river to his wife?[8]

The most puzzling thing about the debate is why neither party refers to what the text itself says. When Paul uses this image he tells us exactly what he means by it. We have no excuse for adding our own suppositions. We are not to conclude, for example, that because a husband is to be like Christ he can wash away his wife's sins; such a suggestion would be blasphemous, and make Christ's sacrifice unnecessary (for married women). Nor that he can have many wives, just as Christ can have many members in his Church. Nor that he is necessarily to be in authority over his wife as Christ is in authority over the Church, unless Paul actually says so. We are not to think the husband is to be like Christ in any way we fancy. As C. S. Lewis said, just because we are told to be like doves does not mean we are to lay eggs.[9] A likeness is only of any use if we understand *in what way* it is like the original. Just because a man is his wife's head does not mean he necessarily has her brains.

Paul's teaching has been charged with all sorts of unbiblical ideas and connotations. "Headship" has become the catchphrase. No Christian discussion on marriage is complete without it. Everyone wants to know whether it involves authority, what it means in everyday life, and how a couple (or, more often, a husband) should put it into practice. In fact this very emphasis is not biblical. Even the word is not. Like many of the ideas which go with it, it is never used by Paul. He describes a husband as a "head"; he never talks, as so many do, about some abstract quality known as "headship". So we must stick to the meaning he gives the word, or we will be in danger of imposing totally unbiblical applications onto the biblical image. We must be quite clear what "head" does – and particularly does *not* – mean.

A man is never to be told to be the "head of the household". People with street questionnaires are fond of this phrase; they ask for the "occupation of head of the house", by which one is socially graded. From time to time I have quizzed them as to what they mean by this. They are usually not quite sure. The senior man? Well not necessarily . . . The husband? Yes. At least, if he is in full-time employment . . . Oh, the chief wage-earner? Probably. Unless that's a woman. And then possibly . . . It is all fairly vague. The general idea is of someone who, as we say, "wears the trousers"; the person who holds the purse strings; probably the man unless he is unfortunate enough to be unemployed or have a well-paid, bossy wife.

And sadly Christians are often just as vague. There is an impression that the Bible says a man should be the "head of the home". He should in some way be in charge: earn the basic salary, make important decisions, and be the ultimate threat when the children are naughty. We are often remarkably ignorant about what the Bible does say. Shaun and I went to a party where the guests had to dress as pub signs. He, of course, wittily went as himself (The Nag's Head). When, after three hours, no one had guessed who he was we gave the clue that he was the something's head. People tried everything. The family, the household, the house (which, if one could build such a monstrosity, might win an architectural award), and even, most oddly, the church. No one suggested he might be head of his wife.

The Old Testament does sometimes describe men as the heads of their families. This means that they were tribal chiefs. Their sons and grandsons, though they might be married with children, would not be "heads" in this sense (indeed they would come under their mothers' as well as their fathers' jurisdiction). We should never confuse this with Paul's concept of a husband as "head". The only time he uses the word which could be translated as "head of the household" he applies it to young women; he advises them to marry, have children, and "rule" or "be head of their households" (1 Timothy 5:14).[10] In fact the concept of head (meaning ruler) of the home or family is scarcely found in the New Testament, since tribal society was no longer prevalent. Paul talks of a husband as the head of his *wife*, not his family or his home. He sees every husband as the head of his wife, whether he is the senior male running the household or not. And he does not describe this kind of head in terms of being in charge. The popular notion that a man should be "head of the home", a kind of chief of his nuclear semi-detached two-car tribe, has no basis in biblical fact. Paul is not advocating a partiarchal hierarchy which goes husband, wife, children, dog. He is talking about one person's care of another.

We also ought to be clear that a husband is not told to do anything about his "headship". For one thing he is never commanded to be his wife's head. He *is* her head whether he likes it or not. It is permanently true. Those who tell husbands to "assert their headship" are talking nonsense. A man's headship cannot be asserted or denied: it is fact. It is not the result of certain behaviour but its basis. And the behaviour it affects is not the husband's. When Paul mentions his headship he is not talking to him but to his wife, as the preceding and following verses show (verses 22 and 24). It determines her attitude not his. It is relevant only to wives. A husband's proper concern is not his own "headship" but his wife's "bodyship". His worry should be that she is nourished and cherished. All he needs to assert is his own altruism. A husband's "headship" is, in fact, none of his business.

And, as I hope has been made clear, his "headship" is never linked with authority. The only time authority is mentioned in the context of a man being head it is authority given to the *woman*, as we have seen (1 Corinthians 11:10). Being someone's head is about looking after her, not being in control of her. A husband is to imitate Christ in His death, not His goverment; His selflessness, not His supremacy.

Love like Christ

What, then, is a husband's duty? It is simply and supremely to *love* (Ephesians 5:25). This is how he is to be like Christ. For he loves, not as a man who desires someone or admires her or wants to feel she belongs to him, but ". . . as Christ loved the church . . ." And not as He loves her by governing her, but as He "gave himself up for her".

As the Church on earth lives to serve Christ, so He lived on earth to save her. This is how a husband is to enact the role of Christ. Not by being born in a stable. Not by teaching and healing and performing miracles. Not in leadership and authority, but in self-sacrifice. It is not enough for him to know that he is to be like Christ. He must also know what the point of similarity is to be. It is not by being in charge or leading or taking decisions; these he is never told to do. It is by laying down his life for another. This is the greatest love a man can have (John 15:13), and it is this he is to show to his wife.

And how did Christ do this for us? He gave up everything. He too, like a husband, left His parental home, "who, though he was in the form of God, did not count equality with God a thing to be grasped". He too surrendered everything to cleave to another, and "emptied Himself, taking the form of a slave". And He too became one flesh with the one He came to serve, "being born in the likeness of humanity. And . . . humbled Himself and became obedient unto death" (Philippians 2:6–8).

Everything He did on earth was for us. Every mile He travelled, every breath He drew, every word He spoke was to serve the Church. He put us first in everything. He even put our relationship with God before His own, and was cursed while we were saved. This is the kind of sacrifice a husband is called to make. It is staggering. In taking on the role of Christ he has been asked to give up everything he has. His work, his family, his career, his friends, his very self is to be sacrificed for her. His concern is no longer how to please the Lord; he lives now in order to please his wife (1 Corinthians 7:33).

Most men, if asked why they love their wives, would no doubt answer "because . . ." Because she is clever; because she loves me; because she is beautiful, or has borne my children, or is always fun to be with. But the supreme answer is not because of anything. Christ did not love us "because". He loved us *in order* to clean us, and make us "holy and without blemish". So a man's love for his wife should not depend on anything in her. Happily for us Christ did not love us for any qualities on our part. In the words of C. S. Lewis, "This headship . . . is most fully embodied not in the husband we should all wish to be, but in him whose marriage is most like a crucifixion; whose wife receives most and gives least, is most unworthy of him, is – in her own mere nature – least lovable".[11]

He does not love her, then, because she is beautiful, but in order to make her so. He reverses the natural process. The day a bride marries she is probably young and gorgeous; the day she dies she will look blemished and wrinkled. But lovely as she looked, she was full of sin; and, decrepit as she will one day be, under the influence of her husband's love she can become holier and more splendid year by year. The more a man loves his wife the lovelier she can become.

His model is not simply a man who pleased His bride, but one who sanctified and cleansed and beautified her

(Ephesians 5:26–28). This is the Love he is to imitate. Whereas a wife lives to please her husband (1 Corinthians 7:34) he lives to benefit as well as please her. He must constantly put her interests before his own. He must always be asking himself "how can she best be served?". This must be the reason behind his work, his worship, and everything he does. Every decision he makes should be for her. If he is offered a new job the question he should ask is not whether it will lead to promotion, or be more interesting, or help the firm, but whether it will better serve his wife. If he is asked to join a church committee or play football or stay late at work, his first question must be whether it is in her interests.

Paul's teaching is often turned inside out. We knew a couple who were fairly new Christians. He had been made redundant and was at home looking after their small baby. His wife had a job which was demanding and enjoyable, as his had been. Naturally enough he sometimes found his position trying. He often felt frustrated and depressed, as many housewives do, and was glad of opportunities to be away from the house and the baby. Sometimes when his wife came home he would escape to the pub for a blissful hour of adult company. His wife, although distressed at his difficulties, was otherwise happy and fulfilled.

The elders in his church saw what he was going through and told him to assert himself. He must exercise his "headship". His wife must give up her job, and they must move somewhere where he would have a better chance of employment. It was chilling to hear the passage which calls a man to lay down his life being twisted to make him "assert" himself. He understood what it meant to be the head of his wife. He even had the courage to put it into practice. And his elders had no idea. He gave up his job, his happiness, and even his abilities so that hers could be used instead.

I was telling this story to a friend, when he objected, "A man should work for his wife's holiness, not her happiness," he said; "her sanctification, not her career."

Of course. A husband's supreme concern is his wife's spiritual welfare. This is far more important than whether she is in suitable employment. But I wonder whether the men who say this really have their wives' interests at heart. A wife will be sanctified through making sacrifices, this husband could have said to himself. It could be a most convenient doctrine. But so far we have only been talking about the first part of a husband's duty: loving as Christ loved the Church. He is to lay down his life for her holiness. Then, in case he is tempted to elevate this to a "spiritual" plane (by which we often really mean purely theoretical or even irrelevant) Paul goes on to use a far more earthy image. He is to love her as his body (Ephesians 5:28).

Cherish as a head

She is his flesh (verse 28). As the head lives to serve the body so he must live to serve his wife; as the head cares for the body so he must care for her (verses 29,30). And the teaching is drawn from the essence of marriage, from the fact that they are "one flesh", from love-making itself, so we can be confident it is relevant today. Once before, at creation, man and woman were one flesh: on their wedding night they became one flesh again. A husband has no separate identity of his own any more: his body is his wife. He should be able say, with Charles Williams, "love you? I am you".[12] For "he who loves his wife loves himself".

It is a superb complement to the earlier image. Christ's

love for us was often painful and exhausting. A man's love for himself is natural and instinctive. You seldom have to think about it. You sleep when you are tired, feed when you are hungry, and wrap up well when you are cold. If you are sensible you also make sure your body gets regular exercise and is working as well as it can. If you are treating it as you should you never stop listening to it and caring for its needs.

A husband's love for his wife is the same. He should tend to her needs all the time just as he tends to himself. Like his body, she need not be pampered, but her well-being should never be neglected. If she needs friends her husband should look for them; if she is unhappy he should ask himself why; if she is ill he should care for her; if she has gifts he should ensure she uses them. All these are things one would do for oneself. This is why it was right for the husband I mentioned to put his wife's work before his own; he was doing what any man would instinctively do for himself.

And this is why the church elders were so wrong in their advice. The husband was depressed and miserable. They thought he should swap places with his wife and make her depressed and miserable instead. I know Christian husbands who make a sincere attempt to love in the conventional way, yet whose wives are doing work the men would not dream of stooping to. Their husbands, I believe, think this is all right because it is "women's work". But they are supposed to love their wives *as themselves*. They should never expect their wives to do something they would not be prepared to do themselves.

God calls a husband to be ready to give up everything for his wife. He should put her wishes first in choosing their holiday. He should put her job first when they decide where to live. He should put her family first when they issue Christmas invitations. He should put her judgement first when it comes to the children's education.

You protest. Your wife is as thick as two short planks. You might put her welfare first, but you cannot be expected to put her *judgement* first. And it is true that Jesus did not put our judgement first when he put our interests first. He loved us as He knew to be best, not necessarily as we would have liked the best. A wise head, though it will always listen to its body and usually follow its inclination, will occasionally overrule it.

Honour as joint-heir

This is where we turn to a husband's third duty. He is to honour his wife as an equal; to live with her in the knowledge that she is weaker, giving her honour because she is a joint-heir (1 Peter 3:7). And almost all women are weaker than their husbands, on a purely physical level. In the last analysis a man can usually enforce his wishes on his wife. Even if he never lays a finger on her, he will almost always be capable of bullying her to get what he wants. Ultimately, in a disagreement, he can lay down the law. Whether this is because his muscles are stronger, or his income is likely to be bigger, or society still expects him to have the last word, hardly matters. We should simply face up to the fact, on the basis of Genesis 3:16 and empirical evidence, that a husband almost always has been, and almost always will be, in a position to command and exploit his wife. He can usually get his own way.

But he is to honour her, says Peter, as a joint-heir of the grace of life. She is weaker physically. But she is equal eternally. She is more vulnerable than he is on earth, but she is not his inferior in Heaven. She is co-heir of the kingdom of God, so she deserves his full honour and respect (1 Peter 2:7). He must treat her as his equal. And this is where the analogy with Christ breaks down. The average husband is not infallible. He is no more likely to have better judgement, or be right on any issue, than his wife. On some things she may be far more knowledgeable. It is a Christian principle to "consider others better than yourself" (Philippians 2:3), so he should always be ready to put her opinions before his own.

Besides, if he has such a low view of her judgement, what was he doing marrying her in the first place? Paul is quite clear in saying that a man will live to please his wife (1 Corinthians 7:33). The Bible is quite explicit in saying he must lay down his life for her (Ephesians 5:25). Obviously he should have married a woman he respects enough to honour and nourish and put before himself.

So because of a husband's superior strength or position his wife is likely to be at his mercy. Her welfare and happiness will probably to some extent depend on him. He can of course take advantage of this and decide to be "boss in his own home". But this is not the Christian way. Christ's example teaches him to neglect his own desires and lay aside his power; it tells him to use all he has for *her* benefit; it shows him that any advantage he may have over her is to enable him to serve better. The Fall gives a man a certain power over a woman which he can easily use at her expense. His "strength" can be his wife's enslavement. Christ's life should inspire a husband to make it her liberation.

Suppose they are both doctors. In the normal course of events it will be a wife's work that takes second place. She will be out shopping while he is keeping up with extra study; society will expect this. A Christlike husband will lay aside this "right" and free her to become the best doctor she could possibly be. Or perhaps she is a housewife. Expectations will tell him to put his feet up when he comes in while she continues with her day's work for the next hour or two. Jesus's example tells him to take over from her so she is the one to have some free time. She may be a mother. Normally she will be doing boring chores like washing nappies while he has the fun of reading to the children or playing with them. But a Christian husband should be asking himself how he can free her to enjoy the children and be the good mother she was made to be.

A truly Christian wife may come in for scorn. A truly Christian husband almost certainly will. Christ neglected His power to suffer humiliation for our sake. A man must be prepared to endure the same for his wife. We have a friend who is one of the finest Christian husbands I know. He comes home from one demanding job and immediately starts another. As soon as he gets in he is carrying the baby, putting another child to bed, emptying potties, cleaning up vomit and doing other pleasant jobs so dear to a father. His domestic duties sometimes keep him from church activities. His spiritual "superiors" think he is not "keen". His peers say knowingly "I married a wife" when he declines from some church meeting or other. Everybody thinks he is henpecked. He is the least henpecked man I know. He is making sacrifices for his wife and children. He is freely obeying God's commands. He is living to liberate his wife: he is a truly liberated man.

It is not surprising Paul refers to a husband as a saviour. If men were to give themselves for their wives, the question of their wives' submission would never arise. No one in their right mind can grudge Christ the total submission he demands; He has done so much for us we must be overwhelmed with gratitude. Husbands who behave as Paul tells them to would surely find the same. A man who lays down his life for his wife and frees her to be herself would find himself married to a woman overwhelmed with gratitude too. She would surely *want* to entrust herself to him wholeheartedly and unreservedly. There would be little question in her mind about submitting to him. She would know it was in her interests to please a man who cared more about her than about himself.

Wives

. . . (21) Submitting yourselves to one another in the fear of Christ; (22) the wives to their husbands as to the Lord, (23) because the husband is the head of the wife as Christ is also the head of the church, and is himself the saviour of the body. (24) But as the church is subject to Christ, so also should wives be to their husbands in everything . . . (33) . . . let the wife make sure that she fears her husband. (Ephesians 5)

(1) In the same way, wives, submit yourselves to your husbands, so that even if any disobey the word they will be won through the behaviour of their wives, (2) seeing your pure behaviour in fear . . . (5) For indeed in this way then the holy women who hoped in God adorned themselves, submitting themselves to their husbands, (6) as Sarah obeyed Abraham, calling him Lord; you became her children, doing good and fearing no terror. (1 Peter 3)

There is no doubt about it. A wife is to submit to her husband. Having seen how he should behave towards her, however, we should hardly be taken aback. He is her head (verse 23), caring for her needs all the time; of course she should trust herself to him just as a body trusts its head. He is even her saviour (verse 23), putting her interest first in everything he does; of course she should submit to such sacrificial love even as the Church submits itself to Christ.

This is not culturally relative, as many people try to argue nowadays. As we have seen, he is not her head because of any legal or social set-up. He is her head because they are one flesh. His love for her as his body springs from the essence of marriage itself, from love-making; her submission to him as her head is argued from the same principle.

Nor is it dependent on his sinlessness, as others sometimes try to tell us. It is true that there is a sense in which a wife's behaviour is prompted by her husband's. She submits to him because he is Christlike; she obeys because he loves. So, one sometimes hears it said, if he is not a Christlike husband she need not be a submissive wife. (In which case, of course, we would all be off the hook!) But in Peter's letter a wife's submission comes in the context of suffering, turning the other cheek, and obeying even oppressive governments and masters and husbands. Both before and after his words to wives, Peter stresses that submission does not depend on kind treatment. "Servants," he says (1 Peter 2:8), "submit yourselves to your masters in all fear, not only to the good and forbearing, but also to the perverse." He tells the wives to do so even though some husbands do not obey the word (3:1). In fact this is one of the reasons he gives for submissive behaviour. Even if it involves suffering you are to do it, for "if indeed you do suffer because of righteousness, you are blessed" (3:14).

Peter even suggests a further reason for submission; a wife may win her husband over to the Lord (1 Peter 3:1). When he sees her submission to him he sees how he should submit to Christ. When he sees her reverent and chaste behaviour he sees how his behaviour should be reverent and chaste. She is a living reminder of what he should be. If this can be true of a non-Christian husband (as Peter says) how much more must it be so of a Christian one? He will recognise the allusion; he will know what she illustrates; his conscience will tell him he should be as she is.

But what does Paul have in mind when he tells wives to "be subject"? What does it mean for a woman to submit to her husband? There are a number of things it does *not* mean. Unfortunately much of the behaviour advocated for wives in the name of submission is nothing of the kind. We tend to think of the submissive wife as quiet, domestic, passive, and – dare we say it? – rather dull. Yet no qualities could be more irrelevant to true submission. Who was more obedient to God than Elijah or John the Baptist? Who more submissive to Christ than Paul? Indeed, who has ever submitted more humbly than Jesus Himself? These people should be our models for submission; yet they were tough, outspoken, unconventional, and courageous in the extreme. There is nothing soppy about submission.

Nor does submission mean silence. 1 Corinthians 14:34 does not mean you stop talking to your husband (indeed, it contains advice to the contrary). If you hate spending Christmas with your sister-in-law, say so. If you think pink kipper ties are not the thing for the eighties, tell him. If his job keeps him away from home too long and you believe he should give it up; if the family needs to move house so you can get better employment; if he does not look after the children properly or the meals he cooks are disgusting, then explain what you expect of him. This is not inconsistent with submission; David spends much of his psalms moaning about God's treatment of him, yet he was "a man after God's own heart" (Acts 13:22).

Obviously there is a difference between communicating and nagging; the latter in a wife is like rain on a wet day (Proverbs 19:13, and 27:15). But again we have a matchless model for submission: Jesus asked if the cup might pass from Him, but He was well prepared for the answer no. This is how a wife should be.

And submission is not financial or emotional dependence. The submissive wife is not necessarily the one with the helpless little girl image. Obedience to God should never mean abandoning all thought of earning a living or making decisions or growing up. Similarly, submission to your husband should not mean these things either. It is not necessarily unsubmissive to earn a bigger income, get a better degree, have more intelligent opinions or correct a man when he is wrong.

Nor does submission mean domesticity. It is not a "job" in this sense. Submission does not mean you keep a beautiful home, or give up your job, or become a housewife when you have children, or cook the meals, iron the shirts, do the dishes, or plan the shopping. A wife is a picture of Christian discipleship; since when has this entailed full-time domestic service? She submits to her husband as to Christ; since when has this meant darning His socks? Her supreme model is Jesus Himself; since when do we look to Him for examples of housewifery? The truly submissive wife is not necessarily the domestic one.

And submission is not manipulation. This is a disgraceful abuse of Paul's command which is popular at the moment. People do this with God as well as their husbands. "How to pray to get what you want" is the thrust of much of our teaching on prayer.[13] This is not prayer at all; how to pray to get what God wants should be our concern on our knees. Similarly, how to submit to get what you want is the substance of a number of books for wives. Say yes to everything he ever utters, scribble sexy messages in his lunchbox, greet him at the door in high heels and not much else and you will have him wrapped around your little finger. Such advice is degrading to husband and wife alike. Submission means doing his will, not tricking him into yours.

For just as a man has power over his wife which he can use for his own self-importance, so a woman can have enormous influence over her husband which she can employ for her own ends. She can dictate many of his opinions; she may make or break his career; she is likely to shape what kind of a father he will be. And I have frequently heard women suggesting one should exploit this. It is the power behind the power; the "hand that rocks the cradle". A woman is thought to have a "right" to get her own way through subtlety; to persuade her husband to a certain course of action and make him think it was his idea. Again, this is not the Christian way. The Christian way of submission is to give up all thought of self altogether, to put aside any devices one might use for one's own profit, and to put one's entire life at someone else's disposal.

But there is a more subtle form of "submissive" manipulation which is just as erroneous. It is often thought that a wife's submission implies a husband's leadership. This is not so: Christians submit to one another, but this does not make every Christian into a leader. There are husbands who do not particularly want to govern their wives; a man might have good reason for wanting his wife to take decisions or discipline the children or run family prayers. A submissive wife will see what he wants and fit in with it. There is nothing wrong with this. Those who think "headship" means "authority" will say he is abdicating from his role. Men must take a lead, they say, or women cannot submit properly. So women have to manipulate men into leadership; they are told that on no account should they undertake anything which might be a man's responsibility, and eventually their husbands will be forced into their "role". I have heard the same idea applied to the Church in general; if only women would stop taking part in Christian work men might come forward and fulfil their duties. I very much doubt if this theory works anyway, but even if it does it is no more submissive than wearing skimpy négligés to manipulate your man into taking you to the Bahamas.

Occasionally there may be exceptional situations in which a wife should not submit. Women can be raped, robbed and beaten by their husbands. They can be asked to steal or lie. They can see their children abused. Where must they draw the line? Our first allegiance is always to God. Any obedience in the Bible, whether to masters or parents or governments, is subject to this. If a woman's husband wants her to do something contrary to the Word of God she must stand up to him. Sapphira failed to do this when her husband attempted to deceive the other disciples, and "immediately she fell down . . . and died" (Acts 5:10). Her sin, presumably, was the same as Adam's (Genesis 3:17): she listened to the voice of her spouse. She did not oppose her husband when he was doing wrong. She submitted to his plan and, like Adam, received fairly speedy judgement.

If a man is doing something which is *without any question* wrong, then his wife should not submit to him. This is also the one situation in which a husband should oppose his wife; Eve's suggestion to Adam was clearly contrary to God's command. But this does not include instances of mere disagreement or difference of opinion between husband and wife. A woman may think her husband mistaken, but this is not the same as seeing him obviously going against the written word of God.

I know of a woman whose husband beats their children fairly regularly and without any signs of repentance. This is clearly wrong (Ephesians 6:4). I believe she should take them away from him, and I deplore the pressure being put on her, by Christians, to stay by his side. I know another whose husband has run her into debts of thousands of pounds. Again this is obviously wrong, and she should not allow him to continue to do so. Wives of men who are violent or unfaithful, criminal or mentally ill, may all have cause to oppose and sometimes to leave them. Christians must be entirely supportive. Such women are already in a distressing position: their consciences as well as their husbands may torment them for what they cannot choose but do; the last thing they need, and sadly often the first thing they receive, is condemnation from Christians.

Happily most husbands do not come into this category. To the ordinary, run-of-the-mill, imperfect, selfish, sinning husband a woman should submit as she would to Christ Himself.

But what is submission? One might as well ask what is Christian discipleship. It is everything. This is why marriage is, in some ways, the most supreme example of sexual interdependence. How should a wife submit to her husband? "As the church submits to Christ", Paul says. And in case we should miss the point, he continues ". . . let wives be subject to their husbands in everything (verse 24)". In fact it is the same kind of behaviour that he says slaves should give their masters (Ephesians 6:5).

The Church's *raison d'être* is Christ's service. Her ambition is His pleasure. Everything she does must be to gratify Him; every decision she takes should be according to His will; every work she undertakes ought to be to His greater glory. Every course the Church ever follows should be the one which will most please Christ. If a wife is to submit to her husband as to Christ she must submit her whole life to him. There is nothing she will do without conscious or unconscious reference to her husband. The work she does, the friends she has, the clothes she wears, and the hobbies she pursues will all be in keeping with what he would want for her. Being a wife is like being a Christian: not so much a matter of performing particular duties as of embracing a completely new attitude. There is no self any more. There is only living to please another. This is what it means to be one flesh: total and absolute surrender.

Such is a wife's submission. Everything she does will be in order to please her husband. Consistently we find she should treat him as if he were Christ. Her model is Sarah, who called Abraham "lord" (not merely "sir" as is sometimes claimed, but the word used throughout the New Testament of Christ Himself); who submitted to him and obeyed him. Her proper attitude is to "fear" him (not "respect" as gutless translation would nowadays have us believe), and then she need fear nothing else (1 Peter 3:6). And her concern is to please him (1 Corinthians 7:34); her proccupation is his pleasure when once it was only Christ's. Her submission to her husband is to be like her submission to God himself. It is astonishing. If it were not there in front of us in the Bible we should think it blasphemous.

Great mileage is often made out of the fact that the Bible never tells wives to "obey". Strictly speaking this is true – although Peter suggests wives should take Sarah as their model, and she "obeyed Abraham" (1 Peter 3:6). The word used for wives is "submit", which is also used for the mutual giving way to one another which all Christians do (Ephesians 5:21). But this does not mean a wife is living to please her husband any less than if she were told to "obey". On the contrary, submission is far more all-embracing than mere obedience. Obedience simply means doing as you are told (and by careful manipulation you can often be told the right things!) but submission to Christ, the image Paul uses, is total. It involves not only our actions but also our attitude. It is willing and joyful and cheerful, like our trust in the Lord.

Now of course this is not always easy. We do not take kindly to submission. It means putting someone else's will before your own. It sometimes means making someone else's mistakes instead of your own. It may occasionally mean doing things you think are stupid. And in fact many people will not respect a woman for submitting to her husband. For there is a movement abroad at the moment which says people have a primary duty to themselves. If your husband is not allowing you to be fulfilled or reach your potential or "be yourself" it is unreasonable to submit to him. A husband is an ordinary sinner; it is possible that submission to him may occasionally involve frustration, annoyance, or even a waste of his wife's abilities. It would be deceitful to claim, as some books do, that the reward for submission is a fully guaranteed bed of roses, and a husband so gratefully doting that he strews his wife's days and nights with Black Magic. Peter took it for granted that righteousness can involve suffering (1 Peter 3:14). No doubt some women submit to their husbands and are taken for granted, or even treated badly, in return.

However, the balance of scripture, and experience, tells us the opposite. Usually when we make sacrifices for each other we find a glorious fulfilment; we tend to be happier people ourselves, and our marriages are much more rewarding. Peter clearly takes this to be the norm. A wife's submission may disarm her unbelieving husband without a word (1 Peter 3:1), and she will have nothing to fear (verse 6). Submission can be extraordinarily liberating. Instead of being enslaved by our own desires, we are free to live our lives for another. Instead of worrying about our own requirements, we are able to spend our lives pleasing someone else. A married woman is indeed in a privileged position. She never needs to think of her own happiness, because someone else has been commissioned to think of it for her. She never needs to be concerned about her own fulfilment, because he has been charged with taking care of it. All she needs to do is to make his task of loving her possible by giving herself to him without reservation.

It is indeed like being a Christian. Submission to Christ often involves a struggle. He calls for a surrender on our part which seldom comes easily. If he asks us to give up a particular course of action, or take up another, we often go through agonies at the time – which is partly what makes the reward afterwards such a blessing. A wife who submits to her husband is sometimes going to find it difficult to put his wishes before her own. But unless she does so how can his love find full expression? Unless she puts herself in his hands how can he care for her? Unless she trusts herself to him completely how can he dedicate himself to providing her with the fullest possible liberation?

LOVE & AUTHORITY – 1 Corinthians 7:4

There seems to be something missing. We have discussed a husband's and wife's respective roles, but we have surely left something out. What about authority? Where is the husband told to have authority over his wife? Where is he told to be in command? Where indeed?

It is nowhere in the Bible. He is never told to rule over his wife or command her.

Surely, some say, it is *assumed* in all the biblical teaching. It was so taken for granted at the time that the Bible did not need to mention it. This kind of teaching is very dangerous indeed. If we start drawing things out of the Bible because we think they were assumed at the time we can draw out anything we like. If it could be taken for granted that husbands had authority over their wives it could also safely be taken for granted that wives had to submit to them. Nonetheless, Peter and Paul both saw fit to tell them to.

As it happens there is talk of authority in marriage (1 Corinthians 7:4), but the only mention of it is mutual. Paul recognises that a married couple have authority over each other. A married person has no power over his own body, he says; it is governed by his spouse.

So husbands are not *told* to have authority over their wives. Paul does not command it; he simply recognises it. ". . . the wife must pay the debt [of sexual intercourse] to the husband, for the wife has not got authority (or power) over her own body, but the husband has . . ." (1 Corinthians 7:4).

At first glance it looks as if Paul is just talking about sex. What he is saying seems to amount to no more than this: whenever a husband wants sex his wife should make sure he gets it. It seems fairly sound marriage counselling.

But he is saying far more than this. The *reason* she is to give her body to her husband whenever he wants it is *because* she has no rights over it herself. Paul has just established that we do not own our bodies. "Do you not know," he says (6:19), ". . . that your bodies are from God, and that you are not your own? You were bought with a price . . ." The price was Jesus's body, which was exchanged for ours. Our bodies belong to him. But when a woman gets married, her body, which by rights is Christ's, is handed over to the husband for his care and enjoyment. She does not own it. She owes it to her husband.

Surely, though – one could argue – the husband has authority only over her body? He does not have authority over her mind or her soul. He has no say over what she thinks or says or does, other than in bed. This kind of thinking is unbiblical. A man or woman cannot be broken up into body and mind and soul. What a man thinks will affect his behaviour. The God he worships will change his mind. What he says is an indication of what he believes and who he is and how he feels. The idea of dividing someone up into compartments is a Greek one and is foreign to the biblical view of humankind – indeed, the thrust of much of Paul's message in chapters 6 and 7 is that our bodies matter because our bodies *are* ourselves. The commandment to love God with all your mind and soul, body and strength, does not imply that it is possible to do one without the others. It simply means that you are to love God in every possible way. You cannot worship God "only in your soul".

So if a man has power or authority over his wife's body, he has power or authority over his wife. This is common sense. If he commands her body he commands what she says, how she behaves, where she goes to church, and even what she feels. He has power over every area of her life. This is fairly comprehensive authority. A husband, then, *does* have authority over his wife.

Those who know the Corinthian letter will see where we are heading. So far this teaching about the husband's authority may not be surprising. "Reactionary", perhaps to some people; "chauvinist" or extreme, maybe. But since Paul is supposed to be such a frightful misogynist, not particularly astonishing. But we have not yet finished the sentence. It is very revolutionary indeed; powerful stuff, even today: "the husband should pay his debt to his wife", he says, because ". . . in the same way also the husband does not have authority over his own body, but the wife does". In other words exactly as the husband has power or authority over his wife, so the wife has power or authority over her husband. Everything we have just seen about the wife's body is true also of the husband's. He too was bought with a price. He too is not his own. When he got married, he too was handed over to his wife for her pleasure and use as long as they both live. She has authority over him just as he has authority over her.

When it comes to authority the marriage relationship is absolutely symmetrical. Those who say that the husband has some kind of authority over his wife are right; but they should never say this without also adding that she has the same authority over him: "(3) The husband must pay the debt to the wife, and also the wife, in the same way, to the husband. (4) The wife does not have authority (or power) over her own body, but the husband has, and the husband does not have authority (or power) over his own body, but the wife has." (1 Corinthians 7)

Making love to someone means giving your body to her or him; and giving your body to her means giving yourself to her without restriction. As we saw, the Shulamite and her beloved give themselves to one another without reserve: of course they have comprehensive power over each other's lives. A married person retains no right over himself at all. His wife has authority over him. He has authority over her. And it is absolute authority. If a man's wife asks him to take regular exercise he should do so. If he asks her to go to church with him she should do so. If she asks him to give up his job; if he asks her to stop smoking; if either partner asks anything of the other he or she has no right to withhold it. Our bodies, our very selves, are not our own. We must live every day with that knowledge. The unmarried person does not *own* his or her body, but is in charge of it. The married person has given that charge over to his spouse. It was bought by the death of Christ and made over to his partner. She or he governs it. He or she is in charge of it. Each has authority over the other.

This is why the erotic relationship is the ultimate in mutual dependence. Indeed it is more than mere dependence: it is complete loss of self. A friend of mine criticised this idea as an "idolatry of marriage". And that is almost what it is: not for nothing does a groom say amongst his vows, "with my body I thee worship". God has allowed marriage this astonishing status. This is how we become "like a god and goddess".

People will of course object to this. We all have very convincing reasons for not giving ourselves to our partners.

A woman may say, for example, that she tries to submit to her husband. For his part, though, he does not seem to recognise his duties. He would never give up his job, or even his bi-monthly duties on the PCC for her, and would not dream of doing anything she says. This is probably true of most Christian marriages to some extent since one half of this teaching has been stressed much more than the other for the last two thousand years. (Everyone talks about "headship", and a wife's submission; no one mentions bodyship, and a husband's sacrifice.) But this is no reason not to submit, as Peter's letter makes clear. A husband's obedience to scripture is his responsibility, not his wife's. She need only answer for her failings on the day of judgement, not his. She should do her part and submit. If he fails to lay down his life for her it is ultimately between him and God.

A man may say his life's work is more important than

giving himself to his wife. He is, perhaps, ordained to
serve the gospel – if he behaved as she would like him to
he would be less effective for Christ. He should have
thought of this before he married. Marriage is demanding as well as fulfilling, and the cost should be carefully
weighed up beforehand. After all he had no excuse not to
do so. This particular result of marriage is quite clearly
spelt out by Paul: "The unmarried man cares for the
things of the Lord, how he may please the Lord; but
he who is married cares for the things of the world,
how he may please his wife, and he has been divided."
(1 Corinthians 7:32)

Others will say that this teaching will result in anarchy.
You cannot *both* have authority over each other. Someone
must be in charge or there will be chaos. If this is all the
faith we have in God's specific commandments our faith
is worthless. You could say the same of throwing your life
away, or seeking only the Kingdom of God, or any of
Jesus's sayings which involve a little risk. You might
expect them all to end in disaster. Followed half-
heartedly they are almost bound to. All I can say is, I dare
you to try. Taste and see that the Lord is as good as his
word. There are many strange and thrilling visions in the
Bible, and this revolutionary idea of marriage, in which
two people have total command of each other, is surely
one of the most inspiring.

Applications

People sometimes ask how this kind of teaching works
out in practice. What does it mean in terms of disciplining
the children, spending money, housework, washing up,
careers, and all the other heartaches the married flesh is
heir to? As I hope was clear from chapter 5, there are no
sexually prescribed roles in these areas. It simply does

not matter who takes on what jobs. They are the responsibility of both partners; how we share them out is up to us. Sadly, as Patricia Gundry points out, most people "never even consider that *they* can determine what kind of marriage they want and then create it themselves".[14] Yet God has left us free to decide these things. The couple in the *Song* are by no means conventional or even socially acceptable, yet they are the biblical model of erotic love.

The scriptural guidelines for marriage do not concern themselves with divisions of labour. They are far more radical. They will affect our behaviour more than any external structures, but not in such predictable ways.

I knew a couple who were married for several years without children. She was not ready for them. Her work was important to her, and it would have been jeopardised by pregnancies and small children. But he had wanted children for some time. One or two Christian leaders I know would have told him to "assert his headship". As it happens this is exactly what he did; Christlike, he put her welfare first and never mentioned the subject.

Eventually she realised he wanted to start a family. She was apprehensive at the idea, but realised that "a wife has no authority over her own body but the husband has". She believed she should submit to him in everything. She told him so. She left the matter up to him, and put herself in his hands.

He took her at her word and they stopped using contraception. She then discovered she was so apprehensive about pregnancy that she found sex physically painful. So she asked God to help her submit in feelings as well as actions. It was not until then that she was able to make love to him willingly, despite the risk of pregnancy. As a consequence she found the experience more liberating and exciting than ever before.

As it happens she did become pregnant. The struggles started again. She was depressed at the thought and sometimes found herself antagonistic towards the baby. Again she prayed. Again she eventually won through. Now she has several children, and loves being a mother. It is sobering to realise that if she had had her own way they might never have been born.

A story like this is in danger of sounding saccharine but it is a first-hand example of the surrender God asks of married people. It is bound to be painful at the time. My friend put her entire future in her husband's hands. Total trust in someone involves risking everything: losing our lives for Christ can be just as frightening. Yet this is also how we find that freedom from ourselves which she found so intoxicating.

Her children now give her undreamt-of happiness. Her husband, because he made the decision to have them, takes responsibility and care for them in a way which is still fairly unusual for men, and which frees her to enjoy them to the full. And when it came to a decision about his future he put himself in her hands in the same way. He was due to change jobs, and in his turn realised that "a husband has no authority over his own body but his wife has". For various reasons he asked her to choose his employment. He too risked his future, his work and his happiness. He too was prepared to hand her complete control of his life, and gave her *carte blanche* for the next decade of his life.

This is where the biblical teaching applies itself. Not who does the shopping, but who owns your life. A friend of ours married someone who was not as secure a Christian as he. After a few years of marriage she was not going to church regularly any more. Children, or Sunday lunch, or cleaning always seemed to get in the way. So he stayed behind to help her instead of going himself. Many would see this as a recipe for disaster; he ought not to let his wife disrupt his spiritual life in this way. But he was imitating Christ who gave up everything for the sake of our relationship with God; she realised he was making a sacrifice and eventually organised herself to go to church with him again.

This kind of love, however, should never be forced from one partner by the other. A man, for example, is never called upon to insist on his wife's submission, or even to ask for it or expect it. Parents are to rule or govern their children (1 Timothy 3:4), so if their children are unruly they should discipline them; their unsubmissive behaviour should not be tolerated. But husbands are never told to rule or govern their wives. They are not responsible for their wives' submission in the way that they are for their children's, so they are not to ask for it. A wife's submission is much more of a glad and willing thing – a voluntary placing of herself under her husband's love and care – than is always possible for employees or slaves, or even sometimes for children. For a man to try to force such behaviour from his wife would be as inappropriate and ineffective as a woman trying to insist that her husband lay down his life for her.

We know a couple who disagree about abortion. She, if she gets pregnant, will want amniocentesis tests to see if the child is normal: she does not want to carry a handicapped baby. He believes abortion to be wrong and would be unhappy with any such tests. Perhaps one day she will say to him, "my body belongs to you; you make the decisions". Until she does, it is not his place to ask her for such a sacrifice. If he is wise he will allow the tests (and pray they will not be positive!).

This is how marriage works out in practice. She will do anything for him. He gives up everything for her. Both give the other complete power in every area of their lives. It is total interdependence.

I have often heard an explanation of the husband's "headship" which goes something like this: by and large a couple should decide things together but if they simply cannot agree the husband has the casting vote. This always strikes me as a very sad and impoverished picture. It also makes little sense. Paul specifically draws the doctrine from Genesis 2, *before* the Fall (Ephesians 5:31 and 1 Corinthians 11:8,9). However, presumably, before the Fall Adam and Eve were in perfect agreement. They never would have needed "deciding votes" or "emergency measures". *In practice*, Adam would not have been Eve's head at all; if "headship" means having the final word in a disagreement, a couple who always see eye to eye are not head and body at all since he never needs the last say. To continue the anatomical metaphors, a husband who is always putting his foot down, on the other hand, is very much the head of his wife according to this interpretation, as he is constantly needing to insist on his casting vote. Surely this is wrong. Headship, like bodyship, is a continuous not an occasional thing. It means a husband is constantly loving his wife before himself.

People often ask whether husband and wife perform the same roles. Are their functions identical? And in a sense the answer is of course not. A head and body are not the same. (The head does all the talking, and the body does all the work!) The Church and Christ are not the same. She submits: he loves. So a wife does everything in her power to please her husband. He gives up everything, not only to please her but to make her beautiful, holy, happy, fulfilled, and reaching her maximum potential. They are like an actress and her agent: if she has a good agent she will put herself completely in his hands; if he is a good agent he will spend his time developing her talents and furthering her work. He exists to serve her. She recognises this and submits to him. Small wonder a woman is her husband's "glory"; we will know he is a good husband by the beauty of his wife. (1 Corinthians 11:7)

There has been an attempt lately to say that the marriage relationship is symmetrical. In the interests of women's equality some claim we must reinterpret the scriptures to present a wife's and husband's duties as identical. We would be well advised to leave the scriptures as they are. Though she was made for him, he is now to live for her. Though Adam was formed first, he lays down his life for Eve. If we are worried about women's equality we would do better, not to change what God has said, but to expound it truthfully.

Yet there is something remarkable about this asymmetry. It is like lovemaking itself. Of course it is not symmetrical: a woman and a man have different sexual functions. Yet in true lovemaking there is little difference between the way they make love to each other: both woo, both win, both surrender authority to the other. And perhaps the most important thing about the head and body imagery is not their difference but their mutual dependence; a separation at the neck means instant death for both.

Indeed the more fully we accept our separate roles, the more we realise they are much the same. The distinction between the Church's behaviour and Christ's should be lessening every day: the difference between a wife's attitude and her husband's also fades as they both become more like Christ. After all, there is not much to choose between total submission and total self-sacrifice. Body and soul, mind and strength, are given over to someone else. And this is what both lovers do.

EIGHT

Singleness

"Sing, O barren woman,
  you who never bore a child;
burst into song, shout for joy,
  you who were never in labour;
for more are the children of the desolate woman
  than of her who has a husband,"

says the LORD.

(Isaiah 54:1)

"Virginity is . . . a blessed thing . . . if conferred to
those frequent incumbrances of marriage."

Robert Burton

There is no doubt whatsoever in the Bible that being
unmarried is good. Single people can have fewer worldly
preoccupations, be more single-minded Christians, and
even be happier than the married (1 Corinthians 7:32–34;
40). Small wonder Paul advises them to stay as they are
(verse 27).

Yet we find the teaching shocking, or simply incompre-
hensible. We seem to think everyone wants to be
married. The idea that anyone could be happier single is
something we refuse to believe. And although in our
society it is allowable, if eccentric, to choose singleness,
our attitude to the single life is negative. Though we

never ask ourselves, "Why on earth would Josephine want to get married?" we often say to each other "I wonder why poor Jane never found a husband . . . after all, she's very attractive." It never seems to occur to us that perhaps "poor" Jane believes the Bible, enjoys being single, and prefers to stay that way.

This pessimistic view of the single life is unbiblical, unchristian and faithless. Paul, by contrast, is very positive about staying unmarried. He stresses the values and joys of the life, and he practised what he preached: he chose to stay single himself, although this was quite contrary to Jewish practice at the time.[1]

He addresses himself to the issue in 1 Corinthians 7:

"(1) Now, concerning the things you wrote about: it is good for a man not to touch a woman, (2) but because of sexual immorality each man should have his own wife, and each woman her own husband . . ." (He then talks to married people about sex) ". . . (7) I would like everybody to be like myself, but everyone has their own gift from God: one this, another that. (8) Now, I say to unmarried and to widows, it is good for them to stay [as they are], as I do, but if they are not controlling themselves they should marry, because it is better to marry than burn . . ." (Paul goes on to talk about being married to non-Christians) ". . . (17) Only everyone should live the life the Lord has given him or her, as God called him. I command this in all the churches." (He discusses being called in different situations, circumcised or uncircumcised, slave or free.) "(23) You were bought with a price; do not become slaves of people. (24) Brothers and sisters, let everyone stay with God in the state in which he was called. (25) About virgins I do not have a command of the Lord, but I give my opinion as someone who, by the Lord's mercy, is faithful: (26) so I suppose, because of the inherent need, it is good for someone to stay as he or she is. (27) Have you been bound to a wife? Do not try and be free. Have you been freed from a wife? Do not try and find one. (28) If you marry, though, you are not sinning, and if a girl marries she is not sinning; but you will have worldly troubles and I would spare you that. (29) The time has been shortened though, brothers and sisters . . ." (and we are to live in the light of this) ". . . (32) I want you to be without anxieties. The unmarried man cares for the things of the Lord, and how he can please the Lord, (33) but the married man cares about the things of the world, and how he can please his wife, (34) and he has been divided. Also, the unmarried woman, the virgin, cares for the things of the Lord, so that she can be holy both in body and in spirit, but the married one cares about the things of the world, and how she can please her husband. (35) So I say this for your advantage, not to put a restraint upon you, but for good order and undistracted attention to the Lord. (36) However, if anyone is not behaving properly towards his virgin, if their passions are strong" (or possibly "if he/she is past the bloom of youth") "and so it ought to be, let him do what he wants; he would not be sinning; they ought to get married. (37) He who does not have this need, though, and stands firm in his heart, and has his will under control and has decided in his own heart to keep her as she is, will do well. (38) So both the one who marries his virgin does well, and the one who does not marry does better. (39) A wife is bound as long as her husband lives, but if he sleeps she is free to be married, only in the Lord, to whom she wishes; (40) but she is happier if she remains as she is in my opinion, and I think I have the Spirit of God as well." (1 Corinthians 7)

Oddly enough some people think Paul is being a kill-joy, laying down the law with impossibly difficult teaching. Nothing could be further from the truth. He wants us to be without anxieties (verse 32). He bends over backwards not to burden or restrict us. Although he suggests we stay single he insists we are free to marry. And he specifically says his advice is "for your advantage", and "not to put restraint upon you"(verse 35). He is offering us Christian liberation. He wants us to be free to enjoy our situations to the full, and to live the particular lives the Lord has given us (verse 17).

LIBERATING COMMANDS

Freedom from marriage

This chapter in its entirety is not addressed only to the single. It is relevant to us all. And central to Paul's message is a command he gives everywhere. "Let every-one live the life the Lord has given him" (verse 17). This does not just apply to the question of being married or single but, in context, this is one of its major applications. God has given you a way of life. Live it to the full.

What is my way of life? Perhaps I have a strong desire to be married. I feel sure this is my "gift". If God would hurry up and give it to me I would enjoy it to the full. Or perhaps I am not sure quite what my "gift" should be. Some days I like being single; some days it drives me mad. If God would tell me what my particular life is to be, what my special "gift" is, I would do my best to enjoy it.

This kind of thinking is unbiblical. We have already been given a gift, a particular situation is not the same as a "calling". Our calling is to God. We are called to serve the gospel. The only Christian vocation is the vocation to be a

Christian. And our calling never changes; it is the same for all of us. This should never be confused with our individual way of life or our particular occupation; our "gift".

Quite simply, our "gift" is the one God has given us. Our way of life is the one we have. If you are single your gift is singleness. If you are married it is marriage. And our gift, unlike our calling, is not particularly important. It does not actually matter whether we are slaves or free, Jews or Gentiles, married or single. It matters very much indeed that we are godly. And of course our gift may change. Just because God gives you one gift now does not mean He cannot give you a different one later. I have been given marriage. Tomorrow I may be widowed. I would then be given a single life. Perhaps you have been given singleness. In five years' time you might be married. But now, whether you are fourteen or forty, you have been given a single life. Live it.

On reflection this may seem an absurd command. "Live the life you are living." Surely we have no choice. Why are we told to do something we cannot help but do? The point is there is a way of life appropriate to each gift. The single life, like the married life, is easily spoilt.

The first way to spoil it is not to see it as a gift. All too often people are persuaded to think of the single life as a curse. Paul tells us repeatedly it is good. Yet people refuse to believe it. The culprits are often not unmarried people themselves; the real culprits are those who assume everyone wants to be married. I am constantly hearing people say, "If only poor so-and-so could get married . . ." This kind of comment is offensive in the extreme. It assumes on the part of so-and-so a disobedience to God. He has given single people a gift and told them to enjoy it, but it is difficult to do this if everyone keeps telling you to change it.

A friend of mine has recently become engaged. A

member of her congregation congratulated her, saying
"I'm so glad you're getting married at last: you've got so
much to give!" This unbiblical well-wisher would do well
to study Paul. The idea that one is more useful, or even
better off, with a partner is contrary to his teaching.

So the first freedom Paul gives us is freedom from
marriage itself. In most societies – including, I imagine,
Corinth at this time – it is assumed everyone will be
married. In many Moslem countries, for example, there
is little choice: it is the men's duty to marry, while the
women are considered useless if they are not bearing
children. Jews were under the same kind of obligation.
But in Christ there is a new freedom! There is no such
pressure on us. We can do as we like.

We need not be "slaves to people" (verse 23) in this
way. Paul clearly sees the single life as a kind of freedom
(verse 27). And this it can certainly be. Those of us who
are married know that it "ties you down". It is a glorious
captivity, but it is one all the same. You can no longer be
undivided about the cares of the Lord. Once you are
married you also live for someone else. But Christians are
free to choose another way of life.

Many people are so determined to idealise marriage
they refuse to accept Paul's attitude. His words were only
for the Corinthians, they say, and are no longer relevant.
(Why we keep them in our canon of scripture is anybody's
guess.) "The inherent need" (verse 26) is translated as
"present distress",[2] and interpreted as first-century
persecution; in which case they would have had good
reason to be thankful for singleness.

Admittedly a country under persecution is the worst
place to be married. Your partner and your children may
be tortured for your beliefs. But as it happens, there was
no persecution that we know of in Corinth. Paul may
mean, by "present distress", the restrictions placed on all

of us. We are bound to find tensions in life. We will have trouble and distress before we get to heaven. None of us lives in ideal circumstances: it is necessary, common sense, and normal Christian practice to rejoice in whatever we have. And even if you take Paul's words here (verses 25–31) to be only for those under persecution, he has already laid down the principle that we are to lead the life God has given us. Corinthian or not, we accept what we are given.

We are to enjoy and appreciate our gift. Paul goes further. We should not even try and change it. Whatever your gift was when you were called as a non-Christian, stay in it now you are a Christian. If you were circumcised when called, stay circumcised; if you were uncircumcised, stay uncircumcised; if a slave, stay a slave; if free, stay free (verse 18–22). "Brothers and sisters, let everyone stay with God in the state in which he was called" (verse 24).

"Are you bound to a wife?" (or, we can assume, a husband). "Do not try to be free. Are you free from a wife?" (or husband). "Do not try to find one" (verse 27). If you are free, stay free. Do not look for a partner.

This makes sense. There is nothing which detracts from enjoyment of a single life more than trying to get rid of it. The most successfully single people I know are those who have no thought of marriage. Someone we know, when he was a young man in his first curacy, used to waste considerable emotional energy assessing the nubile fauna of his parish. "Is *she* the one?" he was constantly tempted to ask himself, before deciding her nose was too long or her legs too short. It was not until he put this thinking behind him that he was able to enjoy his job and his situation. Now he loves being single. He has more friends, more time, and far more freedom than a married man could have.

It is only when we forget marriage that we can make

true friends of the opposite sex. A friend of mine in her twenties was plagued with thoughts of finding a partner. Every possible man was assessed as soon as she met him. This made true friendship with any man next to impossible. Those who were ineligible were dismissed as no good. Those who scored higher were only seen in terms of future partners, not cultivated as present friends. Again it was not until she freed herself from this attitude that she could enjoy the opposite sex. We are all tempted to do this, and it tends to cripple our chances of deep fellowship with either sex. I could have had far better boy and girl friends as a teenager if I had not been trying to pair myself off.

So Paul sets us free from the need to find a partner. This is the first way to enjoy your particular life. See it as a gift. Do not look for marriage. Live the life God has given you.

Freedom from sex

The second way to enjoy singleness is to embrace celibacy. For Paul also sets us free from the tyranny of sex: "It is good," he dares to say, "for a man not to touch a woman" (verse 1). Again we find this teaching so repellent many try to explain it away. The most common excuse given for it is that he was repeating some crackpot idea of the Corinthians. Now it is quite possible he was quoting something they had said in an earlier letter, but if so he endorses their statement; he qualifies it by ruling out abstention for married people, but he does not contradict the initial idea. It is good to go without sexual experiences! It is actually good to be celibate. It is not necessarily superior to marriage, but it is certainly not second-best. This is liberating stuff. It means the world is wrong. There *is* life without sex. We are free to live without it.

This is most unconventional teaching. Our society tells

us we need sex, and cannot be fufilled without regular sexual expression. I saw a headline in a paper the other day which ran: "Too much sex can be as dangerous as too little." That too little is dangerous is taken as accepted fact. It is considered essential: without it we cannot be normal, socially acceptable, or psychogically healthy. It is inconceivable to the world that anyone who has a choice in the matter could use it to abstain. And, from what we know about first-century Corinth, I doubt if it was very different.

Paul's comment is not only liberating for single people; it is also a doctrine of great freedom for homosexuals, for the impotent or frigid, and those who are unattractive to the opposite sex. Society tells them they have failed. A single person may one day marry, but Christian gays are "doomed" to life-long sexual frustration if they want to be obedient to God. This is not failure, says Paul. It is good to live without sex. There is no need to think of this as disaster.

No one is pretending it will be easy. We are designed to make love, so those of us who are celibate are bound to feel tempted and frustrated. There is no convenient answer to this. Some find it a life-long struggle; others are hardly bothered at all. But contemporary "liberal" attitudes to sex tend to render the struggle far harder.

Paul tells us in no uncertain terms to "flee immorality" (6:18). He wants us all to be like him (7:7): we are all to be sexually pure. Some of us have one gift and some another: some are married and some single (7:7). But we are all to be like Paul: we are all to flee immorality. Married people do this by giving themselves to each other; single people do so through stringent self-control (which the married, of course, will sometimes need as well). We are all to be alike in our chastity, and we are to achieve that chastity through our different gifts.

This has been made difficult for single people in our society. Paul tells us to flee immorality, but he does not tell us how far to flee. He tells us to use self-control, but he does not tell us how much of ourselves to control. Nowadays it is possible to dip one's toes into sexual intimacy without taking the plunge. Teenagers can kiss. Couples can canoodle. Young people can disappear into cars or quiet corners at parties for a little physical self-expression. And none of this is seen as "having sex".

Nevertheless these things are all erotic, and the biblical picture of the erotic is one of unconditional surrender. There is no reserve in lovemaking. Everything is given to one person and one alone. If you want erotic intimacy with a woman you give yourself to her, body and soul, for the rest of your life. We have somehow divided the erotic into various degrees of seriousness. If you are under a certain age or president of your Christian Union you will not go far; if you are engaged, or not such an exemplary disciple, you will experiment a little more, and so on. This would appear to be our current "Christian" ethic. If you are married you go the whole way but only with one person; if you are single you can go part of the way with anyone you like. The problem then, of course, is knowing when to stop.

Non-Christians are at least consistent. Secular society now more or less allows anything with anyone. We Christians practise double standards: two men would be frowned on for kissing and cuddling in the dark, as would two people married to others; but unmarried teenagers are told to indulge in any amount of slap and tickle as long as they are not "having sex".[3] Yet these things are all sexual; and sex belongs to marriage.

This supposed liberality does not help the unmarried. Paul's advice is compassionate. Celibacy is hard. Abstention is never made easier by tasting tiny morsels of a dish we want to devour. Lovemaking is designed to be enjoyed without restraint. Sampling it is likely to be more frustrating than avoiding it altogether.

Obviously, in the present climate we all want to know how far we can go with immorality before we have gone too far. But Paul tells us to flee it. In normal usage that means to run away from it, to have nothing to do with it all. The erotic is for marriage. If you are married enjoy it; if you are single flee it.

It would be easy to make Paul's words sound hard, but he is not being legalistic or unfeeling. He knew from personal experience what tensions single people can be under. As he says, he is telling us something for our benefit; he does not want to put restrictions on us. If we find it impossible, and other options are open to us, he suggests alternative advice. His "strict" teaching is indeed liberating. I know several people who wish they had heard it when they were younger: it never occurred to them they were free to save themselves for marriage; they never realised they could go through their teenage years without even kissing a girl. As Paul has already said, "All things are lawful", but not all things are *helpful*; all things are lawful, but we do not want to be enslaved to them (6:12).

Nor is Paul trying to burden us with guilt. He is telling us how we should live, not telling us off for how we have lived. Sexual folly, like any folly, can be repented of and forgiven. We are rare if we have no regrets about previous misconduct. The answer is simple "Go, and sin no more" (John 8:11).

"Flee immorality." But this never means flee the opposite sex. Unfortunately those churches which encourage young people to be truly celibate often encourage them also to shun half their peers. This is a pity. A teenage boy, for example, should have among his friends several girls to whom he can talk quite openly. A single woman in her late thirties ought to know a number of men of her own age, married or single, well enough to call them good friends. Much of the frustration single people experience is because they are often not allowed to make real friendship among the opposite sex.

This is surely another reason why Paul tells us to flee immorality. I knew a teenager who worked through a long succession of boyfriends. No one had told her she was free to do anything else; it had never occurred to her that she could choose "not to touch" a man. All these relationships were frustrating. None lasted. They were pale shadows of marriage rather than honest friendships in their own right. The only relationships which survived from her teenage years were of the kind we tend to call "platonic": with her girlfriends, and the only boy who was not a "boyfriend". This is common to many people's experience. As soon as we begin expressing physical attraction towards a member of the opposite sex we start a course which must either end in marriage or nothing. It will seldom end in friendship. Yet deep friendships with members of the opposite sex are just what we need. By and large we are only free to make them when we have ruled out erotic possibilities.

Single people, particularly teenagers, sometimes ask about "girlfriends" and "boyfriends". Can I go out with a non-Christian girl? Is it right to have a boyfriend? The questioners usually assume that any close relationship with the opposite sex must be pseudo-erotic. But a pseudo-erotic relationship is not a real friendship at all. Anything truly erotic belongs to marriage; any imitation is merely a mockery. We should all have male and female friends and Christian and non-Christian friends. Some of these should be intimate. But if any is an erotic friendship it is time to question whether we should still be single.

Freedom to marry

For this is the third freedom Paul gives us; freedom from
singleness itself. People always seem to go overboard
stressing one half of his teaching or the other. Either
single people are made to feel that they have not "made
it", or married people are made to feel they have fallen
for "second best". Because Paul emphatically says the
single life can be better, people somehow assume the
married life must be worse. Yet he repeatedly says this is
not the case. Those who say it is "second best" are
contradicting him. Marriage is not a sin. Paul stresses this
several times (verses 28:36). A man who marries a
woman is doing a good thing (verse 38). Just as some
people do better to stay single (verse 38), some do better
to get married (verse 9). This is why Paul, twice, tells
them to do so.

But if you have been told to enjoy and stay in the single
life how will you ever know to leave it? It is sometimes
thought that if we were really faithful to Paul we would
never marry. If we were keen, hard-boiled, strong-willed
Christians we would steel ourselves and remain celibate
for life. The human race would quickly and obediently
expire. Because we are not all perfect, it is suggested,
Paul allows a counsel of compassion for the fallen: if you
simply cannot live without sex you might as well give up
and look for a wife. In other words, despite the fact that
you are unmarried, have no available partner in mind,
and all appearances point to your being at present well
and truly single, you may come to the conclusion despite
the evidence that your "gift" is marriage after all.

This interpretation does not make sense for a number
of reasons. First, it is in utter contradiction to Paul's
main argument. We have established that those who are

single have the gift of singleness. If we start thinking it is not our gift simply because it is sometimes difficult, we make nonsense of Paul's teaching. I imagine some of the Corinthians with the gift of slavery did not always feel like being slaves.

In addition Paul tells us to enjoy the life we have. Suppose you decide you have too much libido to do so. You start to look for a spouse. Unfortunately it takes you a decade to find one. You have then wasted ten years – or two, or five, or even half a lifetime – hankering after marriage when you could have been enjoying the single life.

And, finally, sexual frustration is not the only or even the chief reason many people long for marriage. Some want companionship, or children. Why are those with uncontrollable lusts to give in while those with other equally difficult desires stay frustrated? Besides, if we followed this interpretation we would probably find that more men than women would be getting married. The situation would be laughable: it would be the beginning of Christian polyandry. This cannot be how we should understand Paul's advice to some of us to marry in verses 8 and 36.[4]

For one thing about Paul's advice is absolutely clear. He is addressing those with a particular partner in mind. The situation is this: a couple are free to marry; they very much wish to; their passions are strong, they are behaving badly, and they feel as if they are on fire. They are longing to give themselves to one another in the fullest possible way. In short, one could safely say they are a couple in love. In which case, Paul says, as any sane man would, "it ought to be, let him do what he wants . . . they should get married".

But he only says this to those *who have a prospective spouse already*. The couple have a well-established relationship.

They are already committed to one another. There is even a suggestion that they are going too far sexually (verse 36). This is very different from someone rather disliking living alone. Deciding to marry because you are in love is sound. Deciding to marry because you do not like being single is no reason at all. This is how to destroy your peace of mind and throw away your gift. Once in the Bible, it is true, a man went looking for a wife (Genesis 24). But the situation was hardly normative. He was not seeking a wife for himself. The idea was the groom's father's; the search, choice and proposal were his servant's; and the girl accepted the offer without meeting the man himself. He was the only person who had no say in the affair at all. His courtship is hardly a model for us. So we are not to go looking for a partner (verse 27). If you are in love, consider marriage. If you are not, do not. You will never enjoy being single if you are trying to find a mate. If you want to marry a particular person Paul suggests you do so; if you simply want "marriage" he does not.

So it is good to stay single, and if you can "stand firm in your heart" you will find the rewards very great. But it is also good to get married, and if you are burning with passion for someone you are probably well advised to get on with it. If you are both in love, go ahead. Get married if you want to.

But there is a problem here. It seems probable that the Corinthians were all betrothed by their families from an early age anyway; Paul's advice is appropriate for those who only have to decide between marriage and single-ness, not between one future spouse and another.[5] People thinking of marriage often tie themselves in agonising knots over this question. "Is he God's man for me?" "Is she the partner the Lord wants me to marry?" For of course it is possible to fall in love with someone quite unsuitable. Paul seems to give little help in such a situation. This is because it would not have concerned the Corinthians; they may have had no say in the selection anyway.

However, there was one group of people amongst his listeners who seem to have been able to choose their future partners: when talking to widows Paul assumes they can select for themselves. If we want advice about choosing the right person we must turn to what Paul says to widows. This is where we find the biblical guidance on the matter. And he gives remarkably little information: a woman who wants to remarry should choose, "in the Lord, whom she wishes" (verse 40). That is all. If you have found someone in the Lord whom you wish to marry, go ahead. Naturally it is common biblical sense that he or she should also be of the opposite sex and free and willing, but otherwise there are no rules or even particular guidelines on the matter.

Now obviously some choices are wise and some foolish. A woman is wise to choose a man she can submit to, since this is what she will have to do for the rest of their lives; if she has no respect for his values and no time for his opinions she is going to find marriage an uphill struggle. And a man is wise to choose a woman he can love and lay down his life for; if he thinks her judgement poor or her ambitions idiotic he is going to find life very frustrating. So there are certainly silly choices to be made when it comes to marriage. However such "mistakes" are hardly morally wrong. We are free to marry, in the Lord, whom we wish. There is no "right" or "wrong" person in an absolute sense. There are people who are likely to make us happy and people who are not. But there is none who can make us ungodly. We can always be obedient husbands and wives even if we are not blissfully happy ones, so we can take plenty of helpful non-biblical advice as to whom we should marry. The only biblical word of advice, however, is to choose, in the Lord, whom we wish.

It is sometimes thought that marrying for love is a totally modern concept. But Jacob worked for fourteen years to marry the girl he loved (Genesis 29:16–30). Samson married for love – not once but twice! (Judges 14:1–3 and 16:4. Both occassions were disastrous . . .) And what is the *Song of Songs* if it is not a love story? Of course other kinds of marriage are valid too: in tribal Pakistan or in Nepal, where marriages are arranged and love matches have never been heard of, the practical implications of Paul's teaching would be different. For us, in our society, this particular application is the appropriate one.

And falling in love is not something you can ever plan. So plan to stay single. Aim to stand firm. One day you may be swept off your feet and your plans will have to change.

PROMISED BLESSINGS

Paul tells us repeatedly the unmarried life is good. Yet for some this may not ring true. You may love being single and not want to change for anything in the world. On the other hand you may often feel frustrated or resentful, and wish you could be married.

Of course. This is natural. In fact it is probably far more common than feeling satisfied and grateful for single-ness. We are created to make love, so most single people will feel sexually frustrated. We are created to have children, so many single (and some married) people will feel their parental instincts are being frustrated. And we are created to be in partnership with the opposite sex, so single people – particularly in our "nuclear family" society – may often feel unsettled or lonely without the lifelong commitment of marriage.

What we often tend to forget is that everyone is frustrated. We are also made to work, so the unemployed are frustrated. We are made to subdue the Earth, so the powerless are frustrated. We are made to serve God, so those of us who are married will sometimes, according to Paul (1 Corinthians 7:32–35), feel frustrated too. I have a friend who works a great deal amongst women, and she finds considerably more frustration in the lives of her married colleagues than her single ones. It is foolish to pretend we are not frustrated, but it is equally foolish to forget that everyone else is frustrated too. Some constraints on our freedom, like unemployment and slavery, are not good in themselves. Singleness is. Paul says so. When we find it trying it is important to bear in mind the advantages it has over marriage.

A single person can be "carefree"

Paul describes a single person as "free" (verse 27). You can be happier (verse 40). You need not have worldly cares (verse 32). The other day a friend and I were discussing Paul's commands in Ephesians 5 on marriage. As we talked of the teaching which is so often neglected, the total self-sacrifice God demands of a husband, his face began to fall.

"She'd better be good," he said. Then he thought a little more. "I think I'll stay single after all."

We saw in the last chapter what marriage means. A husband has given his life away; someone else has authority over him (verse 4); his concern is his wife's pleasure (verse 33). Small wonder Paul describes him as "divided". He is rightly torn between giving his life to a woman and giving it to God.

Shaun and I experience these tensions every day. He works in the evening; he often has meetings to attend. If he were single he would stay talking afterwards, help wash up, walk home with a friend and perhaps ask him in for coffee; then he might do some work at his desk. All this is part of his job. Afterwards he would probably eat, have a bath, go to bed at twelve and read for an hour. He could give himself to his job and live as he liked. Because he is married he comes home sooner than he wants, goes to bed earlier than he wants, and turns the light out before he has read what he wants. If I were single I would go to bed at ten, get up at the crack of dawn, and work for several hours before breakfast; because I am married, I am awake late at night and get up tired in the morning.

This is the small example of the numerous constraints on married people. When I was single I loved my work and gave myself to it wholeheartedly; as soon as I got married it started to suffer. When Shaun was single he was dedicated to his work and found few tensions in pursuing it; since marriage he has often felt called away from it by his family. To be more accurate, our work has changed. Now we have other responsibilities as well as our individual careers, which must often stand aside. So I have lost many jobs because I no longer wish to travel anywhere or work any hours. And Shaun has lost many hours of work in his study because of having children to bath or to play with.

These things are not begrudged; one would not marry if one were not prepared to give oneself to another. But those of us who are not married will appreciate our way of life far more when we realise the advantages it offers. Single people are much freer in their work, their worship, and their lifestyle. They will still, of course, have obligations and commitments to others: some have lodgers for whom they feel responsible; others are looking after parents; all should be caring for friends and other members of their church. Nevertheless a single person has not given himself away in the same way. You have not granted another authority over you, a right to your body, and a claim on your life. As a result you can give the Lord your "undistracted attention" (verse 35). Instead of laying down his life for his wife as Christ did for us, a single man can lay it down for God. Instead of submitting to her husband "as to the Lord", a single woman can submit to the Lord Himself.

Of course it is good to give one's life to someone else; of course it is deeply satisfying to have a lifelong partnership with another human being. But it is far better to give one's life to God; it is far more satisfying to enjoy eternal friendship with Him. In this the unmarried person can be free and undivided.

A single person can have "children"

Unmarried friends have sometimes told me they would like to be married not so much for marriage itself but for children. This is important. Paul says it is good to live without sex; he does not say it is good to live without children. Some people are going to find this difficult. Again, however, in exchange for this deprivation the single person has a corresponding blessing greater than the loss.

The commandment given to us at the beginning of the Old Testament is to go forth and multiply (Genesis 1:28). Consequently, throughout the Old Testament children are seen as a wonderful blessing (Psalm 126:4,5; 128:3,6.) Great joy is the result of obeying God's commands.

In the New Testament we are given a new commandment. " '(19) Go therefore,' " Jesus said, " 'and make disciples of all nations, baptising them in the name of the

Father, and the Son, and the Holy Spirit, (20) teaching them to observe everything I have commanded you . . .'" (Matthew 28). We are no longer simply commanded to bear natural fruit; now we are told to bear spiritual fruit too. Abraham was promised as many descendants as the stars (Genesis 15:5). We, too, are told we can increase a hundredfold (Matthew 13:23). Whereas the Old Testament emphasises the joy of having children, the New Testament recognises a new joy of having disciples born again. Paul constantly gives thanks to God for those he had brought to Christ (1 Thessalonians 1:2; 2 Thessalonians 1:3,4). He recognised Timothy as his "true child in the faith" (1 Timothy 1:2) and he longed to see him, day and night, because of the joy that Timothy brought him. But he could not have given himself to others in this way if a woman had had a prior claim on his life.

We have a friend who has many spiritual children, as Paul had. She prays for them regularly and teaches them the Christian faith. She goes on holiday with them, spends days playing tennis with them, and takes them out to the theatre. She even advises them in their choice of university, or career, or marriage partner. In many ways she cares for them as a parent does for a child. And they in turn look to her for Christian love and guidance. The relationships are deeply rewarding on both sides. Yet she could not do this if she were married: she would have a husband to spend time with and her own children to pray for.

Some may remain unenthusiastic about this. Perhaps new believers do not bring you much joy. You have known one or two people become Christians, but you would hardly look on them as your children or a source of extraordinary happiness. But children are a great commitment. They involve prayer, love, self-sacrifice, expense, and considerable hard work. They also involve a lot of fun. If you want the fun, though, you must be prepared for the rest. Paul went to enormous trouble, suffering and deprivation not only to bring people to Christ but to keep them with Him, as anyone who reads Acts or his letters can see. Consequently, he found his Christian children very rewarding. E. J. H. Nash, the man who brought John Stott to Christ, started on a five-year weekly correspondence with him when he had met him only once as a non-Christian schoolboy. He also prayed for him every day, apparently for the rest of his life.[6] I imagine he was eventually very proud to have such a spiritual son. Having children is a costly and painful blessing. If you want the joy you must first face the hard work. But those of us who are single (or otherwise childless) need not be deprived: Jesus's disciples, his spiritual children (and even probably Paul's) are surely now as numerous as ever Abraham's were.

Marriage is good and offers great rewards, but there are better opportunities and greater rewards available to single people. Partnership with God is better than partnership with any other; new Christians born in the spirit are better than new babies born to the flesh; and eternal life through salvation is better than a lasting name through one's children:

> To the eunuchs who keep my Sabbaths,
>   who choose what pleases me
>   and hold fast to my covenant –
> to them will I give within my walls
>   a memorial and a name
> better than sons and daughters;
>
> (Isaiah 56:4,5)

DIVINE EXAMPLE

The greatest encouragement of all to single people must be the life of Jesus Himself. Whenever we are tempted to think there is something second best, or unfulfilled, or inferior about singleness we have only to think of Him. His life was perfect, yet He never shared it with a woman. He is our example for living, and He stayed single all His life. So we have a great deal to learn from His example as a bachelor.

We can learn from his chastity. Jesus was above reproach in His behaviour with the opposite sex. He was accused of being a drunkard, a glutton and a blasphemer, but He was never accused by His contemporaries of being sexually immoral. This is all the more remarkable when we consider His intimacy with women, and the freedom He allowed them to express their affections towards Him. Yet it was inconceivable even to His enemies that He ever had an erotic entanglement with anybody. His physical contact with men and women was absolutely pure.

We also need to learn from Jesus's partnership with women. He never shunned them, as some bachelors do who are trying to live good Christian lives. He travelled with them, stayed with them, and above all worked with them. We are to enjoy a similar partnership with the opposite sex. It is good for a man not to touch a woman, but it was not good for the man to be on his own. Single people are to be celibate, not unsociable, Christian bachelors should be chaste, not misogynous. They can and should be intimate with women friends and colleagues as well as with men.

And of course we must learn from Jesus's relationship with the Father. His was truly a life of single-mindedness and dedication. We can never hope for the same intimacy with God, but if we aspire to the same obedience we will enjoy some of the same divine companionship.

So single people have an excellent model for their lifestyle in Jesus. If we live as Jesus did we are bound to find fulfilment and liberation in singleness. Our aim is to be as free with the opposite sex, and as pure. After all, in Christ we are all one family; we should treat each other as brothers and sisters (1 Timothy 5:2–3).

As well as having Jesus as our example, though, it helps to know others who lead exemplary single lives. I have a friend I would happily take as my model if I were single. His secret seems to be his readiness to share himself. Because he has no wife he is free to give himself to others. He is constantly available. He is extremely hospitable. He spends his holidays with other single friends. He is often to be found caring for those younger than himself. He shares his life, his time, his money and his house with other people. He is also self-disciplined in his sexual behaviour. He never blights friendship with women by pointless entanglements with them. In every way, he lives his single life to the full. As a result he seldom seems lonely or frustrated.

He also fills his house with lodgers. One of the greatest difficulties for single people in modern life is the way we have structured our families. In cultures where grand-parents, nannies, uncles and slaves also make up part of the household, single people can care for children, help run a house, and be part of a domestic unit. Our society does not encourage this. Families are split up. Teenagers or young adults leave home. Households tend to consist solely of parents and schoolchildren.

One way round this is for single people to live together with some commitment to one another. A friend of mine discovered recently that one of her lodgers is a liar and an alcoholic. Instead of asking her to leave my friend considered it her duty to care for her. Her household is like a loose-knit family, with responsibility for its members.

It is also good when couples and families share their homes. When we were first married we lived in a house with half a dozen single friends. It was not a deliberate choice, but we all enjoyed it and learned from it. We too were like a large family. We ate together, prayed together, and shared our money with one another, as the first disciples sometimes did.

Since we have had a home of our own we have also, for the last three years, always had someone living with us. At first we did not look forward to our loss of privacy, and even thought it might be detrimental to our family life. It has proved exactly the reverse. It is enriching for the children to have a third adult to relate to. It is refreshing for us to have the company and insights of another person. And those who have lived with us have also sometimes told us they have found it a valuable experience.

None of these suggestions is an imperative for single people. But the single people I most admire tend to have these things in common: they share their lives, their homes, their possessions, and even their most private moments with other people; they are sexually disciplined in the extreme; and they show a lasting and prayerful responsibility for others. Of course all these attributes will make them excellent spouses if they ever marry. And all these things were characteristic of the most exemplary single life of all.

Some people think Jesus failed in His mission because He did not marry. Sun Myung Moon has based his religion on this premise. A perfect man, he claims, should have married and left perfect descendants to carry on his name.

Yet as soon as we ask ourselves why Jesus lived like this the reason is obvious. Clearly there were many pragmatic advantages. Like Paul, if Jesus had had a wife He could not have travelled as He did, or given Himself to His followers as He did, or even have been free to die as He did, since He would have given His life to His wife. But there is a far more significant reason for Jesus's celibacy. If He married a woman how could He have been our bridegroom? If He had had natural descendants what would our status have been in comparison? We are his bride, and His true descendants. We are the wife He loves and cherishes, and the offspring He teaches and disciplines. Jesus has indeed married and left descendants to carry on His name.

Obviously this aspect of Jesus's life is no example for us. We are not married to the Church. But it tells us something about the single life. Jesus, as a single person, was free to be one flesh with us; we visualise the relationship every time we take communion. We can be free for the same kind of communion with God Himself. The single life (like marriage) is seldom easy, but it can be a very great privilege.

The Old and New Testaments clearly teach that marriage is a wonderful thing; it is made by God, and good, and the source of a great deal of happiness. You may be given it for part of your life, and it is a gift and a blessing. But the New Testament also teaches that singleness is wonderful too; it is a life of dedication and happiness, with the blessings of spiritual children. We are all given it for part of our lives, and it is also a gift and a blessing.

The single person who lives singlemindedly for Christ need never fear that he or she will miss out. When Jesus told his disciples that marriage was for keeps, they said, presumably in astonishment, that it would be better not to marry (Matthew 19:10). He did not contradict them. Instead, he confirmed that this is true for those who can remain single; there are those, he says, who have done so for the sake of the kingdom of heaven (verse 12). A little later on, Peter points out how much he and the others have given up (verse 27). Jesus reassures them (verse 29). Everyone who has left homes or families, possessions or children for his sake, "will receive a hundredfold, and inherit eternal life."

NINE

Feminism

HELMER: . . . What duty do you mean?
NORA: My duty to myself.
HELMER: Before everything else, you're a wife and a mother.
NORA: I don't believe that any longer. I believe that before everything else I'm a human being.

Ibsen, **A Doll's House**.

"All feminists are angry young men."

Anon.[1]

I was at a party given by a tutor at a theological college. His wife was talking to me about the feminist movement. "What we want," she said, "is a biblical approach. *Christian* feminism is what we need."

One of her husband's students overheard her. "There's no such thing," he said. He showed no hesitation. In his mind Christianity and feminism had no possible common ground.

Many Christians face a hard choice when it comes to feminism. They have two equally unacceptable options. One is a set of "traditional" Christian expectations. Like bygone missionaries, their elders sometimes preach a certain culture along with the gospel. Christian women seem expected to behave in a certain way. There is a suggestion their "femininity" should be rather more demure and domestic than its secular counterpart. I received vivid proof of this in a somewhat backhanded compliment; a Bible college asked me to do the readings for a film they were making.

"All our women are so demure," they complained. "We thought you could be a bit more . . . well, you know . . . aggressive."

Many Christian women find this stereotyping irksome. If they have an ounce of history they will know that the so-called "traditional" roles are not traditional at all; if they have an iota of common sense they see that some of their elders' and betters' assumptions are so much bunkum. Secular society in some ways offers them more respect, more sympathy, and more freedom to be themselves. They feel the gentle stirrings of rebellion against such rigid archaic roles.

But if they leave this cosy and irritating frying pan they may find themselves in the fire. Their fellow Christians may be wrong, but at least they are vaguely sincere. They believe their assumptions to be godly. The world has no such pretensions. Its god is itself. It has no one else to please. Should Christian women, and men, ignore the expectations of people in the Church and risk being moulded instead by the worldly philosophy of "women's lib"?

It is difficult to know what our attitude to these changing trends should be. Undoubtedly, modern mainstream feminism has become secular. This means if we embrace its values we are bound to accept some of the world's assumptions. On the other hand there is also no doubt that feminism has achieved much in our society which is good. It is helping to bring legal, political, and educational equality to women. If there had been no twentieth-century feminism half of us would still not have the vote. Obviously we do not want to reject the entire movement; but we will also want to be wary of endorsing it wholesale.

ANTI-FEMINISM

Many Christians are less than supportive towards the women's movement. The anecdote at the beginning of this chapter is just one of many such examples. Elaine Storkey, in her book *What's Right With Feminism*, illustrates the aggressively anti-feminist position adopted by some leading figures in the Church, particularly in America.[2] Many books have been written by Christians trying to reinforce the "traditional" roles feminism has criticised. For its part feminism is often mistrustful of the Church: Judaeo-Christianity is frequently blamed for sexist structures and assumptions. This ought to give us pause. What is the reason behind this antagonism? Is there something at the heart of feminism diametrically opposed to the Christian faith? Are Christians against it simply because it is wrong?

We must admit there is a considerable lack of knowledge in the Church about the women's movement. Storkey herself says, "it is my firm conviction that most of these authors *have never read* any of the feminist writers they criticise and have little understanding of what they are saying."[3] Elisabeth Elliot, for example, who is most unsympathetic towards the feminist movement, is under the impression that a feminist is someone who believes the difference between the sexes is merely physiological.[4] This is simply ignorance. Many feminists passionately believe there are other differences. Indeed female chauvinism, the hallmark of extreme feminism, would be impossible without it. A vicar told me the other day that the latest feminist wheeze is to give boys and girls the same names. I have never heard such a notion from a feminist herself. One quite often hears people pontificating about feminism without having any clear idea of what feminism is. If we knew more of its history and origins we might not be so scornful. If we bore in mind what it has achieved in our society we might not be so ungrateful. And if we bothered to find out what it stands for, we might not be so antagonistic. We in the Church are often ignorant of the Christian, Evangelical convictions which inspired the feminist movement in the nineteenth century.[5] We frequently forget, for example, the contribution it made to the abolition of slavery. We ignore the feminist protests of Florence Nightingale and domesticate her image until it is acceptable to us. We forget that feminists fought tooth and nail to combat alcoholism; that they campaigned consistently for the poor and inarticulate; that they hated immorality, were intolerant of prostitution, and even discouraged contraception.[6] When we condemn feminism, we ought to realise that we condemn a movement originally built on Christian principles.

We also tend to forget what it has achieved. I wonder how many women who profess apathy towards feminism would really like to live in a society without universal suffrage? How many would want to be without the Married Women's Property Act? How many would genuinely be happy to be paid less for doing the same job of work?

And we show a remarkable capacity to ignore what it believes in now. Feminists are not women trying to be men, as many anti-feminists pretend. Feminists are women trying to be women. "The whole point is that they want to live an oppression-free *woman's* life."[7] Women are equal to men. They have as valuable a contribution to make. They should be granted the same human rights. This is what feminism stands for. A feminist is not someone who wants to abolish good manners or call her daughter "John" or emasculate men. A feminist is someone who believes that women are equal to men and that they should be treated as such.

To a large extent anti-feminist attitudes in the Church spring from ignorance. In truth, most of us have sympathy for feminist causes and respect for feminist achievements, but a horror of aligning ourselves with the feminist name. It has an almost leprous image. When we think of feminism, we seldom call to mind Christabel Pankhurst or John Stuart Mill. Instead we envisage a few braless wonders on the edge of the post-sixties movement, squatting at Greenham Common or demonstrating about abortion. If we are to shun feminism it should be on the grounds of a rather more informed analysis.

So the first criticism we should make of the anti-feminist lobby is its distortion of feminism itself. As far as I know, no one in the Church has attacked feminism from a position of knowledge. Those who are well acquainted with the movement are largely sympathetic. Those who are critical of it seem to be criticising a grossly inaccurate caricature.

Our second charge against anti-feminism is more serious still. It has misrepresented feminism. It has also misrepresented Christianity. Plenty of books have been written from a supposedly Christian position, reinforcing certain sexual roles, which make almost no reference to the Bible at all. The writers invent doctrine out of their own preferences and present it as Christian teaching. Worse still, those who wish to lend credibility to their anti-feminist position are not above a flagrant abuse of scripture to provide a supportive text.

Elliot, for example, in trying to prove that "what is

right for men is wrong for women", not only quotes some highly misleading translations (for example "[women's] role is to be receptive" in place of Paul's injunction to silence in 1 Corinthians 14:34) but also – I can only imagine deliberately – quotes half of 1 Corinthians 7:4 in order to misrepresent Paul. He is being astonishingly egalitarian: "The wife has no authority over her own body, but the husband does; in the same way, the husband has no authority over his own body, but the wife does." Elliot stops the quotation half-way through. This is bad enough. Then she has the gall to say: "There you have it, the contrast between what is expected of men and what is expected of women. The lists are *different!*"[8]

Tim LaHaye does something similar. "All men possess leadership tendencies," he says. "This characteristic is one of the many areas where a man differs from most women." To illustrate the case he quotes Genesis 1:26, saying that man – *he* according to LaHaye – was given dominion over fish, fowl, cattle and all the earth.[9] Yet it is quite clear from the next verse that "man" means men and women. "So God made man . . . male and female." Has LaHaye not read the next verse? Or is he deliberately suppressing the truth? I am not sure which is worse.

The reactionary position of the anti-feminist is not the one we should adopt. It tends to ignorance and dishonesty. But is it wrong on all counts? Should we have no reservations at all about the secular feminist movement?

SECULAR FEMINISM

Feminism is difficult to define. The doctrines of Christianity or Marxism or Islam can be described. They are what the founder (or his immediate disciples) taught. But what is feminism, and who says so? A few extremists can daub the whole movement with their war paint. No doubt one or two feminists hate men or believe in total anarchy (though I suspect they are more myth than fact: I have never met any of them) but this is hardly the essence of feminist belief. What are its fundamental creeds?

The only doctrine to which all feminists subscribe is this: a belief in *the essential value of women*. This is the basis of feminism. Women have an intrinsic worth. Because of this they should not be treated as men's inferiors. And this is the only point of absolute feminist agreement. Some feminists believe we will never have sexual equality without abolishing capitalism. Others believe in sexual separatism because men always dominate a mixed group. Others again are simply asking for scrupulously fair treatment. But anyone who calls her (or him)self a feminist elieves that women should be thought of and treated as human beings of value.

This is not only the common ground on which all feminists stand, but the reason behind most forms of feminist activity. For example, denying women the vote can imply that women are less intelligent or important; the suffragettes were fighting this form of inferior treatment. Or allowing contraceptives can result in women being used for men's convenience; nineteenth-century feminists fought this kind of inferior treatment. And not allowing contraceptives denies women the sexual "freedom" men can have; twentieth-century "libbers" have fought this sort of inferior treatment. All these different battles spring from the same conviction. Women should be treated as men's equals.

And of course this is also a Christian conviction. As John Stott says in discussing the feminist movement, "every complaint of injustice and every cry for justice should make the Christian sit up and take notice".[10] With this, the most basic of feminist ideals, the Christian has the deepest sympathy. Women and men are equal, and should be treated as such. This "cry for justice" is the mainspring of the women's movement. Christians must heartily support it.

So Christians should be behind the feminist cause. Its first goal is also a Christian one. Whenever we hear an appeal for sexual equality we must indeed sit up and take notice. We should go further. We ought to give active help and encouragement. We should feel genuinely abashed at our Christian apathy. Shame it was the world, not the Church, which brought about many improvements for women. Shame it was only women, not men too, who usually caused the necessary outcry. It is time we redressed the balance.

We should also acknowledge our debt to feminism. Sexual equality is a biblical doctrine. Unfortunately in latter decades Christians have done little to make it a reality. As Stott says, the contemporary liberation of women is largely due to Jesus, but "the shame is that it did not come earlier and that the initiative was not taken more explicitly in His name."[11] Feminism has done much of the work Christianity should have taken on.

So far so good. We agree with the basis of feminism. We too want sexual equality. Obviously we will not agree with every application of the principle. Some women say sexual equality means that women should sleep around as freely as men have done. Christians will say the opposite: men's moral standards should be as high as women's have had to be. Some say sexual equality means abortion on demand. Christians will say the reverse: a father, too, should take the responsibility for an unborn unwanted child.

It is on these points that Christians and feminists disagree. But feminists themselves do too. By no means all believe in easy abortion or unrestricted sex. The pioneers of the feminist movement would have been horrified at such a notion.

The fact that these outworkings may be unchristian does not mean we should disassociate ourselves from the movement. It means the opposite. We must involve ourselves. We are in agreement over the aim; we must encourage a godly pursuit of it. Christians have a vital contribution to make to feminism. The fundamental principle is biblical. It is only Christians who will make the outworkings of it biblical too. As was pointed out in chapter 1 it is because our voice has gone unheard that "Women's Lib" does not have a particularly Christian tone.

Thus far, then, we can endorse feminism. We are fully in agreement with its basis; both Christians and feminists want justice. We will want to work alongside the movement in pursuit of sexual equality. We want equal pay for equal work, the same opportunities for the sexes, paternity leave for fathers, and so on. We are in disagreement with some conclusions of some feminists: we do not believe in separatism or Marxism or lesbianism. We do not see sexual equality in terms of a mother's right to kill. However, such considerations do not rule out the possibility of Christian feminism. These are not essential feminist tenets; one can be a feminist without being a Marxist or a lesbian.

But are these the only points of disagreement? Are there, perhaps, more profound aspects of "women's liberation" we may have overlooked? After all feminism has become a secular movement. It was not always so; once there were women with Christian beliefs at the forefront of the campaign. Now its main writers and thinkers are not Christian, and this means they are not likely to argue from within a Christian framework. Christians and feminists are agreed in wanting the job

market to be fair, but we are not agreed on the purpose of
life itself. Yet this is surely more important. Underlying
worldly assumptions about the purpose of our existence
are more dangerous to the unwary Christian than, for
example, outspoken attitudes towards sexual morality.

Any secular movement is ultimately going to be in
disagreement with Jesus's teaching. There is indeed an
essential difference between Christianity and feminism,
but it is a difference we have not just with the women's
movement but with almost any philosophy in our society.
We do not live for the here and now: we believe in a
hereafter. We cannot live to please ourselves: we have a
Lord in heaven. We may not simply work for a just society:
we have a gospel to proclaim which is even more urgent.
This means that we are profoundly at variance with
almost every worthy cause around.

I personally have every sympathy with, for example,
the Animal Rights Movement, the National Trust, and
the fight against world poverty. I believe Christians
should be involved in all these causes. But they must see
them from a Christian perspective. They will seldom, for
example, have justification to break the law; however
concerned we are about vivisection we must think
carefully before jeopardising Christ's witness by stealing
property or using violence. I heard on the radio recently
that the leader of Christian CND has just left his wife; he
regretfully explained that his work for peace had des-
troyed his marriage. Again, I myself support his cause.
But I believe he has it quite out of proportion: in fighting
these lesser battles, for justice or peace or the environment or the arts, we are never called to abandon a greater
war.

Yet this can easily happen. I know Christians who care
more about women's rights than the Lordship of Christ;
who are more concerned to show the Bible to be

egalitarian than to expound it truthfully; who would rather hear a talk on "humankind" than a sermon on God. I heard a lecture at a Christian festival some time ago on the subject of sexual oppression. The speakers spoke eloquently for an hour. At the end a questioner raised her hand. "I did notice one thing," she said, "that worried me rather. You quoted from the following people: Mao Tse Tung, Betty Friedan, the Naked Ape column from the *Guardian*, the *Observer*, an unnamed young woman, a child psychologist, another unnamed psychiatrist. You didn't actually quote once from the Bible . . . What worries me is that you were very clear on what you said women wanted. You didn't make it at all clear whether this is what God wanted."[12] This kind of thinking is bound to lead us into error, with feminism as well as with anything else.

Let us take an example. There is an assumption nowadays that we ought to be "fulfilled". What we mean by fulfilment is a sophisticated form of happiness. Not the instant happiness of having a good meal, but the rather more long-term happiness of being in appropriate employment or living with the person one is in love with. Now a non-Christian is "wise", from the world's point of view, to seek this kind of happiness. If you do not believe in an afterlife you must of necessity want your present one to be good; and it is sensible not only to seek immediate happiness but also a more lasting form of satisfaction.

A Christian is not always wise to do this. We expect another life after this one, and longer-term happiness still. Just as a non-Christian will sometimes put aside instant happiness (going out for the evening) in favour of more long-term happiness (studying to become a doctor), so we will sometimes put aside earthly fulfilment for the sake of eternal blessings. It is not always right, for example, to live with the person you love. She may be married to someone else. So a Christian is sometimes called to forego great fulfilment on earth for the greater fulfilment still of obedience to God's commands.

The society we live in is most unsympathetic to this. It will try and persuade us we have a right to immediate "fulfilment". It will tempt us to believe we deserve temporal satisfaction. We "Christianise" the philosophy by pretending there is some kind of obligation on us to be challenged and stimulated; the parable of the talents, for example (Luke 19), is supposed to be telling us to use our abilities. If you are a good pianist you must play the piano for the Lord. This is not what the parable says at all; a talent is a coin; the coin we are to use and invest with profit is the gospel. Of course if you can give yourself or others pleasure by playing the piano you should do so. But you have no more *duty* to than you have duty to enjoy good wine. You will never find a parable commanding you to do this. It is common sense. It is good to be happy and fulfilled. It is how we are created to be. But it is not a priority. It is not our Christian obligation. And worldly fulfilment is not our overriding ambition. Why, it would leave us nothing to look forward to: Christianity *is* "pie in the sky when you die".

These assumptions about self-fulfilment are not the responsibility of feminism. Everything in our society is telling us to look after "number one". When a man gets bored with his wife he leaves her. When a child finds his parent's authority irksome, he rejects it. Self-gratification is the tyrant of our age. It is not simply feminism which propagates the idea. The supposedly "Christian" anti-feminist position argues along the same lines; a book actually entitled *The Fulfilled Woman* promises you the ultimate in satisfying experiences if you become a doormat for your husband to wipe his boots on. This argument is neither convincing nor particularly Christian. We do things because they are right, not because they will necessarily be satisfying.

This desire for self-fulfilment is a disease of our time. But the point is this: modern secular feminism, being a child of our time, has the idea coursing through its veins – not so much because it is feminism, but because it is modern and secular. This is why we must be wary.

I have a Christian friend whose husband wanted to go abroad. This would have involved considerable sacrifice for her; she had work she loved and was good at. It was quite unjust of him to see his job as much more important than hers; it was absurdly selfish to expect her to embrace unemployment so his work could take the turn he wanted. Being no fool she realised this, and the very realisation put her into a dilemma. The voice of feminism, the voice of sexual justice and equality, told her it was quite unreasonable to give in to her husband's wishes.

And the voice was absolutely correct. It *was* unreasonable. There is compelling logic in the argument. But there is also a deeper, more compelling logic which calls out to any Christian making a decision. Her own happiness, her work, her fulfilment and her achievements are not the only consideration. There is also a matter of love, and respect, and self-sacrifice and submission to bear in mind. In the end she put her husband before herself and gave in to his wishes instead of her own.

This is the kind of pressure we can find ourselves under. Feminism is right to fight for equality for women and men. It is wrong if it ever tempts us to see that equality in terms of our own fulfilment, assertiveness or rights. "For the desire for *self*-fulfilment, *self*-achievement, *self*-growth and *self*-service is what has produced chauvinism in men. For women to travel further down the same road can only make the situation worse."[13] These ideas are bound to make us unhappy and frustrated, and they are the kind of ideas we absorb without noticing.

A couple I know were going out for a meal last week. He wanted to go by car, she on foot. They both found themselves under pressure to insist on their own way. She had heard from friends and colleagues that women are always making way for men. They have only themselves to blame if they are bullied and walked over like doormats. She ought to "assert herself". He had heard, on the other hand, that men should wear the trousers. Only fools are henpecked. Men should never give in to women; he should also "assert himself". In short, they had both been persuaded that they had a duty to be selfish. These ideas are communicated in the most subtle of ways: they come about through a chance word or barely spoken attitude. If this couple had stopped to think they would both have realised that it is Christlike to give in, and they need not have ruined their evening.

I have pursued the question of fulfilment because it is a good example of the many assumptions in our culture which are profoundly anti-Christian. They are starting to creep into Christian thinking: "Love your neighbour as yourself" now tends to be expounded as first "love yourself". This is where we must resist the influence of the women's movement. We are in danger of being convinced that we cannot be happy if we lay down our lives for one another. Yet this is exactly what Christ's example tells us to do. My friend's meal out was spoilt because she was told she must have her own way in order to enjoy herself. This can happen in more serious ways. To take a well-worn example, many women are made to feel guilty for staying at home as housewives; they have often made the decision to do so through purely unselfish motives, laying aside other work they enjoyed because they believe their small children need them at home. And then they are made to feel inadequate for giving up the stimulation and challenge and money of the work they did before. The world tells them they are foolish to have put others before themselves.

It is important to understand, though, that feminism itself is not answerable for this. Indeed it is not really genuine feminism. It is our own selfishness assuming a feminist voice. One can be tempted by it every day. "It is unfair to change more than your share of the nappies." "It is ridiculous for you to tidy away his gloves." "It is not right for your work to be put second yet again . . ." and so on. This is not feminism. It is our own sin and the egotism of our age disguising itself as sexual justice. But because it disguises itself quite well, we must be careful not to fall for it.

There is much in secular feminism that is right: its basic fight for sexual justice puts us to shame. But we will also come across underlying worldly assumptions, in this, as in any secular movement; and it is these we must be particularly wary of.

CHRISTIAN FEMINISM

Christians ought to be prominent in any pursuit of justice. But there are inevitably aspects of secular feminism we cannot endorse. So what will characterise a Christian involvement in the cause?

A biblical outlook

A truly Christian approach will reject all that is false. On one hand this means jettisoning the additions to scripture we have accumulated over the years. Adding to God's word was the first mistake ever made: "Did God say, 'you shall not eat out of the tree?'" (Genesis 3:1). "We mustn't even touch it," Eve replied, going beyond God's prohibition. Additions to scripture are dangerous. Like Eve's, they can be precursors to a fall. Among them we would include all the old wives' tales: women should stay at home with the children; men are natural leaders; husbands should assert their "headship"; men are more objective; women should not be the initiators – and so on and so forth. Some of these are half truths. Some are similar to something taught in the Bible. But none is scriptural, and all are to be found in popular Christian paperbacks. There are still plenty of books being published telling Christian women to be fluffy little housewives. These notions are fair enough as someone's personal opinion or observation, but when presented as biblical teaching, they should be ruthlessly exposed.

On the other hand, Christian feminism will reject the secular assumptions of our age. We are called to be holy, different from the world around us. We will not swallow many of the things our fellow feminists may take for granted. The following should go on the list of new wives' tales to be abandoned: you must not sacrifice yourself for other people; you should be assertive; you must not let your husband or anyone else take advantage of you; you should stand up for your rights; you must be fulfilled – and so on. These lies are just as bad as the others, and may be more likely to deceive us in the years to come.

A concern for others

But what should characterise a Christian alternative above all is a Christian love for others. In the last century, feminism fought for the less articulate. Its battles were for slaves, prostitutes and paupers. Sadly, the feminism of today seems to have lost much of this spirit. The campaign for abortion exemplifies this: the silent protest from within the womb goes unheard by many feminists.

There are plenty of people in the world in need of philanthropic feminism. Millions of girls in Sudan (and even some Africans in this country) are still subjected to the brutal mutilation of female circumcision.[14] Tiny girls of six cannot walk for weeks, or relieve themselves without excruciating pain for months, because of the "operation". They will never feel sexual pleasure. They cannot give birth without being surgically opened and then sewn up again. I have even heard that a frustrated groom may take knife to his bride on their wedding night if her vagina has been made too small. Is this not an appropriate cause for Christian feminists? If we do not care about such issues, who will?

It is probably true to say that wherever men suffer injustice in the world women are likely to suffer more. Wherever there is poor education, women's will be poorer. Wherever there is exploitation of labour, women tend to be exploited far more. And wherever there is starvation women are likely to be fed after their menfolk, and then pass half their portion to the children. Again, if Christians do not concern themselves about such injustices, who will?

Not that we are short of needs far nearer home. One London woman in six has been raped. Half those rapes have included violence.[15] These women may turn to a rape crisis centre, but if they do, they are unlikely to find any Christians there. They will find feminists who are often aggressively misandronous[16] and also often anti-Christian. Clearly this is another place where we need Christian feminists.

We also need to help people to become more aware of sexual abuse. Rape and incest are still not taken seriously in our society. I heard a barrister on the radio recently say that a thousand pounds – less than one would receive for losing a couple of front teeth – was perfectly adequate compensation for "not serious" forms of rape. By this he did not mean a girl who had led a lover on and then changed her mind. He only meant that she had not been beaten up, stabbed to death, or left bleeding in a gutter. This attitude is still common amongst lawyers, judges and even some members of the police. As it is, the chances of any rapist being convicted are less than two percent,[17] and even when rape is proved beyond any doubt and sentence is given, the penalty is often so lenient the victim will still be suffering the effects of her ordeal years after her assailant walks free. There is very little deterrent to protect women from sexual abuse. Presumably this is because those who make our laws do not realise that rape is a serious crime. Christian feminists must put this right, and urge society to treat it with appropriate abhorrence.

An involvement of men

In all these struggles there is another quality which ought to make Christian feminism distinctive. If it is motivated by a concern for others, as it should be, it is a cause which should appeal to Christian men as much as to women. We tend to think of feminists as women. Why? Because women are concerned about women's issues. Plenty of Christian men are happy to claim that their sex have a kind of umbrella "headship" over women which is expressed in "loving responsibility". Why, then, have they not translated this loving responsibility into active feminism? Women tend to be physically weaker than men. This means they are liable to physical abuse. There

is serious domestic violence in our society, and it is not
confined to the secular world; in Christian and non-
Christian homes alike, hundreds – possibly thousands –
of women are subjected to sickening levels of systematic
torture.[18] As we saw in chapter 3, if women are to be
treated as equals, they will sometimes need protection. It
is ironic that those men who shout loudest about headship
(and the responsibility it entails) are often those least
likely to be doing something about this protection.

Many feminists do not welcome men in their cam-
paigns. I believe Christian feminists should. If a woman
suffers violence from her partner she will almost certainly
find it hard to relate to the opposite sex. She will
eventually need loving men as well as loving women
around her. If the only refuge available is staffed entirely
by women, and she is cared for only by women, there is a
real danger she will grow to distrust most men. Christian
men need to care about so-called women's issues as much
as Christian whites should care about racial apartheid.

We also need to do much in terms of campaigning on
behalf of men. As husbands, and particularly as fathers,
men are seriously discriminated against in this country.
A man does not have the right to so much as a day's
paternity leave, whereas a woman having a baby can
claim several months' leave at almost full pay. Many
men's working hours are such that they barely see their
young families at all. We have a number of friends who
leave for work at seven and get home again twelve hours
later; presumably, until their children are teenagers,
their fathers hardly meet them on a normal day. Because
men are seen as "workers", not husbands and fathers,
they are not free to choose a civilised working day and
spend the rest of their time bringing up their families.
Again, Christians should be the ones to be saying that
there is more to a man's life than a large salary.

These tasks may sound daunting. But I know of a church, which is in no way exceptional, which is beginning to take an interest. They have two or three women in the congregation, as most churches probably have, who have been badly treated by their husbands. It occurred to someone in the church when they were going through the worst that they may have had no one to turn to. To tell the vicar would have been difficult; partly because he is a man, and partly because it would feel like disloyalty to their husbands. To tell anyone else might have started gossip. To go to a secular rape crisis centre would never have occurred to them, and they might have been told outright to leave home, and received little sympathy for their Christian convictions; a woman who was still committed to her husband despite his aggressive tendencies would probably be seen as hopelessly oppressed by sexist indoctrination. So it was suggested that a church-based domestic crisis centre was set up. The vicar was enthusiastic, has suggested it to one or two other churches, and I believe they are now in the throes of arranging it. The idea is for a church to provide two or three people – probably a married woman and a married couple – to train together in a small group. Anyone with domestic problems, whether beatings and incest or simply distressing rows, can ring and ask for help. She, or her husband, will be guaranteed confidentiality, anonymity, and a listening Christian ear.

We need Christian feminism. The Church needs it and society needs it. Christian feminists could be exposing what sexual permissiveness does to women. Christian feminists should be asking how abortion exploits a woman. Christian feminism ought to be fighting pornography. Above all, Christian feminism should be distinguished by its concern for others and *their* rights.

A more Christian behaviour

In a sense, however, there are more basic changes to be made. This book has been trying to illustrate some of the unbiblical attitudes we have about the sexes. Those of us who cannot work in the Sudan, for example, to change attitudes about female sexuality can still do a great deal to make our behaviour nearer home more Christian.

At work Christians often need to show far more respect for women. As we have seen, we need women as well as men in all aspects of employment if we are to benefit from God's design in creation. Presumably we have hardly any women MPs or executives or professors partly because we are reluctant to vote for them, employ them, or educate them. Christian employers should ensure that they are not passing over women suitable for positions of responsibility. Christian husbands should ask themselves if they really are promoting and support-ing their wives' work. Christian parents should give their daughters confidence in seeking higher education and more demanding work.

At a more mundane level, we could be setting a better example at work. Christian men are unlikely to subject their female colleagues to sexual harassment, but they are only too likely to show disrespect to female superiors; I have frequently noticed how bad Christian men are at taking orders from a woman. And they are also only too likely to display ugly sexist attitudes. I was working in a company recently with one other Christian. He was the only one who had never made the coffee, washed up the mugs, or made a cake for anyone else's birthday. It proved to be a very offputting Christian advertisement for those who were working with us.

Our Christian homes could also show far more equality

and interdependence. Christian husbands are sometimes not as good as they could be at nourishing and
cherishing. Many appear to think it their duty to put
themselves before their wives. Some do not seem to
recognise their more mundane domestic responsibilities
at all. We knew a minister whose wife, after years of
running the home, had to take on a full-time job because
they could not make ends meet. She was on her feet all
day, but he still expected her to cook all his meals, do all
his washing up, rear his children and do all his housework when she came home in the evening. He would sit
impatiently in his study waiting for her to come home
and make him a pot of tea.

As I hope was made clear, men are seen by God to have
the same duty to the home as women. Women's outside
work is as important as men's. And because husbands
are to lay down their lives for their wives it is their duty to
further their wives' work, encourage their careers and
make sure they are not doing more than their share in the
home. Men whose wives are housewives should be offering just as much support. A friend of ours is bringing up
her tiny children almost single-handed at the moment
because her husband's job keeps him away from home
several nights a week. The chidren are proving difficult
and she is under pressure. Yet recently the church
expected him to be away for an entire weekend on a PCC
conference.

And of course our churches themselves could show
far more sexual interdependence. As we have seen, the
Church tends to divide its responsibilities into men's and
women's work. Whether or not we believe in women's
ordination we should be encouraging far more women to
study the Bible seriously and equip themselves to train
others in Christian behaviour, as Paul says they should
(Titus 2:4,5). I know an Oxford graduate who has sat

through weekly Bible studies for four years and has never been asked to lead one. She is far more competent to lead them than some of the people she has to listen to. She gains nothing from the meetings apart from humility and a deep sense of frustration. If the reason she has not been asked to lead is because of scruples about women teaching men, she ought to be put in charge of a women's group before her mind atrophies altogether.

We should also be more concerned about evangelism to *men* in churches where they are outnumbered. The domestic image of the Church, the plethora of women's activities, and the expectation on the congregation to sit in the pews taking orders while the vicar does all the work, all help to serve as deterrents to men.

Christian feminism, then, should be biblical and altruistic. We should know what God says about the sexes, and be confident in the knowledge. We should show a concern for others who suffer from sexism, rather than for our own rights. We should include among our feminist ranks, and indeed be caring for, fellow men as well as women.

Indeed any Christian behaviour should be all these things anyway. If the church were truly faithful, we would out-feminist the feminists. If we were really loving our neighbours we would be more genuinely concerned for sexual justice than the most militant of feminine extremists. If we were the body of believers we ought to be, there would be more sexual liberation in our ranks than anywhere else in the world.

Liberation

"Women's Liberation", as the name suggests, is all about freedom. And genuine freedom is not so much freedom to choose, but freedom to be oneself. We are not free if we are living in rebellion against God, no matter how much choice we have in the matter, because we were made for His service, the service which is perfect freedom.

The freedom we need is freedom to be our true selves, to be what we were made to be, to be the image of the God who created us. Men and women are different, and should rejoice in that difference and appreciate it. We are equal, and should promote that equality far more than we do at present. We are interdependent, and Christians should always be working in sexual harmony and partnership.

But above all, we are made to love. We are made in God's image, and He is Love Itself. The way we relate to one another should speak of concern and gentleness and humility. This is more important than all the rest. True women's, and men's, liberation is patient and kind. It is not envious or boastful or proud. It is not rude or self-seeking or easily angered. It keeps no record of wrongs. It delights in the truth. It always protects, always trusts, always hopes, always perseveres.

And when it is all these things, it will never fail (1 Corinthians 13:8).

TEN

Back to the Image

> ' "Remember Freud's dying words: 'Good grief, good grief, what do women want?' "
> "Those were Freud's dying words?"
> "Just before his wife shot him." '[1]

Man was digging the garden. He was having a jolly good try, but something was seriously missing. His ideas all seemed incomplete. He would plough up the earth, and then not think to plant it. He would collect up the fruit, and then not know what to do with it. He grew vegetables, and then puzzled over how to use them.

"This is hopeless," God said to Himself. 'This man can't cope. He's not behaving like us at all. This human being, who is supposed to resemble us, is only half there."

So God decided to complete the picture. He would make a perfect counterpart to man, someone who could help him in the work, so that together they would be His true likeness.

He would have to make somebody equal: the animals would not do at all. He would have to make somebody different: another man would simply double the problem. And he would have to make someone who had some deep connection with the man, someone who needed him as much as he clearly needed in return; it would be absolutely no use making him a partner, a different, equal creature who complemented him beautifully, if the two ignored each other and went their own separate ways. No, they would have to be inseparable; they needed to be part of one another.

God had a brainwave. He decided to use a bit of the man himself. That way they would always want to be together. He would only find himself complete in her, and she in him.

God was looking forward to showing the man his new companion. He knew Adam would be excited. "At last!" he would say. "Here's part of me! My other self. My counterpart. I'll call her after me." God anticipated it with pleasure.

He took her by the hand and led her to the man. "Wake up Adam," He said. "At last I've got a friend for you."

The man sat up and rubbed his eyes. Then he felt his side. "Bother!" he said out loud. "I say," he asked God, "you haven't seen a spare rib on your travels, have you?"

"Adam," God said patiently, "I have made a friend to help you. Aren't you pleased?"

He looked at her. Then he looked at God. "What was wrong with the way I was doing it?" he asked crossly.

God was starting to feel discouraged. "You'll do a lot better together," he explained.

Through his resentment, the man looked at the not-quite-man. He could see that the new creature was in some ways like himself. So far he approved. But in other ways she was not like him at all. Of this he disapproved very strongly.

"She seems to have bits missing," he said to God, rather critically.

God thought it better to leave them to get to know each other. This they did, in a manner of speaking.

"Look here, Notquiteman," the man said to the woman. "I've started to work on this garden, and you'll only mess it up, so why don't you find something else to do while I get on with this? Do some knitting or ironing or something?"

The woman looked puzzled. "We don't wear clothes," she said.

"Yes dear," the man said absent-mindedly. "Don't trouble me now, there's a good girl."

He wandered off, scratching his head for the twentieth time over what to do with the cauliflowers.

Sometime later, something wonderful happened to the man. His life was transformed. The woman bore him two sons.

"At last," he said when he saw them. "They are the bone of my bone and flesh of my flesh. They shall be called men because they were taken out of me."

He was thrilled. He took Cain and Abel off to the garden to help him with the work God had given him to do.

God was walking around one day, when he thought he would have a look to see how they were all getting on.

Out in the garden there were three men, digging over the soil, but not thinking to plant it, gathering pyramids of melons which were rotting in the sun, storing sacks of decaying vegetables, building mountains of butter, and digging lakes of milk, and the whole lot was going to waste because they had no idea what to do with it.

It all seemed pretty futile to God. Still, he was glad the earth produced such plenty, as he had designed it to. "At least you won't go hungry," he said to the men with satisfaction.

"Don't go hungry?" Adam said. "We're always hungry! That's why we can never stop working. We never have enough. We're constantly struggling to provide for our families. Now leave us alone. We're busy."

God grew angry. "Why isn't the woman helping you? That's what I made her for. Where is she?"

All the three men burst out laughing. "The women!" they all said in unison. "They couldn't help. If we can't cope, what can they do? What a suggestion. The women! Ha! Ha! Ha!"

God left them, and went looking for the woman. Eventually he saw her, sitting inside the kitchen, talking to her daughters.

"You know," she was saying, "we could cut open those melons and dry the seeds; then next year we could plant some more."

"Yes," said one of the girls, "and if we could think of some way of turning the soil, of digging it over like the men do, we could plant wild grasses, and grow corn, and eat it through the winter."

"You know," said the third, "there's plenty of food here, if only we could organise it properly. We could cook all those vegetables for supper, if they weren't being stored for something, and have fruit for pudding."

The men outside paused for a moment and looked towards the house. "Women!" they said. "They do nothing but gas all day."

The women looked out of the window, and sadly shook their heads. "Men!" they said wistfully. "They never listen."

Notes

Page 8.
1. Exley, Richard and Helen, Ed. *What is a husband?* (Exley Publications Ltd., 1977), p. 4.

ONE

1. M.D.W. July 1984, *A Fully Human Priesthood*, Oliver S. Tomkins, p. 9. *The Ordination of Women to the Priesthood*, "General Synod, a background paper", by Christine Howard (UO Publishing, 1984).
2. E.g. *The Total Woman*, Marabel Morgan (Hodder & Stoughton, 1973); *For Women Only*, Evelyn R. Petersen and J. Allan Peterson, ed. (Tyndale House Publishers, 1974); *Let Me Be a Woman*, Elisabeth Elliot (Hodder & Stoughton, 1979); simply *Woman*, Dale Evans Rogers (Hodder & Stoughton, 1981) and even *Queen take your throne*, Eileen Wallis (Kingsway Publications, 1985) . . . not to mention *Who's Stopping You Being a Woman? Who'd Want to Be a Woman Anyway? Weeds, Wets, Wimps & Women*, etc. etc.
3. See John Stott, *Issues Facing Christians Today* (Marshalls, 1984), chapter 1, "Involvement: Is it our Concern?"
4. For example see Mark 1:32–38, when he deliberately turned his back on Capernaum, where crowds were queueing up for healing, so that he could go on to preach, because "That is why I have come" (verse 38).
5. *Women in the Bible*, Mary J. Evans (Paternoster Press, 1983), p. 17.
6. ibid., p. 16.

TWO

1. Jonathan Cape Ltd., 1979, p. 180.
2. In fact I have been unable to find this quotation in my copy of *1066* – but if it isn't there it certainly ought to be!
3. For example that excellent, and anti-"Women's Lib" book, *The Female Woman*, Arianna Stassinopolis (Davis-Poynter Ltd., 1973).
4. Which is partly what *The Cinderella Complex*, Colette Dowling (Fontana Paperbacks, 1982) is trying to do.
5. Augustine, *De Genesi ad Litteram* ix, 5 cf vii, 3. "I do not see in what way it could be said that woman was made a help for man if the work of childbearing be excluded."
6. *The Female Eunuch*, Germaine Greer (Granada Publishing Ltd., 1981), p. 277.
7. *Voyage to Venus*, C. S. Lewis (Pan Books, 1953), p. 186.
8. Cf. *The Turning Point*, Fritjof Capra (Fontana, 1983), p. 21.
9. Hestia, Hero, Aphrodite, Cybele (or Rhea), Pallas Athena, Artemis, Persephone, Demeter, and so on and so forth.
10. An idea to which feminists – understandably enough – take objection. Cf. *The Second Sex*, Simone de Beauvoir (Jonathan Cape, 1972), pp. 14–16. "He is the Subject, he is the Absolute – she is the Other."
11. 'E.g. *The Times*, Letters, October 13th 1983: "For many women the language of worship is increasingly hurtful and offensive in its use of 'man' to describe us all. The *purpose* has not been to assert the superiority of the male sex, but this has been one of the harmful *results*, as recent studies of language and its effects have established." Ms Jean Mayland.'
12. This, of course, is why Elaine Morgan called her book *The Descent of Woman* (Bantam Books, 1972). See p. 3: ". . . 'man' is an ambiguous term. It means the species; it also means the male of the species. If you begin to write a book about man or conceive a theory about man you cannot avoid using this word . . . before you are halfway through the first chapter a mental image of this evolving creature begins to form in your mind. It will be a male image . . ."
13. E.g. Hosea 1:2; 2:2–13.
14. E.g. Ephesians 5:25–27; Isaiah 54:5–7; Hosea 2:14–16, 19–20.

15.   C. S. Lewis sometimes gets dangerously near this idea, for example in saying: 'God is so masculine that all creation is feminine by comparison." Quoted by Elisabeth Elliot in *The Mark of a Man* (Hodder & Stoughton, 1981), p. 51.

16.   A fascinating study of this has been done in *Gynomorphic Imagery in Exilic Isaiah (40–60)* by Leila Leah Bronner. She quotes a number of striking biblical images "comparing God's actions to that [sic] of a mother bearing, caring [sic], carrying and comforting her children". For example Numbers 11:12; Deuteronomy 32:18 (the word translated "begat" – RSV – more often means "give birth to", while the next line means "to bring forth with pain or sorrow". It is used to describe a woman giving birth.) Deuteronomy 32:11 ff.; Isaiah 42:14; 46:3; 49:15; 66:13.

17.   In *God in the Dock*, C. S. Lewis (Fount Paperbacks, 1979), "Priestesses in the Church."

18.   John Stuart Mill, *The Subjection of Women* (MIT, 1970), pp. 27–8. "If women have a greater natural inclination for some things than for others, there is no need of laws or social inculcation to make the majority of them do the former in preference to the latter."

THREE

1.   Misquotation, of course, from *Animal Farm*, George Orwell (Penguin Books, 1945), p. 114.

2.   "Gratian, a jurist from Bologna, said: 'The image of God is in man and it is one . . . he has the image of God . . . woman is not made in God's image.'" *Not in God's Image*, op cit., p. 130.

3.   The early fathers, for example, often implied that woman was more to blame because she sinned first – Tertullian called women "the devil's gateway" ("*De Cultu Feminarum*", I, i, in Migne, *Patrolosia Latina*, I, cols 304–5). The Victorians did the opposite by suggesting that women were, by nature, less sinful and therefore ought to have higher moral standards than men.

4.   Although this has always been a mystery to me. I am sure pornography can have a very harmful effect on children, but I am equally sure it has a far worse effect on their parents.

5.   *Are Women Human?* Dorothy Sayers (Downers Grove, Ill. InterVarsity Press, 1971).

FOUR

1.   Jose b. Johanan of Jerusalem (*circa* 150 BC), quoted in *Women in the World of Jesus*, Evelyn and Frank Stagg (The Westminster Press, 1978), p. 52. The Mishnah, of course, is not first century – being completed in about AD 200 – but it is a compilation of all the earlier Jewish Oral Law, which would have been extant in Jesus's day.

2.   According to the School of Hillel, ibid., p. 51.

3.   See *God & Women*, Dorothy Pape, Mowbrays (IVP, 1976), p. 22.

4.   Again this (appearing in public with unbound hair) was something for which one could be divorced. See *Women in the World of Jesus*, Evelyn and Frank Stagg (The Westminster Press, 1978), p. 51.

5.   Often without meaning to or realising it, teachers consistently favour boys in science and maths classes, as was shown, for example, in *The Sunday Times*, 6 November 1983, p. 9. "Girls Minus Boys Add Up Better."

6.   Quoted by James Dobson in *Straight Talk to Men* (Hodder & Stoughton, 1981). Though this is a well-known quotation of Steinham's I have been unable to trace its origin and therefore read it in context; I hope I do not do her an injustice.

7.   *The Gift of Feeling*, Paul Tournier (SCM Press Ltd., 1981). Throughout.

8.   *The Turning Point*, op. cit., p. 19, and pp. 18–19.

FIVE

1.   E.g. Catherine Marshall in "A Man Called Peter", quoted in *The Christian Family*, Larry Christenson (Fountain Trust, 1971), pp. 33–4. Also Christenson himself, op. cit., p. 47. And this is James Dobson's assumption in *Straight Talks to Men* (Hodder Christian Paperbacks, 1981). E.g. pp. 101–2.

2.   1 Corinthians 7:32,34–5.

3.   See Dobson, op. cit., pp. 109–10. Though he gives some excellent advice in these pages, he does overlook the fact that we cannot simply go back to the shared labour of previous years by being more friendly with our neighbours.

4.   Praying mantis, I believe, as well as certain spiders.

5. See *Ascent of Women*, Elisabeth Mann, Borgese (London: Macgibbon & Kee, 1963), p. 11. "Amongst fish, in general, the male is more absorbed by the service to the species than the female . . . The male is the homemaker. It is he who builds the nest, takes care of the eggs, and keeps the young in the nest until they are able to manage for themselves." She quotes the three-spined sticklebacks as an example of this among fish; she also mentions the quail, the male of whom goes broody and sits on the eggs to hatch them out.

6. *Equal Woman*, Myrtle Langley (Marshall Morgan & Scott, 1983), p. 24.

7. ibid., p. 169. Interestingly, it is the men amongst the Alor who want to have children, although it is their leisure which is likely to be interrupted. "We men are the ones who want children," they say. "Our wives don't. They just want to sleep with us." Possibly this puts paid to one of those "differences" we have come to think of as innate – that men want sex and women want children. It is easy to see that the Alor men, like Western women, achieve significance through looking after their children because it is the only job they are expected to do competently!

8. See *Housewife*, Ann Oakley (Pelican Books, 1980), chapter 2, "Women's Roles in Pre-Industrial Society". It is not peculiar to modern Western culture to divide labour into men's and women's work, but the *particular* roles we tend to think of as "traditional" or even "universal" are neither.

9. See *Inventing Motherhood*, Ann Dally (Burnett Books Ltd., 1982).

10. The fact that Paul singles out women, rather than men, to support vulnerable members of the Church seems to give problems to commentators. It is no doubt because of this that a few versions render the verse "if any believing man or believing woman . . ." See *A Commentary of the Pastoral Epistles*, J. N. D. Kelly (Baker Book House Co., 1981), p. 120.

11. See K. H. Registorf, *T.D.N.T. vol II*, p. 49. The word "denotes the 'master of the house' who has control over the household in the widest sense." Here, of course, the word is in the feminine form.

12. "Working at home, domestic." *A Greek English Dictionary of the New Testament*, William F. Arndt and F. Wilber Gingrich (University of Chicago Press, 1957).

13. To "be at the head (of), rule, direct . . . manage, conduct . . . be concerned about, care for, give aid." ibid.
14. *Dictionary of the Bible*, J. Hastings, ed. (T. and T. Clark, Edinburgh, 1906), vol I, p. 848.
15. ibid., also p. 848.
16. Which is what James Dobson, in one of his teaching films on the subject, analysed as the most common cause of complaint amongst housewives.

SIX

1. Works of Chrysostom. "Not In God's Image", op. cit., p. 141.
2. *Lysistrata*, Aristophanes.
3. For example C. S. Lewis. Or John Stott, who says, "If all ordained Christian ministry inevitably has this flavour of authority and discipline about it, then indeed I think we would have to conclude that it is for men only." *Issues Facing Christians Today* (Marshall Morgan & Scott, 1984), p. 254.
4. In his *First Blast of the Trumpet against the Monstrous Regiment of Women* (London, 1878), p. 17,ff. God, he said, has taken from women "all power and authority, to speak, to reason, to interpret or to teach, but principally to rule or judge in the assembly of men . . . therefore yet again I repeat that, which I have affirmed: to wit, that a woman promoted to sit in the seat of God, that is to teach, to judge, or to reign above men, is a monster in nature, contumely to God, and a thing most repugnant to his will and ordinance." Mind you, of course, Knox was a zealous Calvinist, and Mary Tudor was on the throne! (Apparently he regretted his Blast a few years later, when her younger sister took over . . .)
5.   ". . . there thou may'st behold
      The great image of authority; a dog's obey'd in office."
                                                    King Lear, IV:iv.

6. C. S. Lewis, *God in the Dock*, op. cit., p. 93.
7. R. E. Clements, in his *Commentary on Isaiah, 1–39* (Marshall Morgan & Scott, 1980) – New Century Bible Commentary series – prefers the NEB and Good News renderings: "instead of women (Heb. *nasim*), we should read 'usurers', as attested by

LXX and Targ." See also the *Journal of Theological Studies 38* (1937), p. 38, G. R. Driver.

8. J. K. Mozley in *A New Commentary on Holy Scripture* (SPCK, 1929), p. 503, says that verse 10 "is one of the most disputed as to its meaning of any that St Paul has written". Hardly anyone dares approach this passage without some reference to its obscurity. William J. Martin (1 Cor. 11:2–16: an interpretation) says "That this passage is difficult no one would deny."

9. This is the implication in *Eve's Story*, Eric & Joyce Lane (Evangelical Press, 1984). E.g. pp. 120–1, and in Larry Christenson, op. cit., pp. 37–8.

10. *Man & Woman in Biblical Perspective*, James B. Hurley (InterVarsity Press, 1981), pp. 182–3.

11. Because of tensions between this passage and some verses later in the letter some throw doubt on this. But this is a very small minority view. Most people point out that Paul's entire argument is rendered absurd if women are not in fact to prophesy. A few suggest that in that case perhaps Paul is talking of private gatherings. The presence of the angels, however, probably implies formal public worship (see M. D. Hooker, op. cit., pp. 412–3; also Dick and Joyce Boldrey, op. cit., p. 14; and J. A. Fitzmyer, *A Feature of Qumran Angelology and the Angels of 1 Cor. XI.10* (New Testament Studies, IV, 57–8), p. 55. Fitzmyer also quotes G. Kurze, *Der Engels- und Teufelsglaube des Apostels Paulus* [Frieburg im B.: Herder, 1915], p. 12.). However, no one, as far as I know, doubts that men are present; so whichever way one interprets the situation, women have authority to pray and prophesy in front of men.

12. Such as Hurley, op. cit., p. 176. For a full examination of the word *exousia* see: *The Epistle To The Corinthians*, C. K. Barrett (Adam & Charles Black, London, 1973), p. 255. Also *Authority on her head: an examination of 1 Corinthians XI, 10*, M. D. Hooker (New Testament Studies 10, 1964), pp. 190–220. Also J. B. Hurley, op. cit., p. 176.

13. *Women in Paul's Life*, Dick and Joyce Boldrey, p. 15.

14. M. D. Hooker, *Authority on her head: an examination of 1 Corinthians XI, 10* (New Testament Studies 10), pp. 410–16, p. 413.

15. *The Cities of St. Paul. Their influence on his life and thought*, W. M. Ramsey (London: Hodder & Stoughton, 1907.)

16. *1 Corinthians 11:2–16: An Interpretation*, William J. Martin, p. 239.

17. Hurley has had great fun trying to work out exactly what it was Paul had in mind to cover the woman's head. A veil? Some other covering? Or simply a suitable hairstyle? See op. cit., pp. 168–71. Also *"Did Paul Require Veils or the Silence of Women? A Consideration of 1 Cor. 11:2–16 and 1 Cor. 14:33b–36"* (Westminster Theological Journal 35, 1973), pp. 190–220.

18. Though, to my mind, the Corinthians' irresponsible use of languages tends to render this interpretation more, not less, convincing!!

19. See particularly Eric and Joyce Lane (op. cit., pp. 101–3) who are obviously aping, though not acknowledging, Hurley (op. cit., p. 188 ff.).

20. See *A Greek English Lexicon of the New Testament and Other Christian Literature*, William F. Arndt and F. Wilbur Gingrich (University of Chicago Press, 1957), where the word in Timothy can be rendered "quietness, rest", whereas in 1 Corinthians 14:34 it is to "be silent, say nothing, stop speaking", etc.

21. Quoted in C. K. Barratt, op. cit., p. 333.

22. This is Hurley's idea (see above, note 19). He argues that Paul is saying women should not exercise authority by judging the prophets. But if verses 34 and 35 came after verse 40, they are not in the context of prophecy.

23. See Romans 3:27 and 7:21, where Paul himself uses the word law to mean a principle ("On what principle?" RSV) Also Acts 23:29, where it may simply mean Jewish law generally. See also *A Greek English Lexicon*, op. cit., p. 544: "1. gener., of any law . . . 2. *a rule . . . principle, norm* . . ."

24. Cf. *God & Women*, op. cit., p. 132.

25. See *To Corinth with Love*, Michael Green (Hodder & Stoughton, 1982), pp. 159–60.

26. N. J. Hommes, "Let Women be Silent in Church", *Calv. Th. J.*, 4 (1979), p. 19.

27. J. A. Anderson, "Women's Warfare and Ministry", p. 30. Both quoted in *Women in the Bible*, Mary Evans (Paternoster Press, 1983), p. 103.

28. *Women in the World of Jesus*, op. cit., p. 53.

29. ibid., p. 43.

30. Julian C. McPheeters. Quoted in *God & Women*, op. cit., p. 124.

31. ibid., p. 132.

32. ibid.

33. *New Bible Dictionary* (InterVarsity Press, Leicester, Second Edition, 1982), p. 636.

34. See *A Greek English Lexicon of the New Testament*, op. cit., p. 15: "adelphos . . . the pl. can also mean brothers and sisters".

35. *Priestesses in the Church*, C. S. Lewis, op. cit., pp. 88–9.

36. E.g. Michael Green, *To Corinth with Love*, op. cit., pp. 161–3.

37. C. S. Lewis, op. cit., p. 92.

38. *What's Right with Feminism?*, Elaine Storkey (SPCK, 1985), p. 47.

SEVEN

1. The Zondervan Corporation, 1980, pp. 11–12.

2. Perhaps it would be more biblical if the groom, rather than the bride, were given away, by *both* parents . . . ?

3. See G. Lloyd Carr, *The Sons of Solomon*, The Tyndale Old Testament Commentaries (Inter-Varsity Press, 1984), p. 20: "Solomon's name is introduced here in what has been called a 'literary fiction' . . . the 'great lover' in Israel would naturally appear in the poem whether or not he really had anything to do with it. Similarly, Don Juan would conjure up the same picture in later love poetry."

4. *The Four Loves* (Geoffrey Bles, London, 1960), pp. 119–21.

5. See G. Lloyd Carr, p. 88: "One of the unusual features of the Song is the major place the words of the girl have in it . . . Our contemporary attitude where the girl is on the defensive and the man is the initiator, is in direct contrast with the attitude in the ancient world."

6. Wives take note: 80%–90% of men initiate sex almost every time, but 30%–33% wish that women did! *The Hite Report on Male Sexuality*, S. Hite (Macdonald, 1981). Quoted in *The New Internationalist*, April, 1986, p. 10.

7. *The Four Loves*, op. cit., p. 120.

8.   Though, to be fair, those who argue this are saying there is therefore no particular behaviour associated with the concept. The most well-researched discussion of the subject is S. Bedale's "The meaning of *kephale* in the Pauline Epistles", *Journal of Theological Studies* 5, 1954, pp. 211–15. Other treatments of the subject tend to be derived from (and often misunderstandings of) Bedale.

9.   *Mere Christianity*, (Geoffrey Bles, 1952), book III, chapter 10, p. 108.

10.   See Note 10 to Chapter 5. Another use of the same root in the New Testament is in Matthew 10:25 – translated "head of the house" in the NIV.

11.   *The Four Loves*, op. cit.

12.   Quoted by C. S. Lewis in *The Four Loves*, op. cit., p. 111.

13.   R. A. Torrey's book *The Power of Prayer* (Zondervan Books, 1971), actually includes two chapters entitled "How To Pray So As To Get What You Ask", and "Who Can Pray So As To Get What They Ask?"

14.   Patricia Gundry, op. cit., p. 34.

EIGHT

1.   See, for example, *The Life and Times of Jesus the Messiah*, vol I, Alfred Edersheim (Longmans Green & Co., 1897), p. 353. Edersheim explains the "ardent insistence on marriage amongst Jewish society of the time". See also Evelyn and Frank Stagg, op. cit., p. 50: "The Mishnah made the bearing of children a duty: 'No man may abstain from the law *be fruitful and multiply* unless he already has children' (Yeb 6,6)." See also C. K. Barrett, "The First Epistle to the Corinthians", *Black's New Testament Commentaries* (Redwood Press Ltd., 1968), p. 161: ". . . marriage appears to have been obligatory for a Jewish man."

2.   *Greek-English Lexicon*, op. cit., gives the following meaning for the two words:
a)   "be present, have come, impend, be imminent", w. the connotation of threatening.
b)   "necessity, compulsion, distress, calamity, means of compulsion".

3. For example "Sex and that: what's it all about?" (Michael Lawson and David Skipp, Lion, 1985), a Christian book for teenagers, confirms the view that "normal" people must have some kind of kiss-and-cuddle with their boyfriend or girlfriend: "Even these days some of us need to be told that we are allowed to kiss and hug!" (p. 51).

4. These verses (particularly 36 and 37) are quite difficult to understand, and have different interpretations put on them. See, for example, C. K. Barrett, op. cit., pp. 182–5.

5. See Edersheim, op. cit., pp. 149–50. In Corinth – among the Jews at any rate – it would presumably have been standard procedure for the single people to be engaged to somebody by their parents. This amounted to marriage in every legal way, although the couple would not yet live, or usually sleep, together.

6. *Bash – A Study in Spiritual Power*, John Edison, ed. (Marshalls, 1982), p. 58.

NINE

1. Actually this is not anon. at all. It was said at our breakfast table not very long ago.

2. Op. cit., pp. 113–20.

3. ibid., p. 114.

4. *The Mark of a Man*, op. cit., p. 25.

5. See *Faces of Feminism*, Olive Banks (Martin Robinson & Co. Ltd., 1981), chapter 2, "The Evangelical Contribution to Feminism."

6. ibid., pp. 17–25, and pp. 74–5: "the feminists tended to see the propagation of birth control techniques as leading to an inevitable degradation of morals, since it would encourage extra-marital sexuality."

7. Elaine Storkey, op. cit., p. 116.

8. *The Mark of a Man*, op. cit., p. 84.

9. *Understanding the Male Temperament* (Fleming, H. Revell Company, 1977), p. 22.

10. *Issues Facing Christians Today*, op. cit., p. 236.

11. ibid., p. 235.

12. *Sexual Oppression*, Greenbelt, 1983. (Pace Osborne!)

13. Elaine Storkey, op. cit., p. 170.

14. See *The New Internationalist*, April 1986, p. 16, which quotes F. P. Hosken, "Female Sexual Mutilations: the facts and proposals for action", *Women's International Network News*, 1980, and A. Thaim, "Women's Fights for the Abolition of Sexual Mutilation", *Int. Social Science Journal*, vol. 78. "At least 74 million young girls in the world have had their clitorises removed . . . Approximately 70% of women living in N. Sudan, Djibouti and Somalia have been infibulated. (Infibulation is the removal of the internal and external vaginal lips and the sewing shut of the vagina, leaving just a tiny opening for urine and menstrual blood . . .) Deaths due to infibulation . . . are estimated at 6% a year."

15. S. Brownmiller, *Against Our Will* (Penguin Books, 1976). Quoted in *New Internationalist*, April 1986, p. 17.

16. I am sick of there being no counterpart to "misogynous". This is it.

17. As note 15. 1 in 2 rapes are reported; 51% of reported rapists are caught; 76% of these are prosecuted, and 47% of them are acquitted. I make that about 1 in 60 rapists convicted. *The Fulfilled Woman*, Lou Beardsley and Tony Spry (Bantam Books, 1975).

18. See *Family* magazine, June 1984 and April 1985. *Family* (which is designed for a Christian readership) put out a questionnaire in June 1984 asking whether any of its readers suffered from domestic violence. The response they received – from women who regularly experienced extreme violence from professing Christian husbands – was staggering. The report was published in the same magazine in April 1985.

TEN

1. From a T.V. programme entitled *Just Wait Till Your Mother Gets Home*.